I0699322

Law of Aurornova
Cy Harold

CyStorm Publishing

Digital ISBN: 979-8-9907322-2-3

Paperback ISBN: 979-8-9907322-6-1
Hardback ISBN: 979-8-9907322-5-4

Book Cover Formatting by Author H.E. Gober

Book Cover Art by: Monstermind Studios

For Rights and Permissions, please contact: Cy Harold – CyHaroldM@gmail.com

Acknowledgments

Writing a book is no easy feat. Law of Aurornova has been my brainchild for the better part of five years. And, oh, what a five years it has been. I've thought about these characters every day since the story came to my mind, only to push them to the back burner due to all of life's events that have seen fit to hit me repeatedly.

However, the book before you is a product of not just the imagination and inner workings of my own mind but of the helping hands, coaching, coaxing, and, in some cases, threats of some of my most loved people, both old and new.

I am eternally thankful for my wife, Chelle, and kids, who allowed me to spend a little too much time in my office.

My McG-family and extended family (including some friends) for their support and encouragement.

And my writing family. Many of which have had a hand in this book in some way shape or form. Like: Authors TL Combs, H.E. Gober, and Lacy Chantell. My other Enablers, Rochelle and Maeven, and my TWG.

For my mother, who was always in the stands cheering me on, no matter what I had gotten myself into.

Content Warnings

As a courtesy to readers, please be advised the following themes and
actions are present within this book:

Violence

Adult Language

Loss of family

Table of contents

The sun rose on Aurornova at 07:47. Law Everstorm awaited its arrival, as he did most mornings, atop a hill overlooking his home, Fort Kelly, the only settlement on the planet. As the sun continued its ascent, Law's eyes climbed to the sky. The evening lights that swirled around the stars every night began their morning routine—morphing from their nighttime colors of bright purples and deep greens to mixtures of pinks and orange before they finally dissolved in the sunlight to the morning sky's usual red-orange hue.

Watching the sunrise from the hill was Law's favorite part of the day. Recently, it had been a pleasant way to end an early morning shift for his current rotation in the role placement program with the constable division, the colony's peacekeeping corps. For those like Law, the program was standard once an Aurornovan had finished their primary studies and didn't have a mentorship or a plan in place. During his time rotating with the constable division, he conducted late-night curfew rounds and early-morning perimeter checks with Constable Roberts.

Law's gaze fell to the meadow where the colony's habitats or "habs" were scattered like jacks across a blue-green grass tablecloth. He scanned the reflective solar panels atop the domes and cubes before stopping near the eastern edge of Fort Kelly. There sat the hab he shared with his twin sister Jamie. The common-area dome of their hab had three spokes sprouting from its sides, each leading to a personal cube. One for Law, one for Jamie, and until almost one year ago, a cube that used to be for their father, Maxwell.

How was Law supposed to focus on choosing a role within the colony or deciding what he wanted to do or where he wanted to go now that his studies were complete? Jamie was much better at processing her emotions than him. She was like their father, academically gifted and completely dedicated to science, research, and the betterment of the colony. Where Law struggled to decide what he would even be good enough at to dedicate his life to doing, Jamie juggled opportunities that were thrown at her from every division on their planet and others. She received offers from leading exploratory science teams to teaching satellite courses on terraforming.

Law recalled receiving the news that their father had been killed during a "seismic event." It happened while his father was co-leading an exploratory mission on the other side of the planet. Apparently, he was exploring a chasm alone when the quake hit. The structure could not withstand the magnitude of the event and gave way while he was still inside. To this day the exploratory team had yet to recover him. A point that enraged both Law and his sister. He remembered it was a sleepless night for them both. He could not sleep because he replayed his last interactions with his father in his head until it nearly gave him a migraine.

During the months following their father's disappearance, Jamie's incessant demands for answers began to subside. Law assumed she thought she would be better off finding the answers herself. As Jamie's public demands subsided, her questions became Law's. *How on a planet full of scientists and advanced equipment, was no data captured during the earthquake? Why had Dad left his core team to investigate a chasm? What secret discovery kept him away for weeks or months at a time?* The most important question, however, was *Where was Tiberius?* They had not heard from their father's best friend and their godfather since he delivered the news of his death. If Law expected answers from anyone, anyone that would help shine a light on this darkness, it would be him. Instead, there was nothing. Tiberius went dark and returned none of their calls.

Law allowed each unanswered query to crawl back to the forefront of his mind, before a large hand engulfed his shoulder, derailing his train of thought

Charlie, Law's best friend, took a knee beside him with his hand still on his shoulder. "I saw you on the way up. You were a bit zoned out. I thought you were sleeping with your eyes open," Charlie said, chuckling while imitating Law's wide-eyed gaze.

Law nudged him. "Yeah, I guess I was just lost in thought. Early morning."

"Oh yeah, peacekeeper stuff with Roberts, right? Good guy. He plays cards with my dad. Terrible gambler. Rarely makes it out of our hab without transferring my dad a couple U-creds to cover his losses. I think he enjoys the company."

Law agreed. Constable Roberts seemed to take great pride in showing him the ropes over the last few weeks. The constable also didn't shy away from providing any life advice he could conjure up in the moment.

"It's a big universe out there, Everstorm. Don't be afraid to get off this rock, travel, find you a nice girl, even from Proxy B or Earth." Law smirked at the thought. Relationships were far down the list at this point, not just with Aurornova women but also those from other planets.

Law looked down at his communications and media pad. The CMPs were flexible media displays that were fully integrated with most of the technology on Aurornova. Law's, which he had wrapped around his wrist like a small flat screen watch, flashed purple, indicating he had a message. He tapped his CMP twice, prompting a small holographic projection of his sister to materialize between him and Charlie.

Jamie was walking while recording the message. Trees and buildings flashed in and out of focus behind her. "I'm wrapping up now if you want to head this way. Don't be late, Lawrence." Jamie disappeared, and Law rolled his eyes.

He prompted his pad to respond. "Send a message to Jamie," he said, waiting for the device to activate. "I'm coming, sis. Charlie's with me. We'll be there in about 10 minutes."

Charlie stood. "Good, I'm starving. You think she'll be ready when we get to Sci-Rez?" He offered his hand out to Law, pulling him to his feet.

"Probably not," Law replied. If he knew his sister, she would try to cram ten more tasks between the time she received his message and their arrival. Law took in the view one last time. "Let's go. Whether she's ready or not, it'll still be my fault if we're late."

Now that the sun was at its full strength, Law welcomed the warmth. Morning perimeter checks were a chilly endeavor. This morning, the temperature was three degrees Celsius. Law showed up for his shift in two windbreaking jackets, while constable Roberts opted for a modest uniform vest. Law remembered being irrationally angry at the lack of fabric covering the constable. It was as if the inadequate clothing on Roberts would make him colder.

Law could tell the plants reciprocated his appreciation for the sun's glow. He scanned the sides of the path, seeing each flower in full bloom. The myriads of blue-green stems and leaves topped with multicolored flowers were in full effect. It was as if each flower reawakened from a nightly hibernation. The field of flowers ran the entire way toward Fort Kelly.

Charlie broke the silence as they approached the colony's open gates, each flanked by a constable.

"You know, Law, if you wanted to get in with the exploratory core, I got you." A year older than Jamie and him, Charlie worked with the exploratory core for almost two years and established himself as a reliable flight engineer and shuttle pilot. He was also aware of Law's post-studies indecisiveness. "Think about it, you and me, flying through space on a day mission to repair a Comms and Media Relay, maybe a detour or two," Charlie smirked as he grabbed Law's hand and waved it around, imitating flying through the sky.

Law looked at Charlie incredulously. Leave it to him to find a way to bend the rules a bit for the sake of fun. Noting Law's raised brow, Charlie added, "What? They don't care how you get the job done as long as it gets done." Law shook his head with a laugh as Sci-Rez came into view. Charlie stopped abruptly. "Listen, man. The last few months have been..." he fumbled for the right word, "...tough, for you, for Jamie, for the colony! I'm just saying, I'm an only child, but you're my brother, and I got you." Charlie emphasized those last three words a little more this time. Law knew Charlie was not much for words but saw the sincerity in his eyes.

"I appreciate you, Chuck. It's just a lot right now. Finishing our last year of primary studies, thinking Dad would..." Law cut himself off. "I'll figure it out. Just need a little more time."

Law and Charlie approached Sci-Rez. Hexagonal in shape, the structure sat in the middle of the colony as the main cog in a network of buildings that fed off its power. It was a behemoth of a structure, easily towering over the Control building which was a combination of the Admin building and Operations. Even the three ship hangars, or *hueys* as Charlie called them, that held the planets' fleet could not compete. Even if they were stacked atop each other, Sci-Rez would still be taller.

The two walked through the visitor entrance at the southeast face of the building into the receiving area. The cavernous hall was a cold, white and gray semi-circled room. Law could understand why some Sci-Rez employees worked such long hours. Anyone who worked in these windowless rooms would never know the time of day.

A semi-transparent divider stood between them and the frosted door-lined back wall. Law stepped toward the divider first. Once he was at arm's length, the divider sprung to life. Law beckoned Charlie forward, who was still gawking at the size of the room. A pleasant feminine voice spoke.

"Welcome to Science and Research. Scanning..." A faint green light spread from a device at the top of the divider. It quickly swept them both from their heads down.

Charlie whispered to Law as if the faceless reception voice would hear him, "This is the fancy entrance. I've only entered from the north entrance for newly printed parts and upgraded software for the shuttles. That entrance isn't nearly this...clean!" Law shrugged as the reception returned.

"Everstorm, Lawrence J." Law's CMP gave two quick vibrations before displaying a map. ", Charles B." Charlie's CMP imitated Law's showing a similar map. The voice continued, "Level 2 authorization confirmed by Everstorm, Jamie A. Senior Scientist."

Law and Charlie looked at each other. That last part was new. To Law's knowledge, Jamie was still an intern until after the primary studies celebration. Then, maybe a position and title would become formal, but not to the tone of Senior Scientist.

"Please proceed through the designated portal," the divider's voice concluded. To Law's right, the silhouette of a door behind the divider pulsed in a light blue tone. "Your CMP will direct you to your destination." Charlie led the way around the right edge of the barrier toward the corresponding door. He looked at Law.

"Level Two access? I get Level Five at best doing stuff for the core."

Law shrugged, "She's been putting in a lot of hours with Mina and you know he had a lot of respect for Dad. Not to mention, it's Jamie."

Charlie nodded in acceptance as they stepped through the portal. "Yeah, he probably sees her as his protégé or something."

Following their CMPs, they made their way down the corridor toward the heart of Sci-Rez, their steps resonating off the smooth white silicone and fiberglass walls. The corridors of Sci-Rez were not as unfamiliar to

Law as they were to Charlie. He and his sister met their father in his office almost every evening after their studies. Law walked the path in his mind as they passed a ramp to the second level on their right.

The landscape of his father's office was the same each time he and his sister entered. Topographical and geological maps were scattered on any surface flat enough, while marker-drawn charts and calculations graffitied the walls. If ever there was a difference when they arrived, it was a new map or graph his father could squeeze into a nook he had found. Another set of double doors promptly stood aside as Law and Charlie approached, ushering them into Sci-Rez's atrium.

Being at the center of Sci-Rez was like being at the center of a beehive in both activity and sound. The chatter of white coats as they rushed from one point to another meshed with the drones whizzing overhead, delivering cargo to their programmed recipients provided a constant buzz twenty-six hours a day, every day.

A spire that jutted from the bowels of Sci-Rez stood as the centerpiece of the atrium. The monumental structure was the apex of a vertical nuclear fission reactor that fed power to the hive of habs and buildings that made up Fort Kelly. The reactor was a jack of all trades before it arrived on Aurornova. In plain sight, it provided an ominous hum that kept the buzz of the science bees tame, productive, and employed. Behind the scenes, it was the main source of power for the entire colony. A myriad of clean energy sources, solar, wind, and hydro, either served as backups or powered functions deemed non-essential to the mission.

Law and Charlie turned down a hall off the atrium, arriving outside the conference room indicated on their CMPs. Jamie saw the guys from the front of the auditorium-style room and signaled to give her five minutes. Law nodded, while Charlie dropped his head back and let out a distraught moan. With a hand to his stomach, he complained, "I'm starving. Every time man, every time! We rush over here and she's always mid-scientific breakthrough or rewriting some law of physics or something! Just once, can't we find her at her desk waiting or checking messages?"

Law stared at Charlie, unsuccessfully holding back a laugh. Charlie rolled his eyes and admitted.

"Okay, maybe that was a bit dramatic. We had like 800 software upgrades to push out to the fleet. I didn't walk out of Huey Three until about 25:30 and that was hours after I had dinner."

"Okay, okay. I get it. I'm hungry too. She said five minutes. If she even looks like she's trying to start something else, we'll both go in and drag her out kicking and screaming." Charlie, seemingly appeased, looked at his CMP to note the time as he leaned against the wall. Law shook his head and turned back to his sister.

Jamie was in her element, standing at the front of a room full of thinkers. Her clear-rimmed spectacles sat atop her head, temporarily assisting a white headband that struggled to hold back her espresso-brown mane of tight curls. To Law, Jamie looked like their mother. Her wide brown eyes beamed over a full room. The lights at the front of the room cast a golden glow off her brown skin and enhanced the brightness of her jacket.

Had it not been for the fact that they were born the same day, it would be easy to dismiss them as being twins. Law focused on his reflection in the conference room's windowed wall. He was his father. His deep umber skin, shadowed around his jawline. Law turned his face side to side, inspecting the shave he received from the colony's barber along with his haircut. Where Jamie's naturally free hair juxtaposed the organized and prim person it sprouted from, Law's faded high-top gave the impression that he was as put together and clean-cut as his sister truly was.

She presented to a conference room of about thirty people. Most attendees were white coats like Jamie, but Law noticed a few from administration and several volunteers who rotated among Aurornova's vegetable and grain farms.

The colony's chief scientist, Dr. Leeland Mina, sat off to her side, proudly looking on. Law could tell through the plexiglass walls each time Jamie hit a high point because Mina would enthusiastically nod at her, then at the group, and then back at Jamie. The heads of the attendees bobbled in unison with Mina's. Jamie swiped her hand over the projection from an overhead view of a valley southeast of Fort Kelly to an ornate neon pink flower. The pulsating glow emitting from the flower showered the white room's walls with color.

Jamie grabbed the sides of the projection as if she were grabbing an old-school whiteboard and flipped it on its side. Lead lines sprung from each side of the flower like extra leaves sprouting from the stem. Law watched Jamie examine the crowd as they stared in intrigue. Some attendees stood and walked closer to get a better view, others craned their necks from their seat. One in the far back, about three meters ahead of Law, stroked the arm of his glasses. Law could faintly make out the projection increasing in size within the scientist's lens. The same scientist seemed to be the first to speak since Jamie flipped the projection.

Mina's stare matched Jamie's, a smirk inching from the corners of his lips. Whatever the scientist in the back said was precisely what Mina and Jamie were waiting to hear. Mina launched from his chair and clapped enthusiastically. Jamie nodded and clapped as well. The rest of the attendees followed suit, clapping while passing looks of excitement and shock between Jamie and the intuitive scientist, who reveled in his triumph.

Jamie regained order from the front of the room and flattened the projection between her hands so that it vanished. That must have been their dismissal because the attendees gathered their things and marched toward the door. Law retreated against the wall Charlie occupied. His best friend, oblivious to the oncoming traffic, looked up from his CMP for the first time since they reached the room.

"Sweet! She's done. It looks like The Box has a new dish. They're calling it Vasilli." Charlie noticed the indifferent look on Law's face. "I guess it's a perk Feodore gets being the executive chef. They say it's some kind of dark meat fish the size of a moose. It even has antlers." Charlie turned his CMP unit to Law to show the large mauve colored fish. This did not make it any more appetizing than Charlie's initial description. "They're saying it's pretty tender." Charlie said, trying to ease Law's reservations.

Charlie stared at Law pouting his lips while holding his gaze long enough to allow his eyes to glaze over.

Law finally conceded, "Okay, I'll try it." It was exactly what his best friend wanted to hear. There weren't many dishes that Charlie would turn down, likely because he was just north of 200 centimeters tall and built like a rugby forward. If Law hadn't caved, Charlie would have gone into a diatribe about trying new things and being open.

Jamie finally made her way to the door beside Dr. Mina. Law heard him tell her good work before heading off down the hall. His sister turned to the boys with a gratified look.

"Hey guys, glad you're here. I'm starved."

Law cringed, knowing Charlie would be triggered. He looked at Charlie, who responded through gritted teeth, "Well, thank the cosmos we got here thirty minutes ago so we wouldn't hold you up."

"Oh, come off it, Charles! It was fifteen minutes, tops. Plus, had you been paying attention, you would know that we've made an amazing discovery. We've found a new crop, high in starch and other nutrients. It could be the next potato!" Jamie fired back.

Law chuckled at his sister's excitement. fever, was not as amused. He palmed both sides of his stomach.

"Not helping J! I don't want to hear about finding more food, unless you have some 'Nova fries back in that classroom. Shut it, Law!" Charlie hissed at him, cackling in his peripheral. It was routine procedure for Charlie and Jamie to greet each other with a spirited back and forth, and Law's routine was to let it play out.

On the verge of frustration, Charlie backed away and said, "Listen, I just saw Tobey from Admin. I got to talk to him about the next string of drone upgrades. Can you two wrap it up so we can go before all the Vasilli is gone, please?" He left Law and Jamie with one last pleading stare. After Charlie turned the corner, Law turned to his sister.

"Vasilli?" Jamie asked, with a confused look.

"New dish at The Box. I'll let Charlie show you when he gets back. My explanation won't do it justice." That was an understatement, as far as Law was concerned. Charlie's passionate description did not do the dish justice nor did the beady-eyed purple fish with antlers staring at him from Charlie's CMP.

"I should have known it had something to do with food," Jamie said, shaking her head.

Law agreed as he and Jamie began walking toward the atrium. "So, you're getting to be pretty important around here, senior scientist," Law said, changing the subject.

"Oh, whatever Lawrence," Jamie retorted. "Dr. Mina is keeping me busy here. He believes in me and I love the work. I feel like I'm being productive. Maybe even..." Her voice trailed off, but it wasn't hard for Law to decipher where she was going. He decided to change his tone.

"Just like Dad. He'd be proud, J."

Jamie gave her brother a small smile, before pushing him. "I think Dr. Mina's just trying to be supportive since he knows it'll be a year since we lost Dad. He even invited me to his and Daniel's hab for dinner tonight." They entered the atrium and Law saw Charlie talking to Tobey near the door they had entered through earlier. Charlie spotted them and nodded at the pair.

"Well, you said Mina is a pretty good cook," Law said, watching Charlie end his conversation and jog over. Law only half listened to Jamie's debate about if she was going or not. He was paying more attention to Charlie, who had an odd expression as he approached. He looked concerned yet confused. Before Charlie could even reach a distance where he would not have to yell to be heard, he started talking.

Jamie, thinking he was going to reprimand them again, said, "Okay Charles, we know, we took too long, but we're ready to head to The Box. Let's see this *vasuumi* fish Law said you're so excited to taste." Her demand seemed to catch Charlie off guard. Likely because she butchered the name of the new dish. Charlie brushed it off and spoke with a sense of urgency that Law rarely heard from him.

"Listen, we need to put a rain check on lunch and you two need to get back to your hab." Now, Law and Jamie were caught off guard. Law was readying a battery of questions that his sister was already firing off.

"Back to the hab? For what? You were just chastising me about delays and now..."

Charlie cut in before Jamie could finish. "Forget lunch, you need to get back to your habs. Tobey saw me with the two of you and started asking questions...all these questions."

Law was finding it hard to follow Charlie as he waved his arms around. Law cut in this time and said, "But Charlie, everyone's asking questions or giving us concerned looks. It'll be a year this weekend since the..." He still hesitated when referring to it. "Since the accident. I'm sure he's just another curious person who's heard one too many whispers."

Charlie waved off Law and Jamie's answers. "No, this was different, and Tobey has a terrible nidio face. I should know. Half my wardrobe was funded by his U-creds." There was a slight pause as Charlie relished his superiority in Aurornova's premier holo-game that many played behind closed hab doors.

"And?" Jamie said as she pressed Charlie to continue.

"Anyway, I pressed him. He owes me a favor, a couple, actually. Apparently, there's some sort of request. One that Vice Commander Rell wasn't too happy with. It's..." Charlie stumbled over his words as he fought the concern appearing in his face. He looked back and forth between Law and Jamie. Now Law was concerned but losing his patience. As he was readying to find the best way to get Charlie to spit out whatever he was holding back, his CMP went off.

As Law's forearm vibrated from the pulsing red screen, Jamie's pad did the same on her hip. She read aloud the message Law was now reading on his arm.

"Priority message. Please return to your hab to receive a message transfer." Jamie looked at her brother. "Why wouldn't they just send it to us? Or at least mine if they're worried about security. My CMP has more encryption than most of the supercomputers in Sci-Rez."

Law shook his head as he reread the message. He looked up at Charlie and demanded an answer. "Charlie, what is this?"

Charlie gave Law a reluctant look. "It's Tiberius."

It took everything in Law not to break into a full sprint back to their hab as Charlie's words still echoed in their ears.

It's Tiberius.

They left Charlie in their wake, bypassing the electroshuttle outside of Sci-Rez. The shuttle was full of chattering researchers fresh off an overnight shift. Riding it would have meant enduring dozens of stops and drawn-out goodbyes, as each researcher would inevitably try to rattle off their final rebuttals to their colleagues before stepping off and retiring for the day.

So, they set off on foot.

Law's mind churned as his legs stretched to keep up with his sister's stride. They had heard nothing from Tiberius since the teams had given up on his father's search. They heard nothing from their father's best friend, his co-lead, and their godfather in months. And now, as he and Jamie rounded the corner toward the eastern hamlet of habs, Tiberius resurfaced, with a priority one message for him and his sister no less.

"Do you think he's found something?" Jamie asked as she continued to analyze the message. She was rereading the summons on her CMP as she walked. What did she hope to learn, Law thought? To uncover clues hidden between each digitized letter perhaps? Anything that would give her a leg up before confronting the messenger?

Law didn't answer her. He knew the question was more rhetorical than anything. However, he continued to ponder. It was a good question. What, after all this time, after essentially going rogue halfway across the planet, after abandoning Jamie, abandoning him, would prompt Tiberius to reach out. And why now?

Law turned left, followed by Jamie onto hab row thirty-three, breaking stride for the first time since setting off from the Sci-Rez building. They could see their hab just ahead as well as the messenger leaning against the entrance. Law noticed the man was fidgeting and looked impatient. He was their age, likely another participant in the role placement program. It took them about twenty minutes from door-to-door to reach their hab. If they had opted for the electroshuttle, it would have taken at least twenty-five minutes, maybe thirty, but the messenger was likely unaware of shuttle trends.

He lackadaisically addressed Law and Jamie as they approached. "Finally! We sent the priority-one summons half an hour ago."

Law was not in the mood to argue with the disgruntled messenger. It would only delay answers to the queue of questions that were lining up in his mind. He looked at his sister, though, and saw that the messenger's sass was not what Jamie needed right now. Law may not have wanted to engage, but Jamie was more than willing.

She straightened her glasses, craned her head to the side, and squinted her eyes. Law thought this must be so she could get a better look into the messenger's soul. As Jamie began, Law prepared for the worst.

"Oh. I'm sorry, sir. It wasn't our intention to inconvenience you. I'm sure you have more important matters as a participant in the RPP. In the year 2244, you'd think we could find a way to securely transfer a message from one person to another. One that wouldn't waste your valuable time. You should suggest they fax us next time." Jamie's eyes continued to measure the messenger. He looked to Law for help but received no sympathy. Law just wanted him to transfer the message to his or Jamie's unit and be gone. Realizing he was getting no support from Law as Jamie was gearing up for a second pass, the messenger conceded.

"Whose unit?" asked the messenger as he looked between the siblings, likely waiting for one to offer their CMP. Jamie pulls hers from her hip and gives it to the messenger. Her unit was more extensive and more advanced than Law's. It could expand to the size of a small television and allow them both to examine Tiberius' message.

As Jamie offered up her unit, Law expected the messenger to pull his flexible CMP screen from his arm, flatten it, and place his on top of Jamie's to initiate the transfer. Instead, he reached and pulled another CMP from his hip. He pulled the CMP from what appeared to Law to be a silver mesh sleeve. The messenger caught the intrigue on Law's face.

"It's a prototype. CMP security mesh. It blocks hack, visibility from drones, and reduces EMP effects." Jamie passed a look to Law that contained every bit of what she must have been thinking. Law knew the glance well, and he had the same questions. What would cause Tiberius to go to such lengths just to pass a message to him and his sister?

"Transfer complete," said the messenger. He lifted the secure CMP from atop Jamie's and returned it to the holster on his hip. Without another word, the messenger walked off to his electribike parked on the side of their hab. He mounted it and as soon as he flipped the on switch, he rode off.

Law could not think what annoyed him more, the rudeness of the messenger, or how much of a waste of time the whole interaction was. Admin could have easily tracked his and Jamie's CMPs and sent the messenger to Sci-Rez. He sent one last glare with the messenger before turning to his hab. Jamie waved her CMP at the entrance. The door to their hab beeped, clicked, and slid to the side. Law followed his sister in, wondering what their godfather had to say to them after all this time.

The door of their hab slid closed behind them. Law felt the tension let up slightly for the first time all day. He could not decide whether to attribute the release to being back in the hab for the first time in nine hours or the welcoming aromas being diffused throughout the family dome courtesy of Jamie's latest experiment of extracting essential oils from Aurornovan horticulture.

Today, Law caught notes of peppermint and chamomile tea. It made the hab feel homey, something he would never admit out of fear that she would start infusing it into everything within her reach.

Law called out to his sister, "J, come on! What are you doing?" As soon as they walked in, she disappeared to her cube, further delaying them from hearing what Tiberius had to say.

"Calm down, Lawrence," she answered, walking back through her cube's doorway. "I was just changing." Law looked at Jamie, his stance radiating impatience. "Seriously, Lawrence, we haven't heard from him in almost a year. He's probably just giving us some half-hearted apology because he's feeling guilty again. CMP, close skylights 50% and playback secure message from Tiberius Jansen."

The lights in the hab slowly dimmed as the shades in the skylight quietly slid halfway closed. The rest of the main living space transitioned to accommodate Jamie's request. A desk folded itself back into the wall, and the chair collapsed flush into the floor as if it never existed. A rectangle glowed in the center of the wall, gradually brightening until eventually, their godfather materialized in their hab and stared back at them.

Tiberius stood center screen in what looked like the command center the Zoa. Several scientists were behind him, idly working. Others were at a media table surrounding a projection of what looked like a mountain. Law couldn't tell for certain because Tiberius' shoulder blocked a clear view.

Law noticed another scientist behind Tiberius' left shoulder haphazardly carrying two baby drones in his arms. The scientist seemed fidgety to Law. He would not be surprised if he dropped the two drones as he shuffled in place, trying to decide where he was supposed to go.

The most curious case Law noticed, though, was Tiberius. His pony-tailed salt and pepper hair had garnered much more salt than pepper since they had seen him last. It rested on shoulders that had sunk, likely, Law thought, under whatever weight Tiberius must be forcing himself to carry. It's not that Law expected an imposing physique from Tiberius, seeing him next to his father for most of his life had molded Law's expectations. Even in his prime, there was a stark contrast between Tiberius and Maxwell. While they were both academics, Law's father was an avid runner and rower. Habits he kept up to match his shape from his early days in the exploratory core. He often joked he was just trying to keep his body as sharp as his mind was getting in his *old age*. Between that and about fifteen centimeters of height that Maxwell had on Tiberius, Law was used to Tiberius' more wiry frame.

Tiberius shuffled a bit, nodded to someone off-screen as if he had received his queue, and then began, "Hello, Lawrence and Jamie. First, I want to apologize for not reaching out to you sooner. As you both know, I have been working tirelessly to continue the pivotal work your father and I started here in the Zoa."

Law noticed Jamie's attention was solid. Her eyes were squinted, her arms folded, and a finger was on her chin as if she was analyzing Tiberius' every move and every word.

"I am sure you are questioning the need for the precautions I have decided to take in sending this message. Jamie probably more so than you, Lawrence."

Jamie let out a small humph of agreement through her pursed lips.

"We have recently uncovered a lockbox belonging to your father. The lockbox has been encrypted in a fashion that we cannot send you the contents. However, as it is my belief that the lockbox was meant for the two of you, it would stand to reason that you hold the key."

Law and Jamie looked at each other. It was as if they were aching to discuss what just transpired in a movie, but still had another act to finish.

Tiberius pressed on. "As it is also my belief that it would be…" He paused, "…unwise, to send the box in its entirety through shuttle. I have requested that the admin allow you both to be brought to Zoa. You can retrieve the contents of the lockbox, and maybe…maybe we can discuss your plans for post-primary studies." Tiberius was wrapping up. His tone was a little less matter-of-fact. "My request was for both of you to leave on the first shuttle following the Landing Day celebration, which I have as several days following the event. Lawrence, as I would imagine you, both of you, would feel most comfortable having Charlie as your shuttle pilot. I have specified such in my request.I look forward to seeing you two."

Tiberius' electric blue eyes were more muted than they had ever been as he stared at them through his circular glasses. He gave a final nod, and the message ended.

A few moments of silence passed after the message ended. Law was still staring at the wall where Tiberius' head had disappeared. The message had completely caught him off guard. None of Law's expectations had anything to do with something from dad. Especially not a mysterious lockbox to which he and Jamie may *hold the key*. Law looked over at his sister and figured she had already worked through the same thoughts.

"None of this makes sense," Jamie said, rubbing her temples.

"That would be the understatement of the century. We haven't heard from Ty for months, and all of a sudden, he has a lockbox that Dad left, and he wants us to come to the Zoa."

Jamie perked up. "That's just it, Law. Why would he insist on us coming to the Zoa for a lockbox that our father left for us? They could have easily sent it to us."

"He said it wouldn't be wise to send through shuttle. Maybe he wants to protect our privacy. Dad's privacy!" Law waved at the space Tiberius had just vacated.

"I'm not buying that. If he was worried about privacy and suspected it was left for us in the first place, why would his first instinct be to open it?"

That was a point Law had a hard time reconciling. Tiberius always had his reasons. Whether it be for his and Jamie's own good or for the good of the colony, he always put the prosperity and safety of the colony first. But this was not a threat to either. It was their father's lockbox and trying to open it for any reason seemed a bit invasive, even for his father's best friend.

Jamie added, "It is protocol for Admin to inspect any and all transfers made to and from the Zoa." Law was aware of this protocol, having done a rotation with Admin weeks ago. An entire wing of the Admin building was restricted for inspections. Only those with the highest clearance could access that section of the building.

"I know the protocol. We couldn't even use the east entrance of the building because of the inspections wing. We had to use the north entrance and walk through half of Admin just to get to anything on that side of the building. It's the dumbest setup. But what are you getting at? Do you think Ty has something to hide?"

Law watched Jamie chew at the inside of her cheek. "I don't know Law. I just think there's more to it than what he's telling us. We got all of Dad's personal effects after the memorial. It took them almost a year to find this mysterious box with our names on it. What would even be in it that would need to be encrypted?" Before she finished her point, she drew a breath looking her brother in his eyes and said, "I don't think we should go. This all isn't adding up."

Law was still digesting everything, but suggesting they should not go to the Zoa was not what he wanted to hear. Before his sister could recite what Law was sure would be a well-thought list of reasons as to why they shouldn't go, he vehemently disagreed. "I knew you'd come up with some reason for us not to go. Ever since Dad went missing, you've had this vendetta against Ty..."

"Vendetta?" Jamie yelled. "You know what, Law, it's time for you to grow up. I don't have some vendetta against Tiberius. Do I understand that he has a duty to our colony to continue the work he and Dad started? Yes. Do I understand that Dad was just as much a brother to him as you are to me? Yes. But, Lawrence, the fact isn't that I – we needed him to be this doting godfather that stepped in to finish raising us or something. It's that we needed the man our father trusted with his life, that we trusted with his life, to…" Jamie's voice cracked. She turned her back on her brother, her voice softer than before. "I don't have a vendetta, Law. I'm just disappointed."

Law hung his head. He was beginning to empathize with her disappointment, as he wished he had practiced just a little more restraint before accusing his sister of vilifying their godfather.

They rarely ventured too deeply into each other's feelings on pretty much anything. Explanations were not warranted. They just had an understanding. Whether a shoulder or a soundboard was needed, one would slip into that role for the other, sometimes without even realizing. They'd play that role, and then both would continue with their day. No harm, no foul.

Their father was always the more intuitive one in the trio. The one who covered the gray areas that got missed by playing the role. He knew how to calm or refocus each of them. Law thought about what his father would do if he were here now. Seeing Jamie upset, they would often share a piece of candy, butterscotch was his weapon of choice before leading her off to the side and encouraging her to *Speak your mind, my love,* as softly as his deep voice would allow. The interaction would typically end in a hug following a long conversation, and Jamie would be rejuvenated.

Law walked to the other side of the dome. A dish of butterscotch candies sat on a shelf near the door, untouched. He grabbed one and walked over to his sister. He nudged her as he twirled the candy in his hand, eventually holding it out in front of her as a peace offering. Jamie snatched the candy from Law as she sniffled, but he was sure he saw a flicker of a smirk. He decided to make the most of it.

"J, I'm sorry. I know you don't have a vendetta against Ty," Law said as he walked over and collapsed onto the sofa, throwing his chin into his hand and bracing his head. He contemplated Jamie's rationale for not going. "And you're right. There's got to be more to all of this. Some motive that he has by not just sending the box to us. But, isn't that all the more reason to go?" Law felt he was finding his point for going the more he spoke.

Jamie looked exasperated, but she didn't say anything. Gaining momentum, Law went on, "You're right, J. Ty hasn't been very forthcoming with anything going on in the Zoa, especially when it comes to this 'geologic phenomenon' that—" Law struggled to say it. "Killed Dad." The words were sour, leaving Law's mouth. Jamie winced at the words. It was something neither of them dared say to this point. Law fought through the lump swelling in his chest. "Going over there is not only our chance to corner Ty, but it's an opportunity to get answers on our own. Not from the dailies, not from a middle man, and not some watered down statement from Admin. And if we can't get them from him. We'll get them from someone."

Jamie cut in, but her tone was more inquiring than incredulous. "From whom Lawrence? Tiberius has run a tight ship in the Zoa since the accident. He handpicks anyone going or coming from the Zoa. And if they're coming from the Zoa, which is seldom, they usually aren't here long before they're '*reassigned*' off Aurornova."

Jamie was right. Almost no one would be interested in talking to them if it meant getting in trouble with Tiberius. He had full reign over the Zoa since the accident. Admin had granted him such power in response to his passionate plea that allowed him full oversight of operations. He argued that it not only preserved the work that he and Maxwell had completed in the Zoa up to that point, but it also prevented everyone from unnecessary harm if he signed off on all personnel.

However, rumors spread throughout the colony that Admin was no longer pleased with the arrangement and had attempted numerous times to reel in Tiberius. Law thought, maybe that pushed the balance in their favor. He answered Jamie, more so by thinking aloud.

"I don't know. Maybe someone over there isn't afraid of Ty. Someone who sees a bigger picture or someone who was more loyal to Dad than Ty?" Throwing up his hands, Law felt like the momentum he was building slowed, until something jumped out in front of his train of thought.. "Jamie!" His outburst startled his sister as she grabbed a second butterscotch candy and popped it in her mouth.

Law asked her, "What if Dad wanted us to go to the Zoa?" He had her attention. "You said it yourself J, we got all of Dad's stuff. Even the few things he considered most valuable."

Law raised his left wrist, which sported his father's watch. Handed down through each Everstorm generation's first born. Starting with their great-great-great grandfather passing it along to their great-great grand-mother. The watch was not particularly useful on Aurornova where the days lasted twenty-six hours instead of the twenty-four on Earth. Like his father though, Law still wore it. As Jamie was technically the firstborn, the watch should have gone to her, but their mom, Autumn, also had an heirloom that was passed down through the women in their family. A black rope necklace. The pendant was a black titanium compass rose with an emerald at its center. Jamie was currently flipping it between her thumb and index finger as Law spoke.

Law lowered his wrist and ran his finger around the bezel. "What if Ty is afraid of what's in the box?" Jamie was mulling the thought. Law was running with it. "It makes the most sense. No one knows the protocols for anything going in and out of the Zoa than the two people who wrote them, Dad and Tiberius. Why else would Dad leave a footlocker that can't be opened and inspected? Why else would Ty's first reaction be to open it?"

Jamie cut in. "Leaving Tiberius with what he believes to be the only viable option. Bring us to the Zoa. We open the box under his supervision." Law nodded in agreement, but Jamie's face remained in a tight, contemplative scrunch. "But none of this answers the question of why? What was so important that Dad had it locked in an encrypted box that we don't even really know we can open? And apparently, it was hidden for months." That question remained in the unanswered column for Law.

Jamie drew a breath before adding another. "Law, what if whatever is in that box cost Dad his life?" she asked with a look on her face as if she wished she never had. But given everything they had discussed thus far, they both knew it was a valid question. It was also, Law thought, the first thing Jamie said that made him question going to the Zoa, seeing their godfather, and opening their father's box.

Law awoke Saturday morning to the smell of gozooberry muffins. Jamie must have heated an extra one for him before she set off to the Admin Building. He pushed himself up to rest on his elbows, having fallen asleep on the converticouch. It was a dreamless sleep, which was unusual for Law these days. But it allowed the events of the previous night to remain at the forefront of his mind.

After Jamie and Law agreed going to the Zoa would yield the most answers, Jamie left Law to gaze at the stars through one of their hab's skylights. She had an impromptu meeting with Vice Commander Kerrington Rell first thing this morning. When Law asked the reasons, Jamie was at a loss. She told Law that one of Rell's admin assistants came to her before her presentation yesterday. All her assistant told her was a time. Law found that to be mysterious of Rell, but not surprising as the Vice Commander had, as of late, been trying to make her presence increasingly known.

Kerrington Rell was second-in-command on Aurornova and ambitious. Commander Conners, Aurornova's current leader and chief administrator, had barely announced his resignation before Rell began posturing to succeed him. At the time, Commander Conners announced his intentions, most of the planet's inhabitants expected Maxwell to step up and lead. Though Rell, second in command, expected to be ordained as the rightful successor, Maxwell Everstorm was personally responsible for many of the innovations that allowed Earthen people to colonize other planets sustainably. Most of all, though, he was popular among Aurornova's inhabitants. Even though colony leaders were most importantly mission leaders, politics could not be avoided.

Rell and Maxwell's relationship was an amicable one that had a history. As Law made his way to the hab's kitchenette to retrieve the muffin left for him, he recalled the stories his father told him and Jamie about growing up on Tellathia II with Rell and her best friend, Autumn Elizabeth. Law and Jamie's mother.

After Maxwell took the mission to Aurornova two years after the death of their mother during the Storm of , He reached out to Rell and persuaded her to join the mission. Law recalled his father telling them that it was what their mom would have wanted. For neither of them to suffer alone, pouring themselves into their work as they both would. It was not an attempt to provide each with an emotional confidant, but more an empathetic presence. Rell put in for the transfer, joined her fallen friend's family, and never looked back.

That was nearly six years ago, just before Law's thirteenth birthday. He plucked the topmost muffin from the basket and took a ravenous bite. The warm bread of the muffin filled his mouth, followed by the tingly juice of the gozooberries. The fruit coupled its sweet ripe flavor with a natural stimulant better than caffeine. Jamie preferred the planet's native berries to coffee as her early morning pick-me-up, adding them to juices and pastries. Law's CMP chimed as he chewed. Charlie was already speaking before he could raise his wrist.

"Bro! I've been chiming you all morning. What's going on? Did you watch Ty's message? I'm getting off my shift in ten. I've got workout clothes with me, so I'll skip the hab and head straight to The Box." Law struggled to swallow the bit of muffin he was still chewing, to respond to Charlie's rapid questions. "Is that Jamie's muffins? Bring those and her with them."

Law finally swallowed the bite of muffin stuck in his airway and jumped in. "She's not here," he said, prompting an inquisitive look from Charlie. He continued, "Meeting with Rell."

"What about?" Charlie asked.

Law shrugged. "No idea. Jamie didn't seem to know either."

Charlie scratched his chin, letting his fingers tangle in the curls of his auburn beard. "Weird," he finally said before getting back to business. "I got to finish post-check. The Box, ten minutes. There's static about Ty." Charlie cut out, but Law's wrist remained in place.

Why had Charlie marinated on the news of Rell's meeting with Jamie? And there was always a scuttle about Ty, the Zoa, and his father, for that matter. Novan's always had a curiosity about anything classified, closed off, or condemned from public knowledge. Law was not oblivious to this, and Charlie most certainly was not.

Like his father, Henry, Charlie was charismatic and humble. Neither he nor his parents took anything for granted. They came to Aurornova to put their only child in the best position they thought they could. Henry was a tradesman and part of the group that brought habs online and maintained them. His mother, Jean, was one of Law's favorite primary studies teachers, specializing in astronomy and his favorite subject, linguistics. Mrs. Sloane would always send a new linguistics text to Law through Charlie for him to practice or learn. Every now and then, Law and Mrs. Sloane would even speak in forgotten and ancient languages at Charlie's hab when he joined them for dinner.

So, when the time came for Charlie to participate in the role placement program, he had no issues lining up mentors. However, Charlie didn't need them. His heart was always into flying, starting at a rising and largely self-taught engineer, before becoming an ace pilot.

Two years later, those same people are more than willing to trade the only other currency of value on Aurornova, information. Pilots who flew classified day missions, assistants who overheard conversations from unsealed huddle rooms and offices, a social hab attendee eager to debrief while closing shop. Charlie had a way of extracting information from people and it was for this very reason Law was certain Charlie knew something and that's why he was eager to meet at The Box after his shift.

Law stepped out into the humidity of Aurornova's summer morning, sliding his hand across the front door of his hab to activate the lock. The whirring sound assured him their home was secure. He then set off toward The Box for what he figured would not be his and Charlie's usual Saturday routine.

For twenty-six hours a day, six days a week, eleven months a year, the inhabitants of Fort Kelly were productive. However, Saturday was the inhabitants' day to partake in personal endeavors and recreation. For Law and Jamie, and at times even Charlie, it used to be time spent with their father, Maxwell. The mornings started with an early protein-heavy breakfast prepared by Jamie while Law ground beans from his sister's coffee plants. Coffee was the life force for the Everstorms, and Jamie's coffee beans were extremely robust. Novans valued them highly, as imported coffee from Earth or Proxima was a luxury, and she was able to yield the most flavorful and abundant beans.

Charlie often joked that the only reason he knew it was time to start the day was because he could smell Law grounding the beans before the rest of Fort Kelly were awake. Whenever he was at their hab in the morning, he was the first to make a cup. With three sweeteners and just as much cream as there was coffee.

However, when their father was around, Charlie's reverence kept him at bay, not daring to grab a mug before *Mr. Storm*. He, like Jamie and Law, marveled at Maxwell's ability to drain a cup, more often, two cups, black and scalding hot, while scrolling through the morning briefs without flinching. This was especially superlative when it was made from Jamie's foraged and planted beans.

When they were younger, their mom would often joke that if her husband ever died, his spirit would still have to jog every morning. However, she wasn't sure if it would be because Dad was such a creature of habit or because his spirit would need to work off the years of caffeine intake. Both of Law's parents often joked that it was the two unwritten rules of being an expeditionary ranger. Autumn felt her husband took the rules more as mantras than she did.

Law mouthed the first, mimicking his father's voice in his head as he walked.

A ranger has two speeds, explore or prepare for the expedition. This explained the lite morning jogs' that Law felt more to be marathons. The second, *the elixir of life was discovered long ago, and it was called coffee.*

Law wasn't as reproachful of that mantra as he took a sip from the travel mug, he poured before walking out of the hab and after devouring his third muffin. Jamie's latest blend had subtle hints of vanilla and was extremely earthy. So much so that Law would not have been surprised if Jamie mistakenly switched her soil samples with her coffee grounds. He licked his teeth as he continued up the path toward The Box.

These days, Saturdays were different. Jamie kept the morning marathon routine going, having given up trying to get Law to run with her. Though Law ran a few times with her following the news of their father to be supportive. The jog for her usually ended at the lab where she would clean up, change, and work on any number of her personal projects or whatever she and Dr. Mina were trying to get a jump on. Law would return to the hab and take to delivering some of her coffee beans to inhabitants before meeting up with Charlie.

For Law and Charlie, Saturdays often meant a few rounds on the virtucomp courts. The courts housed in The Box provided simulated recreation areas for Auronovan inhabitants. It was not feasible for colonies to haul material for and much less try to build basketball courts, soccer pitches, and each popular pastime of their diverse group of pioneers. After all, ancestors of the more than 2,000 colonists of Aurornova alone were rooted throughout more than forty Earthen countries and this was one of the smaller expeditions. It was, however, indisputably necessary to allow colonists a means for recreation and exercise. There were ten small group courts and three large group courts in The Box.

They often joined a Galactabattle match, the universe's most popular virtual reality competition that put hundreds, sometimes even thousands, of players against each other in the latest battle scenario. Two weeks ago, there was a two-and-a-half-hour alien invasion. Charlie was the game's top scorer, leading the game's air squadron attack, naturally. Law was a ground soldier, garnering a spot at number twelve in the rankings.

Today, however, it would be the gym. Whenever Charlie wanted to talk, share the latest static, recap a date, or check on his friend, it was while lifting weights. So, Law took the path toward the entrance closest to the gym. The path made a wide loop toward the east end of the heaping rectangular structure that was The Box. Just as Law rounded the corner, Charlie greeted him at the entrance.

"You know me too well, bro. Figured I'd want to work out today," Charlie said as he playfully bumped Law's arm.

"Yeah, well, I know you won't rest until you can rip that flight jacket you got on with a sneeze." Law joked. He tossed the muffin he had brought Charlie, who in turn caught it with the tenderness of someone handing him a newborn. Charlie hoisted the muffin to the sky before shoving half of it in his mouth.

"Ooh, stinger, mate," Charlie mumbled with his mouth full. Crumbs fell from his mouth as he mimicked being punched in the ribs. They both chuckled before Charlie began walking back around the winding path.

"Oh, come on man, I didn't hurt your feelings, did I?" Law asked, wondering if Charlie was carrying out their back and forth. He had to admit, a workout would be good after yesterday. "Come on Chuck! I was just messing with you."

"Oh, I know," Charlie said, glancing back at Law as if to question why he was not following at this point.

Law acknowledged and followed in his wake. "So, we're not working out and we're not heading toward the virtucomp courts?" Law asked, trying to follow where Charlie was leading.

"We're changing it up today?" Charlie responded, "We're going to see the guy with the static on the Zoa I told you about this morning, IQ."

Law had almost forgotten. "What kind of static?" Law asked. Most static that passed around Fort Kelly was just noise: conspiracy theories and idle gossip of bored colonists. But occasionally, if you listened close enough, the static had useful information buried deep within. Law wanted to know which kind this IQ guy held.

"We'll both see when we get there. IQ's very, uh, picky, I guess, when it comes to who and where he passes static along." Charlie sounded just as much in the dark as Law. He nudged Law's shoulder, causing him to have to regain his balance. "Dude, tell me about the message from Ty! What's going on? Why is your sister meeting with Rell?" Charlie inquired as he beamed at Law, eagerly awaiting to be caught up.

Law began his recount of Tiberius' message, noticing Charlie was leading him back to the hab village.

"So, you and Jamie have made up your minds. You're going to the Zoa off vague information from Ty, who's doing who knows what over there, for a box Mr. E. never told you two about?" Law found himself slightly annoyed by the conciseness of Charlie's summary. After almost not so successfully justifying it to his sister, the last thing he wanted to do was to convince Charlie.

"It sounded suspicious enough without you adding the mystery and suspense brief to it, Chuck," Law said, with a glare at his friend. He figured Charlie must have caught his annoyed tone as he backtracked.

"Listen Law. I'm just saying, I understand where you're coming from. Going to the Zoa probably is the right move. They barely let anyone go over there now without Ty's blessing. By going, you can put a lot of static to rest and possibly even get things back on the right foot with Ty." Charlie was deploying his trademark *pilots-eye view*. As Charlie put it, no one is better at seeing the bigger picture than a pilot. Law appreciated the reassurance and thanked Charlie before starting back up the path.

"Chuck, where are we headed?" Law asked as they walked further into the hab village. They had completely bypassed the path back to Law's hab block and walked further north into the older blocks.

"Block six," Charlie answered.

Block six was part of the hamlet where some of Aurornova's original habs had been set up in the planet's earlier days of settlement. Law gazed at the nearest hab they were walking past. It was a patchwork of older panels tinged to a dirty off-white color, showing its defense against the planet's harsh summers.

Newly printed panels gleamed in the sun, laced with the latest solar absorbing technology. Tech that had not made its way to Law and Charlie's side of Fort Kelly. This was not unusual, as this hamlet typically received all the latest and greatest technology the planet's engineers offered. These habs were originally the property of some of the first settlers and now, their descendants if the family stuck around. The inhabitants here were part of Aurornova's self-proclaimed '*high-class*'. They viewed themselves as trailblazers. Touting the names of their grandparents and parents as if they themselves discovered Aurornova and built the settlement. Law rolled his eyes at the thought, which made him think about this IQ guy they were going to see.

"Charlie, what is IQ doing in block six?" Law asked.

"His grandparents raised him. The two of them were some of the planet's leading scientists, and practically discovered the Zoa, before it became the large operation it is now. I'm sure your dad knew about them." Charlie said the last part a bit more somber, giving a quick side-look toward Law. As if he was still gauging how much he should bring his father up.

"You're probably right." Law agreed as they made the final turn onto the path leading toward IQ's hab. At the corner, they started past a hab whose inhabitant was at work in her small vegetable garden. A postage stamp among the rest of the yard.

As the two passed, she peered up at them, her jaw clenched, and face smudged at the sight of them. Law felt her eyes boring into him. Each step that progressed them up the path was a notch her neck rotated to keep them firmly in her sight. Charlie must have felt it too, because at this point, he rotated his head almost 180 degrees to stare at her as they continued up the path. Law turned and watched her shake her head in disgust at Charlie's audacity. Law nudged Charlie as his continued gaze at the lady began to drive Charlie into his path.

"Geez, does she think we're coming to steal her cucumbers?" Charlie asked shaking his head.

"There will always be those few," Law said. "It'll only get worse as the settlement gets larger," he added before pointing to their destination.

"Yeah, well, they still need to know I got time whenever they're lacking." Charlie grinned as he returned Law's nudge. "Let's see if IQ has his finger on the Nova's pulse, as much as he thinks he does. The sooner we get back to our side of Kelly, the better."

Law and Charlie started up the path to IQ's hab. Before they were even an arm's length from the door, a beam ignited from the top of the frame and began scanning them.

"What in the cosmos!" Law exclaimed.

"Typical IQ. Of course, his hab is upgraded to the max," Charlie said, holding his arm in front of Law, signaling to let it finish. After the beam reached their feet, it switched off and was followed by a digital voice, "State your business, Everstorm, Lawrence and Sloane, Charles."

Charlie cleared his throat. "I have a 2221 baseball card that I would like to trade for a 2150 football card?" Charlie said, sounding a bit confused at what he had just said. Law, just as confused, started to ask a question but assumed Charlie knew what he was doing. The digital voice responded.

"One moment, please."

A few seconds passed before an ascending chime played and the hab's door slid aside. A pleasant young woman greeted them on the other side, whom Law immediately recognized as Nahdine, one of Jamie's best friends.

"Hello, Charlie, Lawrence," Nahdine said with a pleasant smile. "IQ's expecting you. Follow me, please." She beckoned them in with a wave of her hand as she turned, leading them into the bustling living dome of IQ's hab. Upon walking in, Law was overcome with a thick haze smelling of...was it juniper? Whatever it was, Law thought, sent him reeling as he waved his hand in front of his face, attempting to wade through the fog. As they traversed the living dome, slithering through what had to be dozens of people, Law noticed a group of about six hovering over a nidio table as the two opponents were locked in. The spectators whispered to each other, likely expelling how they would handle the next move or several. The translucent pieces moved simultaneously on the holotable as their masters furiously scrolled and dialed in commands from their CMPs.

Looking to his right, Law noticed almost a dozen people in the kitchenette, the source of the haze, blowing multi-colored puffs from thin translucent tubes connected to their CMPs.

"Is it me, or is this dome bigger than ours?" Law asked, not directing his thoughts toward either Charlie or Nahdine.

"No, you are correct, Lawrence. The domes were typically larger for the first settlers of Fort Kelly." Nahdine answered as she turned, whisking her long jet black hair over her shoulder. "Novans spent more time in their habs back then. It was before The Box was built, so they did not really have–umm—what is the word?"

"Recreation?" Law supplied.

"Yes! Recreation. Thank you, Lawrence." The assistant said with a smile. Law watched as she placed a strand of hair behind her ear. "I still struggle at times." Nahdine looked at Charlie, "Law is nice enough to speak Tellathian with me sometimes when I visit Jamie."

"You sound just fine to me! Plus, I don't get to speak it as much anymore. Growing up Mom and I would use it a lot with each other. It was her native language. Dad and Jamie never really grasped it."

"You're sweet, Lawrence," Nahdine said with a smile before leading them deeper down the hall to one of the hab's cubes.

"Yeah, he is, isn't he?" Charlie agreed. He barely noticed Charlie beside her, grinning from ear to ear before she pressed the small pad screen next to the cube's door. A chime played like the one from the hab's main door.

"The door will open when IQ is ready for you," Nahdine informed the two. "C'zeto Lawrence."

"Oh, C'zeto Nahdine!" Law said hastily as he broke from his daze. Nahdine giggled and disappeared back into the crowd within the living dome. As Law continued to gaze at the cube's door, Charlie slapped his chest with his large hand. He attempted to mimic Nahdine's softer tone.

"C'zeta-toe, Lawrence." Charlie tried to lock eyes with Law, but he slapped Charlie's arm away.

"What are you doing?" Law asked, laughing at his friend's awkward behavior. "And, it's *C-Zet-Toh*. It's Tellathian for goodbye."

"That's beside the point. What's important is, you need to ask her to Landing Day."

Law shook his head. The Landing Day celebration was the last thing on his mind, much less securing a date for it. "She was just being nice. She's always that way when she comes over to hang out with Jamie."

"I wonder why that is," Charlie retorted, placing his thumb and forefinger on his chin and pretending to search the hall's ceiling for answers. "She's gorgeous, man, and if she's hanging with your sister, then she's probably some kind of genius. Do. Not. Fumble!"

Law rolled his eyes and waved his friend off. Charlie did have a point though; Landing Day was fast approaching. The celebration almost served a dual purpose. It was a day of migration for inhabitants coming to and leaving Aurornova. It was also a day of celebration for the young adult inhabitants finishing their primary studies. It had become customary to have a date.

Nahdine was always kind to him. And Charlie wasn't wrong, she was very attractive. One night, while Jamie and their father were running late getting back from Sci-Rez he'd gotten unusually close to her when she asked a question about one of the linguistic books. He was met by one of the most pleasant smells of peony and moon lily blossoms. When he looked up at her he just stared as she brushed her long jet-black hair out of the way of her almond shaped eyes. As he examined her smooth cream-colored skin, he forgot what she had called him over for. She became self-conscious thinking he saw something on her face, to which he apologized profusely. It was the first time Law remembered looking at her as a woman and not as one of Jamie's friends.

Just as Law went to join Charlie and lean on the hallway wall, a voice came from beyond the door.

"Enter!" The sliding partition opened, revealing what looked like a small Sci-Rez conference room. This cube, like the living dome, was larger in size, featuring a conference holo-table at its center with multiple projections encircling it.

Law was able to catch several U-cred counts and charts with names and numbers before IQ must have caught his head on a swivel. He tapped the CMP on his wrist and all the projections dissolved immediately.

"Gentlemen, gentlemen, gentlemen! Welcome to Chez-de-IQ!" he said, with his arms stretched wide. He had CMPs clasped around both of his forearms. IQ walked around the conference table toward them, outstretching his hand to shake Charlie's.

"Thank you for coming Mr. Sloane. I think this will be a fruitful endeavor for us all." IQ clasped Charlie's hand with both of his before letting go and extending a hand to Law. "And to you, *Prince* Everstorm. I am so sorry for your loss. Your father was a true asset not only to the colony but to many a solar system over his lifetime." Law hesitantly accepted his handshake with an eyebrow raised.

"Uh, thanks," Law said, as he felt IQ maintained the handshake and eye contact well beyond what felt comfortable.

"Right! Let's get down to business." IQ turned to the others within the cube and nodded his head toward the door. Without question, each stood, collecting their pads and CMPs, and exited the cube. IQ's eyes followed his associates until the last crossed the threshold and the door returned to its shut position.

"Now, Charles, as I mentioned, you have come to the right place. As you know, I have eyes and ears all around The Nova as well as the Zoa." Law snickered at the audacity.

"I highly doubt that," Law said with cynicism in his voice. Charlie cut in before he could say anything else.

"What Law means to say is, what happens in the Zoa is very hush-hush. It's been that way since...since." Charlie's voice trailed off.

"Ah ha! That is the question, isn't it? When did things become so secretive about the Zoa? Why did it become that way? There was no reason for things to come to a virtual halt unless..."

"Unless what IQ?" Law asked, cutting him off. "It was made clear that comms with the Zoa have been dicey since they moved their focus to a new site that shows geologic promise. It was thought they found something..."

"Exactly!" Now it was IQ's turn to cut in. "Aurornova is the seventh planet populated since the first mass exodus just shy of 100 years ago to the Alpha Centauri system." Law scoffed at the impromptu history lesson. Unphased, IQ continued. "Our communications instruments have encountered everything a planet has to offer, from super-magnetic poles to eternal electrical storms and everything in between."

Charlie chimed in this time. "Well, yeah. IQ, but that doesn't make it–what did Jamie say the other day—infallible?" He looked at Law with a raised eyebrow. "Anyway, I go on CMR repair runs all the time. There's always some new issue that the engineers I shuttle encounter with all these new metals and materials we're using to boost our tech."

IQ shook off Charlie's rebuttal. "Yes, and how long does that typically take you, Charles? A matter of hours? A return trip or two, maybe? Surely, almost two years as it has been with the colony being in the dark with the Zoa?"

"Two years is a bit of an exaggeration," Law said with annoyance. "Plus, since it seems you're keeping score, I'm sure you know the protocol. They are always hesitant to share the details of their findings on any planet, much less here! Think about the gem rush on Tellathia One. Even the gold rush back on Earth. Scavengers are quick to show up and they will ravage the planet as soon as they think there is something of value."

"I would believe that, Mr. Everstorm if your father was still the man in charge in the Zoa," IQ said.

Law shifted in his seat, his eyes darting around IQ's face as if he had lost his place while reading a novel. IQ's reverence toward his father threw Law off.

"As I mentioned before, Lawrence. Your father was a great man to the colony. Conners was a puppet. Everyone knows your father and Rell ran things behind closed doors. Your father was his brain, while Rell was his fist." IQ declared before allowing a slight smirk to break. Charlie looked at Law as he scratched at his jaw.

"Okay, IQ..." Law relented. "What are you telling us?"

IQ waved his hands toward two chairs around his conference table, inviting Law and Charlie to sit. His voice noticeably lower. "I believe you are correct that something has been found deep in the Zoa's mountains, Mr. Everstorm. Something that Tiberius may already be sharing with a—third party."

"That's impossible!" Law exclaimed. It was one thing to imply that there were secretive or unsanctioned activities going on in the Zoa, especially since his father had gone missing. But to insinuate what felt like treason, facilitated by Tiberius for that matter, felt absurd. Even Charlie had some questions about this point.

"A third party? Like who? Scavs?" Charlie pressed. He was all too familiar with the scavengers. They roamed from planet to planet, claiming none to be their home as they traveled from solar system to solar system like parasites. They wait for the hard work to be done to find anything worth value before dropping in and taking what they could.

"Not so sure, Charles. My little *birds* have not been able to get close enough to find out whom. But what I do know is Tiberius has been doing a lot of *'scouting'* in the mountains by himself. Seems awfully below his pay grade, don't you think?"

"You've had someone following him?" Law asked. This time, his query was much less skeptical. It was becoming increasingly clear that the more IQ talked, the less Law wanted to be in a backroom in his hab. IQ himself was treading very dangerously on

"Not someone, Lawrence. Something." IQ fumbled between which CMP to tap on either of his arms before he settled on the one on his left.

A projection of a sleek drone rose from the holotable as lead lines sprouted from it, pinpointing different areas in the projection. He grabbed the projection and waved his CMP over Law and Charlie's, so a smaller version hovered over their arms.

"The latest in drone tech, gentlemen," IQ said, beaming at Law over the projection like a proud father monitoring their sleeping baby. "With some enhancements yours truly came up with."

"You really do get all the best toys!" Charlie said as he beamed. He expanded the projection to see some finer details, and Law did the same, reading each lead line. The drones were collapsible to the point where they could be stored in the port of one of the larger CMPs, like Jamie's. Because of their size, they were virtually untraceable.

"Does this say an invisibility projection?" Law asked, slightly blown away. He'd never seen anything like this technology before. He was sure that if Jamie had been there, she would have marveled at the possibilities. Though she would probably be less thrilled about the circumstances.

"Are you using the same sort of stealth tech they are adding to the omnijets?" Charlie asked as he looked over, trying to get to the line Law was reading.

"Experimental, actually. You probably won't see this on your jets for another five to eight years, Charles." IQ nodded with a smile as wide as his face would allow. Charlie was clearly impressed.

Law had to admit, he was impressed as well. Maybe not as much at the tech as Charlie was, but more so at IQ's ability to get things done. Get answers when he so desired and utilized the resources at his disposal to do so. Something Law wished he could do. Which reminded him.

"Ok, so you've been–spying on Ty, for what? What's in it for you?" Law asked.

"Well, Mr. Everstorm, it's something I think you would appreciate. I want answers. Our colony deserves them."

"Answers? To what? My father's death? I appreciate that, but you don't seem like the…" Law hesitated as not to offend the man. "…altruistic type."

IQ cackled. "You know Lawrence, I misjudged you. A man down to his business. I respect that. Although, I enjoyed much more freedom to learn things about our quests around the planet and discoveries there while your father was in charge. I have not had that leniency with Tiberius Jansen at the helm. Which is proving to be bad for business."

"And what business is that IQ?" Law asked.

"I'm in the business of acquisitions. I thought that was evident. In whatever form that may present itself. Sometimes information, sometimes materials, getting the things people need to them, through whatever channels present themselves," He answered with a slick smile on his face. Law had no interest in playing another of his word games. So, he pressed on.

"So, you think Tiberius is mixed up with some off-world buyers or scavs?" Law asked, trying to piece all the information together. "The unified criminal database is pretty extensive. If one of your drones picked up someone Ty was dealing with that he shouldn't be, I'm sure they'd be in there."

"Well, that's assuming I actually have my drone on the necessary networks. However, that is beside the point." IQ's index finger pointed as he turned to face them. "My drones cannot get close enough." His hand went to his head. He grabbed a tuft of hair, giving a slight tug to his jet-black curls. "Every time we're monitoring him at these secret rendezvouses, my drones get closer and closer. But just as they are getting close enough to provide any sort of useful audio or visual, they are knocked out." IQ sent his fist through his drone project and into the holotable, causing it to flicker slightly.

"How?" Charlie inquired. "From everything I can see, these babies are more durable than our omnijets. They should be able to withstand an EMP."

"Among other things," IQ agreed. "And we could detect that, Charles. EMP, ESD, or anything of the sort. Although," His voice trailed as he looked back toward the holotable.

"What is it?" Law pressed, as he felt like he was finally getting closer to answers.

IQ hesitated as he looked at Law from his periphery. He rocked back and forth slightly like he was holding something back. He eventually relented. "From what we've been able to tell, it's as if they're more affected by a CME."

Law struggled momentarily, feeling like he had heard the acronym before. "You mean a solar flare?" he finally asked.

"Exactly, a coronal mass ejection. At night—at every single instance." IQ arched a brow at them, studying their faces like a child trying to decide whether his parents were accepting his story.

"That doesn't make sense," Law said, after trying to comprehend what he had just heard. "If that's true, you're saying Tiberius, or whomever he's meeting with, has the power to create solar flares at will...at night?"

"Right!" IQ agreed with an almost manic laugh. "Trust me, the evidence looks as wild as it sounds. Regardless, I will not continue losing drones to whatever it is that's frying them over there, nor do I give up easily. Hence the attachment to my little babies here. I need to get this tech into the hands of my associates as soon as possible. I suspect the sooner I do, the sooner we'll figure out what your godfather has been up to. And even more importantly..." IQ paused and stared intently at Law. "We may even figure out what really happened to Mr. Maxwell Everstorm." IQ pursed his lips before dropping his gaze. He then double-tapped his CMP, making the drone projections dissolve back into the desk and away from Law and Charlie's CMPs. Law couldn't help but think about the possibility of having one of them at his disposal. Going to the Zoa would provide unlimited opportunities to get answers, with no ability to get them without being obvious.

"Which brings me to the end of what I know and my last order of business I need to discuss with Charles. I bid you well, Mr. Everstorm," IQ said, extending his hand to Law. Law accepted it, as he stared at Charlie, puzzled at what additional business he may have with IQ.

"Maybe your trip to the Zoa will yield more answers than my little babies ever could."

Law craned his neck, but he knew better than to question how IQ found out about his impending trip. He probably knew about it long before Law received the heads up from Charlie that a message was coming.

"Now if you will excuse us." IQ motioned toward the door.

Charlie merely nodded. Law knew this meant that it was best to let him handle it and that he would get him up to speed at a more appropriate time. Law returned a subtle nod and made for the door that opened prior. He didn't care for being dismissed so unceremoniously; however, Nahdine was waiting at the threshold, likely to escort him through the throngs of people that were in the living dome.

Nahdine wore the same pleasant smile as she turned to lead Law away. He complied and walked toward her. Just as he reached the threshold of IQ's office cube, Law stopped before exiting and turned back toward the room.

"Hey, IQ!" The man broke from his conversation with Charlie to look at Law. His best friend squinted his eyes and raised an eyebrow. Law inquired in a hushed tone as the door was open. "You think you would be willing to part with one of your new little babies?"

IQ's eyes brightened as his ears perked. "Ah, a man about his business indeed," IQ answered, still beaming at what he likely believed would be a good business opportunity.

"Well, my father taught me to stand on it whenever it was necessary," Law replied, his brows furrowed as he tried to portray his seriousness with the situation.

"I am able to part with anything, Mr. Everstorm. For the right price." IQ slowly left Charlie in his wake as he approached Law. "It just depends on what you're willing to pay." Now IQ's excitement melted away so that his business demeanor remained.

Law could make out Charlie in his peripheral, shaking his head. However, Law was locked in. He kept his eyes on IQs. It was time he started finding the answers he was after. Today's hunt was only an appetizer. The beast was awakened, and it was hungry. If he were going to get what he needed, it would be a lot easier if he had the right tools in his arsenal. One of those tools was one of IQ's stealth drones.

"Name your price. I'm down," Law said as he swallowed the lump that held instant regret at what he may be signing himself up for.

IQ drew back a little and dropped his chin, likely taken aback by the gall he did not register with Law. However, Law noticed him reset as he crossed his arms, raising one to twirl at his baby goatee.

"How about this, Mr. Everstorm? I think, to an extent, our interests align." IQ's tone suggested he was trying to convince himself of this point just as much as he was trying to convince Law. "So, I will do you one better. I'll grant you two of my drones. The price?" IQ stopped dead in his tracks to return his gaze to Law. "How about we say you'll...owe me a favor." Law drew back a bit. He knew the price would be more than he was willing to pay and his generosity was very likely not for Law's benefit as much as it was for his own. However, as far as favors go, how much could IQ really ask for? Yeah, he proved that he knows a lot more than most as far as the Zoa was concerned, regardless of how questionable the means. At the end of the day, he was just another gossiping inhabitant whose knowledge carried a little more weight than most. What could be the harm?

"Fine by me." Law held out his hand to shake.

IQ snatched it in his, shaking it vigorously before answering the last question he knew was on Law's mind. "My associates will take care of getting the drone to you prior to your trip. I suspect you'll want it ported with your sister's CMP-X as hers is larger and my drones require the higher model."

Law shook his head. At this point, IQ was showing off just how much he knew about what was going on in the colony.

"That will be just fine," Law said. IQ nodded, and they dropped hands. "Want me to wait for you up front, Charlie?"

Law asked more to gauge Charlie's thoughts on all that transpired more than to get his opinion of whether he should wait. He knew his best friend well enough that he tended to stumble over his words when he was uncomfortable or caught off guard with something. His answer, in this case, was precise.

"Sure. Shouldn't be more than five minutes. Right, IQ?" Charlie asked, nodding toward their host.

"Of course. Just a few more particulars, and then he'll be right out." IQ walked toward Charlie with his back turned to Law.

"Right this way, Lawrence," Nahdine chimed behind Law, surprising him in the process. He almost forgot she was standing at the door.

"Of course." Law followed her across the threshold of the cube door and back toward the living hab.

Either they walked more slowly this time or Law was too lost in thought to realize. He tried to recap all he had learned. Though the hope going in was to have more answers, he felt like he was left with more questions. For now, those questions would have to serve the dual role.

Law listed out what he left with after talking with IQ. Tiberius had more eyes on him than just admin. He's been going off the reservation on his own for unknown reasons. Lastly, there is a likelihood he's meeting with a third party. That piece of information was the most concerning.

Each of those points only offered several corresponding questions. Who else was watching Ty without his knowledge? How far off the reservation had he gone? Most importantly, though, who could this alleged *third party* be? And did this have anything to do with his father going missing? Law fought that thought. Tiberius would never. That was his dad's best friend. Maxell had trusted him with his life, with his kids.

It was merely speculation. The answers would come, and he just secured his first tool that would help in that endeavor. Jamie would have questions, but he would cross that bridge when he got there and—

"Lawrence," Nahdine said softly, pulling him from his reeling thoughts.

"Wait, what? I'm sorry," Law said, not realizing she was trying to get his attention.

"It's okay. I'm sure you had a lot on your mind. Typically, the people who meet with IQ do."

"Yeah. More or less," Law said as they reached the front door together. He stepped aside and held his hand out to let her go ahead of him.

"Such a gentleman, as always," Nahdine acknowledged before stepping outside of IQ's hab. Law followed closely before the hab door slid shut behind them.

The pair sat on the landing of the hab in silence for what felt to Law like an awkwardly long amount of time. He welcomed the fresh afternoon air into his lungs after having to walk back through the multi-colored smoke that polluted the hab's living dome.

"So, are you planning on attending the Landing Day festival this year?" Nahdine asked, breaking the ice. "I'm sure, like Charlie, you've secured a date and all?" All the time she had been to the hab, he had never noticed how alluring her eyes were. The midday sun gave the hazel in them a golden tinge. Law snapped his gaze to his feet.

"Oh yeah, I guess I didn't think about that." Law said. The Landing Day festivities were a yearly event, but he never really thought about asking for a date. He peeled his eyes from the pebble he was rolling around with the tip of his shoe back to Nahdine's almond-shaped eyes before her gaze dropped.

"Yeah, I'm so sorry Law. I'm sure you have so many other things on your mind. How are you?" Nahdine asked as she gazed at Law attentively.

"No, no! It's not that," Law said, stammering over his words. "I mean. I guess. Well, I haven't had time to find a date." He finally managed to get the words out. As he did, he noticed Nahdine perk up, though Law felt she tried to remain reverent. He continued, "But thank you. I'm getting better, I think." He only managed to say that part half-convincingly as he nodded. Nahdine stepped toward Law, getting almost close enough as if she were going to hug him. Instead, she grabbed his hand.

"And if you aren't. That's okay too. You're allowed to take all the time you need," she said as she held his gaze. Law studied her hazel eyes as she held his hand until the hab door slid open. Charlie volleyed his head between the two, looked at their hands, and then grinned as wide as he could.

Nahdine released Law's hand, giving him one last glance. "It was great talking with you, Law. Remember what I said. Now if you'll excuse me. Charles," she said as she walked toward the door to IQs hab. She turned, giving one final glance and a finger wave to Law before she backed into the hab and the door returned itself between them.

Law stared at the door for a moment, trying to ignore Charlie, staring a hole in the side of his head with the same grin he put on when he caught them holding hands.

"You going to wear that shit-eating grin the entire time?" Law finally said as he rolled his eyes before turning and walking away from IQ's hab.

"I may. It does wonders for my jawline." Charlie rubs his hand along his stubble as if to accentuate his point.

"Yeah, you've mentioned."

Charlie skipped beside Law as they walked back down the path. Law tried his best not to let Charlie get inside his head, but he had a way of getting Law to talk without saying a word. A smile crept onto Law's face. Charlie was winning. This was exactly how he did it. They continued down the path. Charlie bumped into Law and hummed a tune as he continued skipping. His gaze did not leave Law.

"You know, no one as big as you should be allowed to skip." Law tried to act more annoyed than amused.

"Everstorm, I will do this the entire way back to our habs and you know it. What did I witness after my meeting with IQ back there?"

"Nothing, we were just talking. She asked how I was doing with everything going on and if I...if I had a date to the Landing Party." Law tried to decide whether that really was what she was asking. Charlie stopped in his tracks.

"So? Did you ask her?" Charlie asked, his shoulders hunched, waiting for the answer in anticipation.

"Well, no. I told her I hadn't thought about it. Then she asked how I was, then you popped out of IQ's hab," Law said. Charlie threw his head back before running his fingers through his hair.

"Come on, man! She practically gave you an open invitation!" he said as the momentum for skipping died. Charlie trudged past Law, down the path like a sad puppy who had just been denied a treat. Law thought for a moment and realized Charlie was right. Why had he not asked Nahdine to be his date to the Landing Day festivities? Even a no would have been less costly than the ominous owing of a favor to the colony's underground kingpin. Which now that Law thought about it.

"Hey, Chuck! What *'business'* did you and IQ have to go over that was so secretive that I had to step out?" Law asked as he contemplated the scenarios. "He tells me he's been spying on Ty at the Zoa with his drones, but I have to leave so you two can talk business?"

"It's nothing, man. Like you found out with the guy, he's not the charitable type."

"Exactly!" Law said, now grabbing his friend by the shoulder. "Chuck, please tell me you didn't get mixed up in anything wild with him just to get some info for me." Law looked at his friend, wondering what he may have done.

"Nothing I can't handle, bro." Charlie slung his arm around Law's neck.

L aw walked through the door to his hab after parting ways with Charlie, who had promised his parents he would grab some supplies. Before dapping each other up into a hug, he made Law make a promise of his own; that he would send a comm to Nahdine and ask her to the Landing Day celebration.

"Nahdine," said Jamie, strolling into the living dome, causing Law's cheeks to flush.

"Huh, yeah, no, I'm going to," Law said, wondering why he let the words slip. Jamie looked up as a figure dissolved into her CMP.

"Going to what, Lawrence?" Jamie asked, her eyebrow raised as she stopped in her tracks.

"Um, nothing. I was talking to myself." This was enough for Jamie as it was not uncommon for Law to catch her doing the same thing on days she worked from the hab rather than going to Sci-Rez.

"Cool. I was waiting for you to return. You and Charlie are usually done with your workout by now."

"Well, we had a change of plans today. And I wanted to talk to you about it." Law was trying to navigate how he would re-approach the subject that ended icily the previous night.

"Good. You and Charlie must have talked. Our shuttle to The Zoa will leave Tuesday after things settle down from tomorrow's Landing Day celebration. Charlie will be commanding it, as Tiberius has requested." Jamie finished with her matter-of-fact tone as she handed him a mug of coffee and sat on the converticouch. Like a buoy bobbing in the sea, she left Law in her wake. Suddenly, he remembered her morning meeting with Vice Commander Rell.

"Hold on! What the heck happened with you and Rell?" Law demanded as he walked toward the armchair that was next to the converticouch.

"Last night you had all but convinced me we weren't going to suddenly turn a one-eighty to get my shit ready. The omnijet is up in 52 hours?" Law's frustration was unexpected to both himself and his sister as she eyed him for lashing out.

"Sorry, this whole mess is just. A lot J!" Law apologized, sipping his coffee. The roasted aroma of the castlenut centered him, likely as Jamie expected it would.

"I couldn't agree with you more, Law. At the end of the day, we must be on the same page if we're going to have a chance of getting through this unscathed." Jamie took a sip of her own coffee and leaned forward to rest her elbows on her knees, palming her coffee and letting the steam waft toward her nose. "You're right, talking to Rell changed my mind. But only a bit. It was more what you said last night that made me reconsider. Something doesn't smell right in the Zoa. It's nothing for me to question Tiberius' motives but for you..." Jamie ended with a quick backhand to Law's knee while adding a sarcastic look.

"Fair enough," Law agreed with a smirk.

"Before we get into my meeting with Rell, you said something about a change of plans with Charlie this morning?" Jamie asked.

Law went into the information they had learned from their meeting with IQ. How he followed Tiberius as well as the possibility of securing them their own drone. After hearing Law's recap, Jamie placed her mug on the coffee table as she analyzed the new information.

"Well, I'll give it to IQ. He really does have his finger on the pulse. Probably even more than Rell."

"Yeah, I said the same thing, before he dismissed me to talk only with Charlie."

Jamie's eyes narrowed. "Oh, what has Charlie gotten himself into?"

Law shrugged at what he was sure was a rhetorical question.

"Either way, IQ is certainly onto something, because Rell has all but recruited me to spy on Tiberius during our trip."

"And you agreed?" Law asked quickly, holding his hands up in defense when Jamie narrowed her gaze at him. "Put differently, we were going to spy on him anyway, but for our own agenda," Law finished.

"Well, *spy* feels a bit loaded for what we were going to do. We're just a brother and sister trying to respect their father's last wishes. In the interim, if we found answers, we found answers."

Law shook his head menacingly. "You know, you always have a way of framing things in a way that is a lot easier to digest. Did Rell select you be her new Vice Commander?" Law asked.

Jamie rolled her eyes. "Aurornova could be so lucky, Law." She grabbed her mug to take a quick swig before she returned it to its coaster. "Rell is convinced that Tiberius is off the reservation. IQ's insider information all but confirms that. It appears the people in his pocket are a lot more inconspicuous than the people Rell is using to keep tabs on Tiberius. Rell claims he can't get close enough because Tiberius smells his informants from a mile away."

"Why would that matter?" asked Law. "If people are being sent from command, doesn't Ty have to respect that?"

"In a manner of speaking," Jamie answered, jabbing a finger in Law's direction. "Doesn't mean he can't have them chasing their tails. "Rell wants me to keep tabs on Tiberius. She suspects he will let us get closer to him than he would anyone and let his guard down. Especially..." She paused.

"With me." Law finished.

"The two of you have always been close. And I have made it no secret that I am unhappy with him. So Rell was hoping anything he shares with you I would be privy to."

"She wanted you to spy on Tiberius *and* me," Law said with a scoff. His animosity for Rell using this opportunity for her own agenda grew.

"Basically," his sister acknowledged. "To which I told her to sit on a comet and spin."

Law's eyes widened. "Okay, sis!"

"Wipe that smirk off your face, Lawrence," Jamie said, smirking herself. "It's one thing to feed her information about Tiberius, but I wouldn't do that to you, little brother." Jamie ended by taking another push at Law's knee.

"Well, I appreciate that, sis, but you know I would tell you anything I found out. Like you said. We got to be on the same page." They nodded in solidarity as they both reached for their mugs simultaneously.

"What I don't get is why don't they just pull the plug and reel him in? They're the ones in charge, right?" Law asked.

"Well, there are a lot of things going on. Conners has decided to retire early. The planet will receive its largest migration since discovery almost directly after a *'seismic'* event. The same *event* took the life of who was supposed to be the colony's next commander, as well as twelve other souls. The Zoa isn't right around the corner," Jamie said.

Law agreed, though he enjoyed flying, especially when his best friend at the helm, he was not looking forward to the ten-hour trek across the planet.

"But most importantly..." Jamie said in a hushed tone that made Law look around as though someone had entered their hab he had not noticed. "Rell seemed to hold back a bit. Like she had more information than she was letting on. But she mentioned something about not wanting to push anyone into hiding." Jamie's eyes continued to scan the room for some invisible intruder Law had not yet placed.

"Hiding who? Tiberius?" Law asked, confused by the notion.

"That's what I thought at first until you just told me IQ believes Tiberius is having these secret meetings with some third party," Jamie whispered

"Which would explain why she's not trying to haul his ass back here and make him answer for everything that's happened," Law said before he lurched back into the armchair.

"That's not all. When I was walking up to her wing in Admin, she had multiple projections up of the site of the geologic event. It was flagged similarly to how we saw it on the dailies we watched the morning we got news of Dad."

"Ok?" Law said, more of a question for her to keep going and leaned forward.

"They cleared everything just as I had walked in, but I'm pretty sure I saw something a bit different from what we saw on the dailies."

"Like what?" Law asked, trying to think of ways to help her recollect what she saw.

"It would be better if I showed you," Jamie said. A mischievous smirk crawled across her face as she tapped the sides of her clear spectacles with her index and middle fingers.

Law was astonished. "You didn't!"

Jamie merely nodded to acknowledge her brother had surmised exactly what she had done. "I was able to snap it with my glasses," said Jamie as she was already up, making her way to the holotable. "It also helps that before I left, Rell had my pad upgraded with the latest encryption software. It allows me to securely transmit information directly to her that would be unbreakable and untraceable at the Zoa. The drawback for her, it also makes my personal files more secure, and it also protects my personal files from prying eyes. Including the files, I snap with my glasses." Jamie sat her CMP on the holotable to get the projection to rise. The projection that had been featured on the daily news going over the event that took their father was now hovering in front of their eyes.

"You notice something different about this?" Jamie asked, ignoring the projection and staring squarely at Law, egging him on to find the hidden clue. Law squinted, trying to see what he was missing and recall what he had seen over a year ago.

"I mean, it's been a bit J. It looks pretty much like what they showed on the daily." Law continued to study the projection while Jamie said nothing. Just as he was about to give up and request her assistance, it came back to him.

"Wait..." Law said as he grabbed the projection on both sides and flipped it over before widening his hands to expand it. "Are these tunnels?"

"Yes! Those were most definitely not in what they showed us in the dailies the day of the incident!"

"Well, why would they leave those out?" Law asked.

"That's the question. Why leave what would seem to be such a trivial thing out? What are those tunnels being used for? The questions are endless when you withhold answers."

"So, Rell is holding back and asks you to spy on Tiberius. Is anyone going to be straight with us and tell us what the fuck happened to our father!" Law shouted as he slammed his fist on the holotable as he pushed to his feet. The projection fizzled before reconstituting.

"Law, it's frustrating. I know, but we are getting somewhere. We know more than we knew last night. We at least have somewhere to start now." She pointed toward the projection while her other hand was on Law's shoulder, gently massaging it. "The only thing that matters now is how far we're willing to go to get the answers we need."

"However far we need," Law said without hesitation. Jamie nodded as she heard exactly what she wanted to hear. "We've got Charlie with us too, and some tools to start." Law updated his sister on the details of IQ's drone he secured and the ominous favor that was requested in return. Jamie's nose wrinkled. Law was indebted to IQ now, and it was her pad that would be needed to integrate with what he considered 'contraband', but they both agreed that was a bridge they would cross when they got to it together.

Jamie discontinued the projection of the site map and catacombs. They both finished their coffee together before Jamie grabbed the remaining gozooberry muffins from the morning for the two of them to finish. After a few moments of silence and savoring, Jamie spoke.

"So, are you all set for Landing Day Celebrations?" she asked before popping the last bite of her muffin into her mouth.

Law hesitated. "Yeah, I guess. I mean, it will be all of us at a table together. Charlie will sit at ours this year instead of his normal bouncing between ours and his parents'."

"Well, you know, I'll be presenting this year. The flower I was presenting when you and Charlie came to Sci-Rez! So, I'll be seated at the stage, but will join you once the presentation is over."

"Right! No, I remember. Congrats again. I really meant what I said earlier. Mom and Dad would be really proud of you."

Jamie pursed her lips into a smile. Law did the same before his gaze fell to his empty mug as he massaged the sides with his thumbs.

"Good thing you'll have Nahdine to keep you company until I get done." Jamie's acknowledging smile morphed into a mischievous one. While Law stared at her, his jaw hanging open.

"Yeah, Charlie commed me after your meeting with IQ apparently and filled me in. He told me I needed to 'school my boy on your friend'," Jamie said, reading from her CMP with an eye roll to end it. Law dropped his head back.

"I swear I'm going to kill him. We'll just walk to the Zoa." Law massaged his temples.

"Well, before you doom us to an eight-year walking journey," Jamie said, unsuccessfully holding back a laugh at Law's dramatics. "In his defense, she commed me right after he did, asking if you were going with anyone to the celebrations."

Law immediately stopped massaging the sides of his head and looked up. "What did you tell her?" Law asked, his voice breaking a little bit as he tried to shift it back to a more calm and composed tone.

"I told her I didn't think you were but would ask."

"Well, I'm not, I just..."

"Didn't think about it," Jamie said, finishing his sentence. "I know. That would make both of us. I've been so focused on this presentation for weeks, which really has just been a distraction from thinking about Dad."

"So, you don't have a date either?" Law asked, though he knew the answer.

"No, just third-wheeling with the Minas. He and his husband, of course, wanted me to come over and have a celebratory drink with them for my promotion. They asked if you and Charlie wanted to join as well. I told them we could do so again after the presentation. I'm sure Charles will be preoccupied with his date." Jamie said. Law caught the eye-roll Jamie tried to hold back at the end.

"Anyhow, that doesn't matter," she said, snapping the subject back to him. "I'm done talking to you about this. What you're going to do is you're going to take this..." She placed two fingers on her CMP that she had pointed in his direction and slid them from bottom to top. Law raised his wrist and checked his CMP. It lit up with the notification.

"Nguyen, Nahdine communication code acquired and saved," the robotic voice said.

Jamie smirked at Law, who shifted his weight uncomfortably. "And you're going to comm Nahdine and ask her to be your date to the celebrations." Jamie stood and walked toward her box.

"How do you know I even want to go with her?" Law asked after his sister, not in the least bit seriously.

"Please, I've seen the way you look at her when she comes over. And suddenly, you got all this stuff you need to be doing in the living dome when she's here." Jamie sucked her teeth. "Plus," She stopped and looked at Law. "I see how she looks at you." Jamie smiled, then continued down the hall to her cube before the door slid open and then shut behind her, leaving Law alone in the stillness of the living dome at night.

L aw laid in his bed with his arm raised in front of his face, staring at the comm code for Nahdine. The green *start comm* button pulsed in the bottom right corner of the screen. He made multiple attempts at tapping, but he couldn't commit. His thumb tapped at the idle space on the screen as the CMP shook from his trembling grip. Law took one last deep breath and tapped the connect button.

The CMP chimed as it waited for the receiver from the other side. Just as the third chime ended, Law moved his finger toward the red disconnect button until it disappeared, replaced by the smiling face of Nahdine. The words that followed were jovial.

"Hello, Lawrence!" Nahdine said as she beamed through the screen. Law dropped the screen on his chest before scrambling to sit more upright and appear a little less than the devil may care. He scratched at his high-top to even it back out from lying on his bed for so long contemplating this comm.

"Sorry, sorry," Law said, pushing himself to his elbows to get to a good position. "I, uh, didn't expect you to answer. Um, I mean, I figured you might be busy or something. Um, Hi." Law felt his cheeks flush.

Nahdine giggled, half covering her mouth. Law let out a small laugh at the sound of hers. It put him at ease as the lump in his chest melted away, allowing it to rise a bit with added confidence.

"It was nice seeing you today," Law said smoothly. A soft pink painted Nahdine's cheeks.

"It was nice seeing you, too. So many people come and go from IQ's hab. It's nice to see a friendly face every once in a while."

"So, you're at IQ's a lot?" Law asked. He almost regretted doing so, because he was unsure why he asked. He felt heat creeping up the back of his neck.

"Occasionally. I'm sure you noticed he has a lot going on. Different business dealings and other things. He likes the help and is generous with his U-creds. Plus, he's my cousin," Nahdine said with a shrug.

Law's brows furrowed, having not made the connection between the two. She nodded while smiling as she watched him put the pieces together.

"What brought you to IQ's? I mean, I've seen Charlie there a few times, but I'm pretty sure that was your first, given how surprised you were looking around."

Law scrambled to come up with something that did not sound too suspicious. He figured if IQ had not told her what he was there for, it probably wasn't in his best interest to do so.

"I had heard about the drones he was testing out. I wanted to see if I could get my hands on one," Law said. He tilted the CMP down a bit and tapped his forehead with the brunt of his hand. Was that the best he could come up with? He lifted the CMP back up.

"Excuse me, had to sneeze," he said, knowing the CMP auto-mutes when it doesn't detect a face. Why couldn't he have been that quick to come up with a reason he was at IQ's? Law shook it off and continued. "So, I know it's late and I don't want to keep you. And I know it's last minute, but I was wondering if maybe you would do me the honor of going to the Landing Day Celebration with me?" Law couldn't hold back the audible sigh that followed getting the question out. At that point, regardless of whether she said yes or no, he would count that as a win.

"Of course I will, Lawrence," Nahdine excitedly responded. "If you weren't going to ask me, I would have just asked you, anyway. I was giving you the benefit of the doubt since you called me for the first time since I've known you."

Law was clearly losing his ability to control his body as he let a smile spread across his face. He liked her boldness. It was softened yet made clear it could be defiant.

"You know, I don't doubt that in the least bit," he replied. The two share a moment, staring at each other before Law took the initiative not to be upstaged by his date.

"So, I'll come by your place by 20:30 and we can walk together to Sci-Rez, maybe take a detour or two to talk a bit?" He had no idea what the detour would be or what they would talk about, but he let his brain go on autopilot to see where it got him.

"That sounds lovely, Law," Nahdine said softly. They let a quiet moment pass once again before Law wrapped things up while he was ahead.

"Cool. Well, like I said, I didn't want to keep you up too late. And now, I've got to spend the rest of the night planning the best way to impress you." He hoped a charismatic end was the way to go.

"I don't think you will need long. You've done just fine so far, Law." Nahdine giggled. "I'll see you tomorrow."

"C'nolo, Nahdine!"

"C'nolo!"

Law waited and let Nahdine end the transmission before dropping his CMP to his chest. His heart raced and he let it. It felt good. A smile stretched across his face in triumph. It had been a long time since he had felt this good, and for the first time in almost a year, he didn't feel guilty about it.

"Computer, ambient lighting," Law requested as he stared at the ceiling of his cube. His heartbeat slowed as he rode the triumphant feeling to sleep.

The first half of Sunday was all but non-existent to Law as he was now making his way several hamlets north to meet Nahdine at her hab. He awoke that morning to a frantic sister who was going back and forth between projections on the holotable and her CMP to prepare for her presentation this evening. It didn't take long, witnessing her in her that state, before Law sprang into action, trying to alleviate whatever pressure he could. Once the coffee brewed and he could scramble a few eggs and get some toast for her, Jamie centered herself and took a breath.

She also used the moment to congratulate Law on a job well done. Apparently Nahdine had commed her first thing that morning to listen to her practice her presentation, only after they shared the tea of Nahdine's conversation last night.

Law turned down the path his CMP indicated would lead him to Nahdine's hab. His heart beat a bit faster as he scanned the hab indicators looking for number forty-nine in the big black letters beside the door.

He was two habs away.

Law stopped at the head of the path to Nahdine's hab and slipped his hand in the inside pocket of his blazer for his pick. Raising it to his hair, he picked his hair to get a nice even fluff before sticking it back in his coat pocket. Taking a deep breath, he continued down the path. Law reached the door and pressed the chime before snapping his arm back to his side and standing as tall as he could.

In his other hand, he held a beautiful bouquet of night-lanterns that he had scooped from the meadows just outside of the settlement's walls. As the sun dipped in the sky, the night-lanterns prematurely started transforming from the bold navy flowers that stood tall amongst the Aurornovan grasslands. On nights with a full moon, they went from navy to a brilliant white shade. At full strength, they would glow in the light of the moon. Law did not have to wait long before he heard a beep and the door slid aside, revealing Nahdine's mother, the colony's chief constable.

"Good evening, Mr. Everstorm," she said, with an intense stare. Her voice was stern and matter-of-fact, as you would expect the chief of order within a colony of almost 2,000.

"Good evening, Chief Nguyen." Law swallowed the lump in his throat. He did not expect to be greeted by anyone besides Nahdine. "I'm here to pick up your daughter." The chief inspected Law, before her eyes landed on the bouquet of night-lanterns. The crack of a smile etched across her stone face.

"Night-lanterns. Good choice. A prepared man like your father." She gave a slight nod. The lump Law just forced down manifested itself differently, as it choked him up a bit this time. He appreciated the compliment and wanted to reciprocate in some manner. He thought quickly.

"I try to be, ma'am." Law removed one of the night-lanterns and handed the rest of the bouquet to the chief. "For you." He stretched his arm toward the chief, catching her off guard. Her eyes bounced between the flowers and Law. To his luck, the sun had set. The flowers glowed one by one, casting an iridescent luminosity between them. The chief's smile was now a crevice as she accepted the bouquet just before Nahdine appeared into the hab's door frame. She witnessed the exchange with glee in her eyes.

Law didn't miss a beat.

After he released the flowers, he handed the remaining one he had plucked to Nahdine. Like a wingman understanding the assignment, it lit up the moment it left his fingertips. Nahdine held it to her nose and inhaled. Her face illuminated while her eyes closed as she savored the aroma.

"Thank you, Lawrence," she said. Nahdine wrapped the night-lantern's stem around her index finger before brushing back her midnight-colored mane and placing it behind her ear. Law beamed as he looked at her. The night-lantern was the north star to the midnight blue sky of her dress. As if it sensed its newfound purpose, the flower continued to stretch its petals as it glowed brighter at its new station, holding back Nahdine's flowing hair as it did.

"Gorgeous," Law said under his breath. To his surprise, he said it loud enough for Nahdine to hear. Looking at him softly, she shifted her dress at the hips a bit before wishing her mother goodnight.

"See you at the celebration, Mom!" Nahdine said before placing a kiss softly on her mother's cheek. The chief still eyed Law, but with a softness in her eyes as she smiled.

"You two have a lovely night. Thank you again, Mr. Everstorm." She said as she gave the bouquet an additional whiff before walking back into their hab. Nahdine stepped out, joining Law in the crisp evening breeze. He offered his arm, which Nahdine gladly accepted, wrapping her arm around his and nuzzling in closely before they set off.

Landing Day was Aurornova's premier event, marking the day that the first colonists landed on the planet in 2234. This year would be the

10th Landing Day celebration for the planet and from what Law was gathering, its biggest. If the circumstances were different, it would have been a momentous day for the Everstorm family, marking the day its two progeny had reached the end of their studies and, like many others, would decide their next steps into adulthood. Each year, Law would watch as young men and women before him would announce their intentions to move to other planets, take up jobs here or in the Zoa, or blaze their own trails. Would Law have known what he wanted to do if his father was still here?

"I love seeing everyone get dressed up for today. Everyone's so excited and lovely," Nahdine said. She looked side to side as they walked toward Sci-Rez. Law joined her, scanning the habs they passed. People were standing outside of their domes in their best dress. Parents were leaving instructions for sitters while kissing their young children goodnight. The closer the two got to Sci-Rez, the more crowded the path became until they joined the procession of people working their way to their shared destination. Before they turned to the main path toward Sci-Rez, Charlie waved toward them with two attractive women at his side. One looked up at him, while the other stood next to the first with her arms crossed and a rather smug look.

"Law! Nahdine!" Charlie exclaimed as the pair arrived. Charlie pulled Law in close. "Dude, she looks amazing! Well done." Charlie stepped back and held Law at arm's length. "Actually, you clean up pretty nice yourself, young man." Charlie finished with a laugh before letting Law go and giving him a few brush swipes at his formal suit.

"You don't look so bad yourself, chief," Law joked as he returned the favor of brushing at his jet-black dinner jacket, stopping to straighten Charlie's bowtie.

"Nice to see you again, Charles," Nahdine said from beside Law.

"Likewise, ma'am! Especially since you got this guy out of the hab." Charlie nudged Law, knocking him off balance. "Let me introduce you to my *date*. Jora, this is my protégé Law Everstorm, and his date the incomparable Nahdine Nguyen.”

“Pleasure to meet you,” Nahdine said, extending her hand to shake. Law followed suit.

“Nice to meet you both,” Jora replied. Law looked at the other woman standing next to Jora before looking at Charlie. He began jerking his neck in her direction, waiting for Charlie to get the hint. Jora acted instead.

“This is my friend Amoret. She’s joining us.” Her friend rolled her eyes, raising her hand in a half-hearted wave.

“Charmed,” Nahdine said, her face scrunched, looking at Law from the side. Appreciating seeing eye to eye on Jora’s lackluster greeting, Law and Nahdine exchanged smiles before the five strolled off toward Sci-Rez together.

The short distance to Sci-Rez was spent with interwoven conversation among the group. Law had learned of Charlie’s dilemma with his date’s third-wheeling companion. Charlie had not made it clear to Jora that it was Amoret he was after when approaching them only three days prior while grabbing lunch in Sci-Rez and approaching them in the courtyard. Law could resist the urge to tease Charlie on this point.

“Are you sure you weren’t doing that lip pucker thing like you do when you’re drinking one of your protein shakes?” Law inquired, doing his best Charlie impression of sucking on a straw with his eyes squinted. “Shut it, Storm!”

Law laughed at his best friend’s expense. “Yup, that had to be it!”

“Would you cut it out?” Charlie finally relented with a laugh before landing a well-placed elbow to Law’s rib cage. He hugged his side, struggling between laughing and coughing as he massaged the impact point. The ruckus caught Nahdine’s attention as she continued the conversation with Charlie’s date while looking over at the boys with a raised brow. Law straightened up and offered his arm back to his date, which she gladly accepted before continuing her conversation.

Charlie made his way back to his date's side. Accepting his current situation, he offered Jora his outside arm. He tried to break through her shell with conversation as Nahdine and Amoret conversed in the middle, trying to decipher where they had crossed paths. From what Law could make out, she had frequented IQ's hab on the weekends when he hosted his infamous hab parties almost weekly.

Reaching Sci-Rez, they found a place in the queue leading into the main entrance. The line of Aurornovans wound its way down the path to the main entrance about fifty meters from the front doors. Attendees mingled as they stood in line. White coats of scientists covered tuxedos and evening gowns to not forgo an opportunity to tout their status. While others wore their evening best on full display. Though the colony was small by many standards, the planet had grown rapidly over the last few years. Over the last few years, Law recalled the lines much shorter and the names and faces of people easier to track.

"You remember the line being this long last year, Chuck?" Law asked as he continued to scan the inhabitants, chatting and laughing amongst themselves.

"I think it maybe took like ten minutes tops." Charlie shrugged.

"Last year was the biggest migration Aurornova has seen since we first inhabited the planet," Nahdine said. "Based on what your sister said while practicing her presentation, this year's migration will be almost three times as large. Aurornova is growing faster than any colonized planet before it. Partly thanks to the beauty of our planet, but mostly thanks to the work your father and Tiberius have done in the Zoa." Law thought about the morning his father left for the last time. He and Jamie accompanied their father to Huey One, as they typically did. This would be his longest trip away to the Zoa. He never stayed for more than a week at a time. Tiberius would stay for months, while their father would return to discuss their findings with admin, bring back samples, and present data. This time, however, he would be gone for a month as well.

"I'll be back on the fourth son. Then let's talk about those post studies plans," Maxwell said, with a hand on his shoulder and a reassuring smile.

"Why, again, will you be gone so long this time Dad?" Law asked. Jamie answered for him.

"He and Ty are on the brink of what may be a huge discovery, not just for Fort Kelly, but for every inhabited planet back to Earth!" There was so much excitement in her voice.

"Easy there, Jamie," Dad said in a hushed tone, his lips ticking up in amusement. "Jamie is right. Ty and I believe we're on the brink of something pretty big. Something we'd like to get figured out by Landing Day. This could be a pretty big find for a lot of people and a lot of planets. I can't wait to tell you both all about it." Their father held his arms out, inviting them in for a hug, holding them a little longer than usual. Law watched as his father walked off, Jamie nuzzling herself under Law's arms. He wrapped them around his sister to comfort her as well as himself. As Maxwell crossed into the belly of the omnijet, steam blasted out of the arms that pulled the ramp to a shut behind them.

"It'll be no time, right?" Jamie said, her eyes not leaving the spot on the ramp where the silhouette of their father likely remained. Law chose not to answer. He merely squeezed his sister and rested his cheek on her head, before planting a kiss at the crown of her forest of locs.

"Look! Here they come!" a member of the group just ahead of Law's shouted. The attendants handling check-in pause waving their CMPs and look toward the sky. Law followed suit, as did Charlie and his *dates*.

Nahdine squeezed Law's hand and pointed. Three omnitransports momentarily blotted out the sun. Omnitransports were behemoths. They were ten times the size of omnijets and could carry enough people to fill multiple colonies across several planets. In years past, Aurornova had only been visited by a single omnitransport carrying a handful of people, with the rest being materials, supplies, food, minerals, and livestock. This year was the first time since the colony had existed that there was more than one transport, let alone three.

"I hear that there will be over seven hundred new colonists joining us today," Nahdine said to Law as he watched the transports lower, disappearing one by one behind the Admin building to offload their passengers. Aurornova appeared to be the latest appeal to off-worlders. Law wondered what all the planet held that were so appealing other than being new. Perhaps he would have had a better idea during his visit to the Zoa.

"Hold up your CMPs," an attendant ordered gruffly. Two of his team members awaited Law and his friends to comply.

Law raised his wrist, prompting the lead attendant to wave a detached CMP over Law's wrist unit. It chimed as the rim glowed green on his wrist. Immediately after, the CMP screen displayed a list of food selection details and seating arrangements. This year they were placed at table five, with Charlie and his dates, and two other couples. One couple was from Law's primary studies cohort. He didn't recognize the others.

In years past, the table was filled by Law, Jamie, Charlie, an impromptu date of Charlie's in some cases, and Charlie's parents. Tonight, his parents opted to join some of their friends in the absence of Tiberius and Maxwell. The one absence that was bittersweet for Law this year was Jamie's. Since she would be a presenter, she would be at one of the designated tables with Mina and his husband, as well as other presenters and their significant others. At the time Jamie mentioned this, Law thought nothing of it, but now, not seeing her name beside his at their table, felt heavy.

He was undoubtedly proud of his sister and all that she was accomplishing within the science core. She was brilliant and seeing her success often prompted him to take initiative. Their father often joked this was because of a twin rivalry they kindled, but Law disagreed. He never wanted to be better 'than' only greater 'with'. This time was different, though. With everything going on and with their father and Tiberius gone, he felt a bit neglected.

"Let's go, bro. First round's on me!" Charlie said, swinging his arm around Law as his dates struggled to daisy chain on his arm on the way in. Nahdine giggled at Charlie's enthusiasm and hastily grabbed Law's arm before she missed her chance.

T he atrium of Sci-Rez was a muted clone of itself compared to the usual hustle and bustle. Almost a hive at rest. Rather than the high-energy buzz that was normal for the building's center, it was more of a melodic hum. Servers held trays of champagne-filled flutes, dodging guests and weaving between tables to deliver orders.

The translucent domed ceiling put Aurornova's night sky on full display, allowing the aurora to shine through and dance its way across the tables and floor. Banners and streamers of navy blues, greens, and golds that twisted around the atrium helped transform it from a cold and productive workplace to a warm and festive court accompanied by murals of Fort Kelly's evolution, The Zoa's operations center, and Commanders past and present.

"They have really outdone themselves!" Nahdine said as she marveled at the décor.

"They really have," Law agreed, continuing toward the center of the atrium, eyeing his CMP as he led his date and friends toward their table.

"Oh, look! It's Jamie." Nahdine pointed toward a table near the stage. Law could make out his sister sitting between Dr. Mina and another scientist who appeared to be having a spirited debate, of which Jamie was mediating.

The group arrived at their table and Law pulled Nahdine's chair out, guiding her into it with his hand on the small of her back.

"Such a gentlemen," Nahdine acknowledged, as she gladly accepted. Law felt his ears flush as he forced a more muted smile than what his cheeks wanted to allow. He looked across the table. Charlie was doing the same for his date before forcibly sitting down and eyeing their third wheel contemptuously. She returned the glare in kind and pulled out her own chair, plopping into it with her arms crossed and a humph.

Law chuckled under his breath. Charlie always had a way of making things more complicated for himself. Especially when it came to women. Scanning the room, he noticed several of his cohort mates and those who went before him. Noticeably, though a number were gone, entire families in some cases. This was not an uncommon phenomenon once someone had reached their nineteenth year on the planet. This was when each new adult made one of the most pivotal decisions of their life.

Do they stay on Aurornova and choose a role, or do they leave for another planet, such as Tellathia II, Proxima, or even Earth?

For Charlie, a year ago, he immediately joined the exploratory core as a pilot. Which was not a stretch, as he was rebuilding omnijets from the inside out when he was almost sixteen. And now Jamie was already anointed a Senior Scientist days before today's celebration.

Was Law making things more complicated for himself, too? Should he just join the exploratory core with Charlie? What if he stayed in the Zoa with Ty and found a way to continue his father's work with him? Ty said he wanted to talk about post-studies plans. What did he have in mind? A gentle squeeze on his bicep pulled Law from his spiraling thoughts.

"Charlie's getting you an ale, I hope that's okay," Nahdine said. She eyed Law as if she had noticed him returning from a trance.

"Yeah, no, that's great. Thanks!" Law answered, half understanding and still half considering Ty's request. "What did you get?"

"I got the same. It sounded nice and I'm all for trying new things," Nahdine answered with a pleasant smile. Law was happy he asked her to be his date to the celebration. She had a way of being present, something Law clearly struggled with lately. He found himself staring at her as she was still taking in the atrium while they sat. Her eyes traced the room's perimeter until they landed back at Law's. He delighted in the moment until Charlie returned with their beverages and his own.

"Two ales as ordered." He handed each of them a pint before offering his hand to cheers. Law and Nahdine complied before they all took a deep swig.

"Be right back," Charlie started, looking bemused, "My date has requested I take her on a stroll through the promenade." He finished with a wince before backing away, mouthing the words, *save me*, as he retreated. Law gave a sympathetic smile. Nahdine giggled as she watched him stalk off before taking a sip of her beer.

"Something tells me this is not an uncommon, um, problem for Charlie."

"Yeah, not uncommon at all." Law laughed, sipping his beer, letting the hop-filled citrusy taste flood his mouth. A welcomed sensation that almost felt like it signaled the beginning of the festivities. "You want to see if we can catch up with Jamie?"

"Yes!" Nahdine said enthusiastically. "I hope she is not getting nervous about her presentation. She rehearsed it so many times."

"I'm sure. I've heard it a couple of times myself. I'm pretty sure I could point out a few facts about that flower if I tried," Law teased. The pair shared a laugh and then made their way toward the stage. As they dodged guests and servers and weaved their way around tables, Law could not help but notice the number of people staring. It had not occurred to him how many people he had not encountered since the accident. Perhaps he had not paid close enough attention, but now it was on full display. The looks of sympathy, the whispering as their eyes trailed him passing by. One gentleman gave a firm nod with lips pursed as though he was surprised to see Law at the celebration.

"You okay, Lawrence?" Law barely heard Nahdine ask as he looked up. He looked up into her soft concerned eyes.

"Oh, yeah." He cleared his throat. "Everyone's been staring at how beautiful you are in that dress." Law painted a sly smile on his face, hoping the deflection was sufficient, regardless of why they were staring. She looked amazing. Nahdine smiled and grabbed Law's hand, leading him further through the crowd.

"I think I see Jamie up ahead," she said as she pointed. Jamie must have had the same idea to come find them as she was walking in their direction. She held her CMP in front of her as she approached. It was impressive she had not bumped into anyone at this point.

Jamie snaked around the tables and the people in between them, as she eyed her pad. Law could just make out her alternating between mumbling words to herself and chewing on the inside of her cheek. By the time they were moments away from colliding, Law called out for Jamie.

"Hey, J," he said, not able to get her attention as she plowed forward. "Jamie, look up!" Law finally half shouted toward her. Startled, Jamie's eyes darted away from the keyboard and haphazardly toward where she thought she heard her name. Jamie's glasses fell down her face from atop her head as she was walking, barely being caught by the tip of her nose.

"Hey guys!" Jamie said. As she drew closer, she outstretched her arms and Nahdine did the same. Law caught the high-pitched squeals from each woman as they came into a full embrace. He rolled his eyes and returned to studying the tips of his shoes while they conducted an impromptu catch-up. They wrapped up their discussion as Jamie looked toward Law again with a raised brow.

"He brought a bouquet for your mother, you say?" Jamie scrunched her face and studied Law up and down as if she didn't know him. Nahdine looked at Law with her usual glow, folded her arms, and nodded.

"Sure did. Even grabbed a few for you too, sis," Law lied but made a mental note to grab a few on the way back to the hab later that night. Walking up to Jamie, he leaned in for a quick kiss on the cheek. "How you feeling? Ready for the big presentation?" His sister winced at the question and began chewing her cheek again. He threw an arm around her and quietly said, "You got this. If nothing else, at the end of the night, if Dad were here, he'd be sitting in the front row doing that thing he does."

"Muttering my presentation line by line under his breath," Jamie said with a soft laugh before they both mimicked their father with their chins held high, pretending to mumble gibberish. Jamie added a bit of flare by intensifying her gaze and pointing her index finger at her bottom lip. It was not exactly the pep talk their father would have given her, but Law noticed she was no longer chewing on the inside of her cheek. Perhaps that was good enough. Jamie solidified the point when she took Law's ale from him and took a large swig. She offered no sign that she would return it.

"Hey guys!" Charlie said with a huff as he rejoined the group. He then stood at attention and gave a crisp salute to Jamie. "Senior Scientist, Everstorm. Pleased to be in your presence."

"Thank you, Charles," Jamie replied, bemused by his theatrics. "I seemed to notice you had not one but two dates tonight?" She did not take her eyes off Charlie as she took another deep draw of Law's ale.

"Well, you see," Charlie stumbled. "What had happened was...well it was a misunderstanding, really." Charlie frantically scratched at the top of his head as if he wished to ignite a fire amongst his red curls. Jamie continued to stare daggers in his direction. Charlie stared at Law for a lifeline while Nahdine looked back and forth between the two. Law steered the conversation down more productive avenues.

"They've really gone all out this year, don't you think Jamie?" Law asked. Nahdine stared at Law quizzically for the jarring redirection. All Law could do was offer a quick shrug toward her for his odd attempt. Jamie, still staring at Charlie, who had scanned the room with his glass to his lips as if he had just walked into the celebration moments ago and not what had been over an hour with Law and the rest of their entourage. Jamie kept her eyes locked on him until the very last moment before allowing them to follow her head. "Yes, it is all aimed at celebrating Commander Conners,"

"Really?" Law was shocked. "I mean, I get it, but it isn't like he's out of here tomorrow. He's supposed to continue through the summer, possibly the end of the year even, right?"

"That's just it. He is out of here tomorrow," Jamie said in a more hushed tone.

"What?" Charlie exclaimed. Law's eyes grew as he stared at his sister.

"Since when?" Law asked, a little louder than he intended. Jamie's brows furrowed as she glared at him for his indiscreetness. Law dropped his head and moved in closer, with Nahdine and Charlie on his heels. Jamie continued in even lower tones now that the group was in a small bunch around her.

"I don't know. It must have been something that was kept close until just this morning." Jamie paused as she waved off a server holding shrimp-like cocktails. In this case, the morsels were a bit larger and blue. Charlie groans after unsuccessfully trying to get the server back to grab one. "Trust me, Charles, they're not that great. Anyway. Rell was the one who addressed all of us prior to the celebration while Conners stood idly by. It gave the impression that she was in charge now and going forward. She never came out and directly said it, nor did he, but there was a lot of thanking him for his service, reminiscing, and jokes about him playing more halo golf."

"That's going to be a problem, don't you think, Law?" Charlie asked.

"Not necessarily. She was already sticking her hands into things, asking Jamie to spy."

"Wait, what?" Charlie threw his hands up. Law waved him off, intending to fill him in later. Raising his fingers to his chin, he tried to decide what advantage it may add if any, but gained nothing.

"Let's archive that for now. If she was going to shut anything down or rearrange things, she would have by now. Let's see where it goes. It helps that we have an ace in the hole following our meeting with IQ." Law remembered the sub-network installation for Jamie's pad that would help keep Rell and admin's noses from getting too far into their business.

"Yeah, one of IQ's goons is one of the servers. He brought it to our table with a stack of napkins," Jamie said, patting the pad that was attached to her hip. "I haven't had a chance to go through it yet. He had the instructions written on one of the napkins." She discreetly handed it to Law. He unfolded to reveal a list of instructions covering the entirety of the fabric. "You're going to have to decipher all that," Jamie finished as she scratched her brow. Law refolded the napkin and put it in one of the inside pockets of his dinner jacket. The group continued their conversation.

"Attendees, please make your way to your seats. The presentation will begin momentarily." Everyone in the atrium looked up as if they were searching for the source of the disembodied voice. A holographic countdown appeared above the stage, starting its two-minute descent. The group acknowledged the instructions and parted ways.

"Good luck with your presentation, Jamie! I'll be over to watch as soon as the Commander is done with the keynote," Nahdine said cheerfully.

"Thanks, Deeny!" The two shared an embrace. Law walked up and kissed his sister on the forehead. Staring into her hazel eyes—his mother's eyes—he smiled and nodded. Jamie nodded in return and walked back toward the stage while he, Nahdine, and Charlie returned to their table.

The lights in Sci-Rez's atrium dimmed to where only the aurora provided lighting, aside from the ones that highlighted the stage. As the zeros from the countdown dissolved, Commander Conners ascended the stairs.

"Good evening, Aurornovans, and welcome to the tenth annual Landing Day Celebrations!" As the Commander's voice echoed throughout the hall, a staccato of fireworks exploded directly above the dome. The multi-colored sparks from the explosives danced among the river of the aurora before fizzling out as they rained down on the dome barrier. "We have much to celebrate this year like, for starters, welcoming the largest migration group this planet or any other planet has seen!" The commander outstretched his arms as he nodded enthusiastically before leading the crowd in applause. "Netting almost seven hundred new citizens, our Infrastructure Core is working tirelessly to get vacated habs ready for their new inhabitants and printing out new ones, bolstering the latest we have in materials and technology."

Law thought back to IQ's hab and all the new bells and whistles that these new citizens would be getting. Admin was truly putting on the best showing for this new wave of Aurornovans. Granted, this was the first year the planet had seen more people coming than were going and certainly the first time it was anywhere near the hundreds.

"Since Aurornova was discovered in 2233, it became evident to early settlers and scientists from Proxima and Tellathia II, the planet would quickly become a beacon of innovation and opportunity. Serving as a melting pot of our species who have spread through the galaxy and connected the dots of planets back to the origin or our ancestors on Earth."

Above Conners, a projection of all seven planets that had been colonized, all the way back to Earth displayed with a golden line connecting them all. Law recognized Earth, his birth planet Tellathia II, and several others. Aurornova was the last in the line. It was the biggest and shined the brightest. Conners looked up with a giant smile as he raised his hand to their home.

"Since, colonizing in 2234, this once uninhabited planet's minerals and natural resources have provided viable alternatives to much of what our species have relied on since the dawn of time. The incomparable Dr. Mina leads our science division and, from what I hear, one of his very promising protégés."

The crowd applauded. Law looked over at Jamie's table, where the commander directed his gaze. Dr. Mina had his hand on Jamie's shoulder, giving her a small congratulatory shake. Charlie released an emphatic howl, followed by chanting Jamie's name. Amoret sneered as she looked up at her date, who was standing now. Jamie allowed a smirk while hiking her glasses back up her nose. Law could not help but mirror Dr. Mina's full-toothed grin. His sister was shining, as she should have, during a time when so much had been dim for so long. And even though this was not his own triumph, Law could not help but bask in it. Seeing his sister in all her glory after she had poured herself into her work meant that she would be okay. Law imagined sitting next to their father, who would likely be tearing up right now. Jamie was stoic, like their mother. Law wiped away the tear that slid down his cheek and continued applauding.

"But as many of us know, as explorers at heart, there is no progress with our risk, no service without sacrifice, and no luxury without loss." The commander paused. His head bowed as he chewed his lip. After an audible sniffle, he lifted his head as a holographic mural sprung up behind him.

A tapestry of faces reached toward the dome above some of which Law recognized, but none more than the one at the center. A dreaded ponytail draped over his left shoulder as he stared out into the crowd with the softest hazel eyes that such a stern face could hold. Law stared at the mural with his father at the center, along with nineteen other individuals considered lost during the event that claimed yet another member of their family. Nahdine placed her hand on Law's knee as she looked on.

"The individuals that appear before you make up some of the finest explorers, scientists, minds, and leaders this galaxy has had and will ever offer. Many of which I have had the privilege of calling friends and dare I say" He paused before turning and looking at the holographic mural. "Family. Each and every one of them has placed their threads in the tapestry of our futures. And for that, we shall forever remain grateful." The commander cut and remained silent for a moment. The audience reverently did the same.

"Which leads me to my next point. We must continue to make sacrifices for the sake of our futures. None of which are too small for the advancement of humanity, including our egos. Though I thought it pertinent to keep my position until the end of the year, I think we are at a prime turning point for our colony. It is time for this colony to have a leader who is idealistic, determined, and has enough ambition for herself and for those she has sworn to protect and lead. Not to mention, someone that has just a few less light-years on her batteries." The commander chuckled as he turned to Rell behind him. "Effectively immediately, Vice Commander Kerrington Rell will assume command of Fort Kelly."

Applause cascaded in as attendees accepted the changing of the guard. Charlie slowly clapped as he and Law exchanged looks. Back at the stage, Rell shook hands with Conners before standing at attention and looked over the crowd. Admiring the beginning of her reign. Law couldn't help but think, it was the final move in her game of chess to checkmate Tiberius. She would waste no time shaking things up, likely starting with their trip.

The pomp and circumstance continued for about thirty more minutes. Rell headlined by mentioning the colony's expansion and the possibility of remote sites or mini-forts in other strategically placed areas on the planet. However, the most important point Rell looked to make was reigning in some of the ancillary operations on the planet.

Creating a more unified and collaborative operational structure, she called it.

Law was almost certain she looked directly at him while making that point. But the part that shook Law the most was the statement Rell made immediately following. She said this structure was *something we must return to as it was when Maxwell Everstorm was operational leader over the Zoa.*

Law did not know what to make of this point. The professed loyalty to their father juxtaposed with the skepticism of Tiberius continued to confuse Law. Eventually, *Commander* Rell dismissed everyone to enjoy the festivities, noting that the musical guest would be transported in from Earth within the hour, allowing everyone time to pursue refills and partake in the dinner provided.

As people rose from their tables, Charlie followed suit, mentioning he was going to grab a refill.

"I think I'll join Charlie in getting another drink. May I do the same for you?" Law asked Nahdine. She pondered for a moment before agreeing. Law nodded and made his way to the bar. He caught his best friend with several drinks, sliding across the bar in his direction.

"Save some for the rest of us," Law joked, grabbing one glass that looked similar to what he was drinking before. Charlie turned on the spot with a drink in each of his hands.

"One for Jamie and one for Nahdine." Charlie said before shoving them both into his friend's hands.

"How did you know Nahdine was going to get more?" Law asked as he took the full glasses.

"I was going to get her one regardless and if she didn't want it, I was just going to give it to you." Charlie took a large swig from his glass, emptied it, and got another.

"Two more ales for Sloane!" The bartender slid the beers in Charlie's direction. Law was still holding the refills for his date and his sister walked over and grabbed one while palming the other two at their base, trying not to spill. Just as Charlie placed his empty one on the bar, he picked up the other. He waved his CMP over the bar and typed in a modest U-cred tip amount into the holographic projection that appeared. As it dissolved back into the bar, they started back toward their tables.

"Alright Law, what's your thoughts?"

"About what?"

"The presentation! Rell taking over early. Her asking Jamie to spy?" Charlie's tone lowered with each question.

"It would be a hell of a coincidence. That's for sure." Law stared at the rim of one of the beers he was carrying as he approached their table. The golden liquid ebbed and flowed closer to the rim with each step. Just when Law thought he made it flawlessly to the table without wasting a drop. Charlie came to an abrupt halt ahead of him.

"Well, shit! This can't be good," Charlie said, staring straight ahead.

Law grimaced, examining the mess on the floor below. When he looked up, his eyes met his sisters on the other side of their table. Nahdine was in her seat, she too staring at Law with concern on her face because standing next to Jamie stood the freshly minted Commander Kerrington Rell.

Law fought to subdue his reaction by seeing her staring back at him. Like always, she stood at a soldier's attention. Her off-white utility uniform was clean, crisp, without a single ring and permanent creases running down each leg.

"Commander Rell. I believe congratulations are in order." Law locked eyes with her from across the table as he circumnavigated it, dropping off Nahdine's beer on the way. He reached Jamie first, handing her the beer, which she sat down on the table. Law squeezed his sister's arm as he walked around her before extending his hand to the commander. She took it firmly before initiating a single shake and returned her arm to her side. "Cordial. Much like your father, Lawrence. I appreciate that," she said. Law's eye twitched, but he held her gaze. Rell's mocha brown eyes remained steady, and he tried to reciprocate.

"Thank you. The colony will prosper under your leadership. I'm sure of it." Law asserted. It was not fully a petty retort. However, it was a measured response. Rell's brow raised momentarily before snapping back into place. The corner of Law's lips quelled a full smile. The commander looked toward Jamie, then cleared her throat.

"Well, let's get on with it." She seemed impatient and agitated. Law was cautious, wondering where this encounter was headed. "Though it has just come to light that I am taking over the administration of our colony, both here in the Oasis at Fort Kelly *and* in the Zoa."

Law noticed Jamie was still staring at him, beginning to chew at her cheek while Charlie stared attentively at Rell. Law looked back at the commander, whose eyes never left him.

"The reality is Aurornova is going to be the next great hub the galaxy has seen since Earth. The land is fertile and rich with resources and elements and almost five times larger than any other planet our species has populated. So, it is time to stop treating it as the wilds of Proxima and start reigning some operations in." Rell stepped toward Law, her hands clasped in front of her. In his periphery, Charlie closed in on her, his jaw as clenched as his fists. Rell stopped just short of the toes of her boots, touching the point of Law's shoes. Her eyes looked to the side where Charlie stood.

Rell was on the taller side, standing eye to eye with Law. He had heard many comment on her imposing figure coupled with her militaristic mannerisms as being intimidating. Charlie took another step closer to trump that notion. Law followed suit in unison with Jamie to deflate any notion they would be intimidated by her new position as the trio now flanked her on all sides, save for the one she could use to retreat. Rell took her eyes off Law only for a moment to assess Charlie's imposing figure on her right and Jamie's stern expression on her left.

Then, she returned them to Law, who invited air to rush into his lungs. It steadied his heartbeat as he released it slowly. His vision tunneled on Rell, predicting her next move. He studied the darker brown lines etched into her skin by time and experience. A slight curl formed as her cheek pulled at her pursed lips. Her voice was low, her words intentional.

"As it is not my intention to ruin your final night on this side of the planet, I wanted to inform you and Mr. Sloane as I have already informed, Ms. Everstorm, that your shuttle," She nodded toward Charlie, "And your crew as you will be pilot-in-command will stand by anticipating a prompt departure at 0600, *tomorrow morning*."

The sound around Law was muted. All he could hear was his pulse slamming at his eardrum. "Excuse me, commander," Law barely croaked out as his mouth went dry. "We were not supposed to leave for the Zoa for another week."

"I am aware. However, as you learned earlier, things are changing around here." Leaving no time for response, Rell stepped back, removing herself from the center of the trio's semi-circle and turned on point with the precision of a soldier about-facing. Clasping her hands at her back, she looked over her shoulder at Jamie before leaving.

"I will see you at 0500." Jamie nodded and Rell marched off

Law's heart continued its marathon. Searching for answers from his allies. "What the hell was that?"

"That was the new commander setting her expectations," Charlie replied, shaking his head before collapsing in his seat beside his date, who looked on confused.

"Do you think Ty knows?" Law asked.

Jamie shook her head. "I doubt it. Rell is shaking things up. She's doing it fast, but she's being methodical about it." Jamie was staring off at the space Rell had stood moments ago. "She had every opportunity to tell me about the schedule change since she's asking me to *spy*. But she only just told me we were leaving tomorrow when she stepped off the podium moments ago."

"She's certainly keeping everyone on their toes," Charlie chimed in as he was scrolling on his CMP. "I just received the manifest. I've never flown with any of these guys. And most of them have been flying decades longer than me." He went back to scrolling before frantically running his fingers back and forth through his slick, red strands.

"Exactly how she wants it," Law said, barely above a whisper. There was much more at play here than they knew. And Rell was inserting herself in the middle of it as much as she could.

"Well! That's a problem for tomorrow. Like the commander said, this is our last night in the Oasis, and I intend to make the most of it." Charlie stood up, smoothed the front of his blazer, and extended his hand toward Jamie. "Will you join me on the dance floor, Ms. Everstorm?"

The music Law had not noticed blaring in the atrium flooded into his eardrums. He had no idea how long it had been playing since Rell dropped her bomb.

"I'm sorry. Don't you have a date?" Jamie eyeballed him with all the judgment she could muster.

"I counted two, but I do have trouble with the numbers and such," Nahdine playfully joined in on the opportunity to help her friend give him a hard time.

Nahdine, Charlie, and Jamie laughed and conversed in the background. Charlie gestured toward the dance floor. A group of exploratory core members in uniform currently occupied *both* his dates. The blue chevrons on their shoulders signified they were likely the omnitransport crew members who brought in the new citizens to Aurornova. The pilot-in-command was the one with the most chevrons and gold trim around his jacket. He leaned in and played off the giggles from Jora.

"Clearly, they're occupied," Charlie finished. "So, would you at least entertain a sympathy dance?"

"A sympathy dance would imply sympathy for you Charles." Jamie retorted.

"Oh, come on, Law help me out here!" Charlie begged his friend. Law laughed nervously and mumbled a half-hearted response. He wasn't sure why it had shaken him so much that the timeline had been moved up. He should have been happy that they were going earlier, but he was more nervous and confused.

Jamie scoffed with a roll of her eyes that was contradicted by a deep dimpled smile. "Fine. But just one."

"I'll take it." Charlie grabbed her hand and led her off. Jamie managed to hand her ale to Law before they began wading through the crowd.

Law sat the ale on the table. Without thinking, he started walking toward the back of the atrium and out the doors, not realizing he had left his date at the table, alone.

13

Law's head throbbed from the lack of sleep. He replayed the inter-action with Commander Rell in his head repeatedly, until it led him all the way home. From there he spiraled, he thought of the favor he would owe IQ, how he would use the drone, who this supposed third party was working with Tiberius. He analyzed everything in his head repeatedly while pacing the hab, until he finally willed himself to his cube. He collapsed on his bed determined to drift off to sleep, until it hit him with all the force of a rhinophant ramming a tree, he left his date right in the middle of landing day with no explanation. The realization sat on his chest as he got up. He snatched his CMP back of his bedside table. He already had three messages from Nahdine.

Hey, are you okay?

Do you need someone to talk to?

Okay, well, have a good night—

He swiped back and forth between the messages, rereading them, checking the timestamps as fast as his heart was beating. How could he be so stupid?

The staccato beeps of the alarm that emitted from Law's CMP cut the silence of his cube. It was propped up like a sentry alarm clock.

"End alarm," Law commanded, sitting up on his bed, fully dressed. His head was in his hands. The alarm stopped at once, plunging his cube back into silence. Several hours later the text message cursor on his CMP still blinked, with no words to go with it. Law considered running back to Sci-Rez, going to her hab, and calling Jamie and Charlie to see if she were there. Instead, he froze. Fumbled, exactly what Charlie told him not to do. And of all the people he could have done that with, not only was it as sweet of a person as Nahdine, it had to be his sister's best friend.

He stared at the other side of his cube to see a few extra outfits folded on top of his case. Jamie's handiwork, no less. It wouldn't have mattered if Law put enough clothes in for a month and a half. She would have still added things she thought he needed. He was not sure when she had the time as Rell expected her at Huey Three by now and Law was certain that she and Charlie went well over the mandated *one dance* last night.

At the top was an unexpected addition, though.

Law stood up and crossed the cube. He grabbed his father's favorite exploratory core jacket, which had been shipped back as his remaining personal effects. He held it out in front of him for a moment, slightly elevated to his father's height, envisioning his father in it.

Law's eyes traced the navy-blue nylon and polyweave lapels. Amber-colored stripes ran down the front of either side of the zipper like a sash draped over a valedictorian. Law turned it over and threw it around his shoulders, sliding an arm into one sleeve before repeating with the other and shrugging it into place. The sleeves fit snugly around his biceps, but the shoulders were roomy. Law tugged at the bottom of the jacket to form it just a bit more before going over to his bedside and grabbing his CMP, clasping it to his forearm.

An electroshuttle sat outside of Law's hab. The driver, an elderly gentleman who had his feet kicked up on the dashboard, scrolled through his CMP. Turning to the door, Law recited his commands.

"Set to away, duration unknown, Code L-A-W-0-1-2-9."

"Confirmed," said the small square touchscreen beside the sliding door before its rim shined red.

Law picked his bag back up and walked toward the shuttle. He grabbed the middle door, opting to sit in the center even though it was empty. The driver looked in his rearview at the sound of the door slamming closed behind him. He glared before taking his feet down and molding his CMP back to his wrist. The electric shuttle whirred to life and whizzed off toward Huey Three.

As the shuttle picked up speed, passing habs on either side toward Fort Kelly's center, Law noticed the driver staring in the rearview mirror at him. After Law returned his hardening glare for a few moments, he just barely heard a huff before the driver double-tapped the arm of his glasses, and a faint broadcast began playing. "*Good*", Law thought. He had no desire for idle chat or for someone looking for static as to why he was catching a shuttle to the Zoa first thing in the morning before the rest of the settlement had awakened.

Law didn't want to think about much. The fact he was even on the shuttle *today* and not two days from now made him grind his teeth. Especially since it made him cut his night short. If it were up to him, he probably would just now be returning to his hab, much less leaving it. That was likely Rell's intention to spoil their night, Law thought. No one let her abrupt change in plans get to them except Law.

He had done so well the whole night, too. Law made a good impression with her mother and did all the right things the entire night until Rell.

Tilting his head back and closing his eyes, Law wondered how the night could have gone if he had not let Rell get to him. Would he have danced with Nahdine the rest of the night? Could there have been more? Would it have been the start of something?

Whatever could have been no longer mattered. Law dashed all hopes of a future with Nahdine. And what was worse, as much as he wanted to pass the blame to Rell. The blame became solely his own, the moment he walked out of Sci-Rez's atrium.

Law tapped his clenched fist on his leg before he reopened his eyes. The electroshuttle cut left at the fork that led to the hueys.

The shuttle driver pulled Law all the way up to the bay door. More likely to make a final attempt at learning what little information he could versus being courteous to his passenger.

Nonetheless, he was quiet for the five-minute transport, so Law tapped his CMP and hit the notification that the shuttle had arrived at its destination and sent him a few U-creds as a courtesy. The ding pulled the driver's prying eyes from the bay door to his CMP. After squinting down at it, he scrunched his face and nodded before giving Law a two-fingered salute before kicking the shuttle back into gear and driving off.

Walking through the enormous bay doors of Huey Two, Law saw the omnijet that would take him to the other side of the planet. It was like a metallic black albatross eagerly awaiting its passengers before a storm. A dozen ground crew surrounded the giant bird as if they were dancing for rain. They waved and pointed their arms in various shapes in a robotic ballet, signaling to each other in operational confirmations with each mechanical movement.

Law looked on in awe as the jet's wings unfolded. Half of the wings were slowly going from a vertical position to parallel with the ground and spanning what Law felt were at least three soccer fields. Law had a small wave of pride, thinking that this marvel of a machine that could take them 25,000 kilometers to the Zoa in a mere matter of ten hours was going to be under the command of his best friend.

Charlie stood at the nose of the plane, a maestro orchestrating the symphony. The crew members came to him, multiple CMPs in hand, gesturing for him to sign in various places. Others appeared to be looking for directions, to which he looked up, assessed, and then would point to where they should go.

Charlie must have caught Law out of his peripheral. His face went from contorted in concentration to a full-toothed smile as he quickly signed off on the last few orders before dispersing the five remaining crew members that surrounded him.

"Well, if it isn't the man of the hour!" Charlie chided as he walked toward Law, who in turn stopped in his tracks and saluted his friend.

"That would be you, wouldn't it, Captain?" Law laughed as he watched his friend roll his eyes. He dropped his bag at his side before they started their handshake, ending in a hug. The loud crack of their hands coming together caught the attention of the crew members around them. Law could see over Charlie's shoulder some of the crew members staring in their direction. Aside from them, a handful of burly men loaded almost a dozen large black cases onto the conveyor belt that fed into the jet's main storage compartment. Like the cases, they were dressed in all-black jumpsuits, huddled in a tight formation, talking in hushed tones between each other.

"What's with those guys?" Law asked, not removing his eyes from them.

Charlie turned. "Yeah, those guys. Remember when I mentioned the manifest had a bunch of names I've never seen or flown with?" Charlie asked, now standing with his arms folded. "They're the ones I was talking about."

"How is it you've never seen them?" Law asked, genuinely perplexed. Aurornova was growing rapidly, but not enough that there were endless pilots and flight crew that Charlie would not know.

"That's because they went directly to the Zoa on Landing Day last year. And they rarely set foot in the Oasis. At least not beyond the hueys."

"I wonder how Rell feels about that?" Law asked, shaking his head.

"I'm sure you could answer that question, considering how much she's been inserting herself even before her promotion." Charlie declared through pursed lips. "Enough of that, though. What happened last night? Nahdine was looking for you, and then we all were. Then she and Jamie spent the night on her doorstep in tears."

Law shook his head as he looked up at Charlie. He couldn't begin to figure out a concise way to explain away what happened.

"Later, man, I – I just can't." Law as he felt his cheeks flush.

"Well, don't be surprised if you catch hell when you see your sister." He said, looking around as if he were making sure she wasn't nearby. Charlie's mention of his sister jogged his memory.

"I'm guessing if you know that, you two went wait beyond the single pity dance I recall overhearing you beg for?" Law raised an eyebrow. "How long did you two stay?"

"Uh, not long. We had a few more dances, talked a bit about the trip today, and then I walked her home. Or at least I started before having to redirect her to Nahdine's"

That would have been straightforward enough if it was not so easy to tell when Charlie was blushing. His red hair was nothing compared to the flush of his skin when he was stumbling over himself, though Law rarely saw him at a loss for words.

"Mmhmm." Law hummed incredulously.

"Look, I was just taking care of another member of my favorite family. Plus, you were otherwise occupied, *frolicking through lily fields*, was it?" Charlie returned Law's incredulousness as he eyed him before they both broke out into more laughter.

"Prepare for departure in T-30 minutes." The announcement rang over the PA in the Huey.

"Well, that answers my question about our ETA. Where do you need me, Captain?"

"You can go ahead and board. Jamie should already be in there somewhere," Charlie said with his hands on his hips as he looked around. "Drop your crap over near the sketchy guys and we'll get it weighed and loaded. If I can make that departure time closer to T-minus twenty, I'll be happier. I want to see the sunrise," Charlie finished as he squatted down, trying to see the sky through the hangar's bay door.

"Aye, Aye, Captain!" Law gave the stiffest salute before picking up his bag. Charlie gave him a playful kick to the backside before walking away to continue his preflight checks.

Law looked after Charlie for a minute, impressed by his command of the situation, as he pointed and yelled out to his crew. He didn't get to see Charlie fully in his element often. Maybe he was onto something, encouraging Law to join the exploratory core. Between Jamie's promotion and taking on bigger projects within Science & Research and Charlie being the pilot-in-command of this trip, it was time for Law to start thinking about where he would plant his feet.

It may even be right for him to follow in his father's footsteps.

Perhaps Law could blaze a trail like him, merging the science and the exploration, picking up where he left off with Ty. Could that be what Ty wanted to discuss? Did he want Law to work with him? Is that why his father was bringing him and Jamie all the way across the planet? But what about Ty's shady dealings? Law would have plenty of time to think all of that through over the next thirteen hours of flight time it would take to get to the Zoa.

Law dropped his bag where Charlie had directed him. Turning to make his way toward the ramp at the back of the omnijet, he saw the compartment where the mystery men had been loading their cases was cracked open.

Law scanned his surroundings, looking to see if any of the crew members were nearby. The crowd of people around the hangar was thinning. Law continued his search, looking for Charlie, but he was also not within immediate view. Law's heart switched to anticipation mode and slowly thumped in his chest as he sidestepped closer to the compartment and opened it further. He was not sure what he was going to find since all he saw the crewmembers loading were containers that were likely locked.

The closest crate within reach was also the largest. With one last glance, Law grabbed his bag off the ground and climbed in further. The top of the black metal crate had an electronic pad covering its right side. Law tapped it, causing a bright glow to flood the compartment before it adjusted, dimming to its surroundings.

"Please present CMP for authentication." The command came loudly from the screen.

"Shit! Too loud," Law hissed, his heart racing. As he pushed off the case to get to his feet, his CMP beside the crate's screen chimed. In a noticeably lower tone, the case's screen complied.

"Access granted. Safe mode transfer. Maxwell Everstorm."

"What the hell?" Law whispered under his breath. Law was having trouble functioning. His pulse pounded in his temples and his vision pulsated from the contrast of the screen on the case and the darkness around him. Law looked to his CMP for answers, but the screen merely returned to its dark state. The case's screen did the same, returning Law to the darkness of the omnijet's storage compartment. Outside, Law heard the deep voices of the mystery crew growing closer.

"Do your last check and then lock it up!" one of them ordered.

Law grabbed his bag and took a final glance around before stalking his way back out of the compartment's door and landing back on the concrete floor of the hangar bay. "What the hell were you doing in there?" a burley crewmember asked gruffly. Law recognized him from the group earlier. Thinking quickly, he gave the best answer he could conjure.

"The captain told me to stow my bag somewhere over here. I assumed he meant the compartment with the door that was wide open." Law scratched his head, trying to drive his obliviousness home.

"This ain't it. Get lost."

"My bad man! You know what happens when you get pointed in a direction and see an open door to a compartment with a bunch of crates." Law shrugged, feigning innocence.

"You didn't see anything," the crew member growled as he crossed past Law and slammed the compartment shut. The crew member stepped toward him without removing his eyes from Law until they were almost toe-to-toe.

Law closed the few millimeters' worth of space that remained, refusing to be intimidated by a crew member. The leather straps of his duffel groaned as his fist clenched. He let the cool morning air fill his chest as it did nothing to quell the flames igniting behind his rib cage.

"You sure about that?" Law growled, his brows furrowed. The crew member's hands darted from his sides toward the lapels of Law's jacket.

"Let me tell you something, you little. . ."

"Is there a problem?" Charlie cut in with impeccable timing. The crew member dropped his hands at once. Law realized he had grabbed the crew member's jacket. He let go, though his eyes remained on his adversary as he half squatted to pick his duffle back up that he had dropped.

When had he let go of the bag and grabbed the crew member? Law rolled his shoulders and the muscles in his jaw jumped.

"No, no, captain," the crew member stuttered. "All items are stowed and compartments are locked on this side."

"Then you should be on the flight deck preparing for departure. Don't slow me down April! If my departures aren't early, they're late.

And I don't care much for being late." Charlie crossed his arms as he advanced, standing just off to the side of Law's right shoulder, ensuring that his leather flight jacket strained covering his physique. Though the burly crew member had just a slight height advantage on him, Law was convinced he could hold his own training with Charlie as much as he did. And where Law was maybe in the same weight class, Charlie was not—a heavyweight to their light-heavies. The crew member likely made this discernment along with the chevrons on Charlie's shoulder and decided against any further aggression.

"Aye, Captain," the crew member finally relented and stalked off, but not before levying a passing glare at Law on his way to the omnijet's ramp.

"Care to tell me what that was all about?" Charlie asked while his eyes followed the crew member up the ramp before turning to Law.

"Later. Let's get going." Law tapped Charlie's chest and made his way toward the ramp.

Law entered the omnijet as many of the passengers took their seats. The belly of the jet was spacious and convertible. Most of the time when Law rode with Charlie on missions to service relays or transport parts, the seats were gone, and the space was open so that cargo could be latched down to the floor and scientists and maintenance teams could work at the terminals that lined the walls of the jet.

Law would be on the flight deck with Charlie, where he spent most of the time listening to him explain flight patterns and techniques, hoping to imprint a love for the craft on him. Other times, on the more routine trips like transporting exploratory teams to drop zones, Charlie would just put it in auto-pilot and they would catch up on the static of the day, or more commonly a date that went awry from the previous night.

Today, there was a mixture of passengers. Law noticed three scientists from Jamie's presentation who were huddled up looking at a CMP projection of the flower she presented. The sketchy crewmembers were toward the front of the jet's belly, just behind the flight deck. Law's new *friend,* Crewmen April, was on the flight deck hovering behind a woman who was flipping latches and cycling through projections, hovering over her CMP that she would grab and place into a larger projection being emitted by the flight instrument panel.

He looked away from the projections in Law's direction with a scowl. Law smiled and returned a subtle wave with a wink to drive things home. April's hands clenched the woman's seat, turning a bright shade of red, leaving the area around his knuckles white as he turned his head back in the direction the woman was pointing.

Law held back a satisfied chuckle, just before someone stepped in front of him, obscuring his view of the flight deck.

Law let out a slow, deep sigh, barely hiding an eye roll from the barrier, now staring him directly in the face. Not that he cared if she noticed. Rell wasted no time in speaking.

"I am glad that I caught you, Mr. Everstorm." Law was not. "As I am sure it is no secret that I have asked your sister to—" Rell paused before clasping her hands in front of her. "—Discretely report back to me."

Law cut in, trying to convince her otherwise. "Is that so, Commander? I assure you—" Law began only to be cut off by the Commander's raised hand.

"Your loyalty is commendable. It is regrettable that the former commander and I were off-world during the *incident*. Additionally, not having the ability to make this almost twenty-hour round trip with you, as I am trying to coordinate and accommodate the over seven hundred new colonists, is less than ideal. After pouring over the inspectors reports from the investigation, I'd really like to get over there myself. See things firsthand, but " Rell dropped her head while biting her lip. Law waited as several uncomfortable moments passed before she looked back up. A glaze in her eyes quelled the defiance Law was accustomed to. "The greatest loss to our colony, this planet, and beyond, is the loss of your father. Safe travels, Mr. Everstorm." Rell, returned to her military stature, straightened up, gave a curt nod, and made her way toward the ramp at the rear of the jet. Law remained in the same spot for a minute. He was not sure what exactly made him rethink his feelings toward Rell. Was it her praise of his father? Was it the momentary crack in the armor she worked so hard to adorn at all times? Whatever it was, he thought, perhaps there was more to her curiosity about Tiberius' work in the Zoa than he initially credited her.

"Lawrence! Good, you made it." Breaking Law's contemplation, Jamie looked over her seat at him from two rows up. He took a seat beside her, collapsing back with reeling thoughts. "Did you remember to set the hab lockdown to an indefinite away time? I see you put on Dad's jacket." Jamie paused her inquiry. "It looks good on you." She said with a soft smile before tugging and smoothing the collar. Law returned a quick smile as a thank you before assuring her he had followed the proper traveling procedures before leaving the hab.

"Good, good." Jamie said. Law took her tone as satisfied, but the fact she was still staring at him alluded to annoyance. The bags Law noticed under her eyes showed she likely got as little sleep as he did

"Uh, did I forget something?" he asked, trying to play through Jamie's normal and extra expectations anytime they were away from the hab for a prolonged period.

"Hmm, I don't know." Jamie said. She placed a finger on her chin for a moment before she started wailing on Law's arm. "Maybe. My. Best. Friend. Who. You. Left!" she shouted, making sure to hit him to emphasize each word.

"Jamie! Stop it!" Law said, scrambling to block some of her blows while looking around to see if anyone was looking. The top of his arm became sore with each focused blow. If he was lucky enough to block a hit, it only enraged her even more. So, she alternated between punching his arm and slamming her fist on his thigh.

"Alright Jamie! Cut it out!" Law demanded. Forgetting discretion for a moment. At this point, some of the people seated were leaning and standing to get a look at the commotion.

"Do you know how long I had to sit with her while she cried, thinking it was something she had done or that you blew her off because you just weren't interested?" Jamie queried. "It was a good thing Charlie had not walked me all the way back to the hab after the celebration was over."

"Wait, you two stayed for the whole celebration?" Law asked. Not only surprised they stayed the entire time, but that they left together. It was a question Law should have saved for Charlie.

"Boy, if you don't focus, so help me!" Jamie said, her finger centimeters from his face. Her mahogany brown eyes were laser focused over the rim of her clear frames. Her curly bushel of hair was pulled back so tightly, Law could see a single vein throbbing at her temple.

"I don't know what happened or how Rell set you off so bad that you ran off, leaving Deeny alone like that, but she was really hurt." Jamie finished. Her tone was much softer expressing how Law had hurt her best friend. Law's face found the position it had spent most of the morning, in his hands. He rubbed at it furiously wishing he could peel it off with the embarrassment he felt.

"I know Jamie. Or I don't know. I just panicked." Law muttered, forcing his voice through his hands. "I guess it was just—We weren't supposed to leave for another two days and then Rell comes in and changes everything. It was just jarring." Law raised his head out of his hands and looked around.

"Why does that matter Law? Up until this point, you've been all about going to see Tiberius, going to the Zoa, going to get answers. I would have thought you'd be thanking Rell for speeding up the process." Jamie said as she leaned forward trying to catch Law's eyes. Jamie had a point. Had it been a day or two ago Law might have been thanking Rell.

"I know, but it finally felt like things were moving in my favor for once. Getting the drones, learning the information from IQ, even Nahdine." Law said. He pushed himself back into his chair. "Then, just like that." Law snapped his fingers in front of them. "I was behind the eight ball again. Once again, I don't know what I'm doing or what's going on. A nidio piece with no direction." He slumped in his chair placing a hand on his forehead.

"Lawrence. I can't help but feel like you're alluding to a little more than just this trip with all that." Jamie said. She turned in her seat and placed her hand on Law's knee. "But unless we start giving ourselves the grace we expect from others, we'll never find our way. We'll only continue hurt ourselves more, and even worse, we'll hurt others." She ended with a few gentle pats to Law's knee. "You're kind, smart, and you have this way of finding a connection with people no matter how different they are from you. It's one of the reasons Nahdine liked you so much. Half the time she came to the hab, it was so she could speak Tellathian with someone other than her parents and Charlie's mom."

Jamie was finally starting to crack through the wall of despair Law felt was becoming ever-present.

"It's also why she gave you the grace you refuse to give yourself. Well, that and because we agreed boys are stupid and Aurornova would be much better off if we shipped you all back to Earth." Jamie added with a roll of her eyes.

"There's that smile." Jamie said, noticing a grin reluctantly creeping across his face. She pinched his cheek before pulling at it a bit and then slapping it after letting it go.

"That said, you will apologize to my friend as soon as we get back or I will start confusing my fertilizer samples with my cooking ingredients until you waste away out of fear of not being able to eat." Jamie's finger was in Law's face again as she cast a reproachful look over her glasses. Law rolled his eyes this time as he sat up straight.

"No, for real, Jamie I will apologize to her as soon as I can. Hopefully I'll get a chance to comm her and explain myself as soon as we land." Law said

"Good. I'll leave it at that." Jamie nodded. Law was relieved. Though the pain was deserved, he couldn't take any more of her heavy-handed blows to his arm and leg. "So, I saw you and Rell had a nice little conversation. What was that about?" Jamie asked.

"Well, it was an interesting one." Jamie's eyes perked up as she half turned in her chair toward him. Apparently, Rell had come aboard to discuss a few additional details of her expectations of Jamie prior to her departure.

"She was positive I knew what she asked you to do. I denied it, though." Jamie waved the statement off with a smile before patting his hand, goading him to continue. That was just it! Why would she feel the need to tell me that? I mean, she also said losing Dad was the greatest loss to the planet, which she seemed pretty sincere about."

Jamie held her chin with her thumb and index finger. She measured her words before she spoke. "Well, Law, Rell isn't a fool. Who wouldn't assume that siblings would share secrets? Especially us." She nudged him with her elbow before continuing. "That being said, I felt as though Rell was genuinely concerned with the events that led up to the incident. Not to mention Dad's loss." Jamie looked out the jet's window. "It's refreshing, really. Everyone else seems to try to move on, while Rell is the first person who is high enough to really start demanding answers she's willing to share. Unlike Tiberius," she said, not turning her head. The words were sharp to Law's ears. He decided not to dispute, though. Even if they were on the way to the Zoa at Tiberius' behest, it took him far too long to make the request, even by Law's standards. He had not considered the different angle with Rell. That, perhaps, it was not as much about spying on Tiberius as it was about rectifying a broken promise she made to a friend to protect their family. A broken promise that was made to their mother.

Law stared at the window with his sister. He could make out Charlie waving off the last few ground crewmembers as he walked toward the jet's rear. Law turned as his friend escalated up the ramp. As he reached the top, the ship's PA computer made its mandatory announcement.

"Pilot-in-command acknowledged. Controls transferred to Charles B. Sloane.". Law saw him smile and wink at the nearest passenger before turning to watch the ramp ascend and collapse behind him, sealing off the rear of the omnijet. He'd once told Law how that sound would never get old. Charlie genuinely loved his career choice. He inspected the rim of the closure, before flipping a large latch down with a definitive clank.

Charlie made his way toward the flight deck, doing his best to throw the symmetry of Law's high-top off by shoving his bear-like hand at the top of his head. Law swung at Charlie's leg, barely missing it as he reached up and tried to smooth out his friend's imprint. Charlie reached the middle of the platform, where the crewmembers already stood from their seats to acknowledge him. Charlie turned to address the passengers.

"Good early morning, ladies and gentlemen. My name is Charlie Sloane and I will ensure you each reach your destinations in a timely manner along with this fine crew by my side." Charlie went on to mention that many of the passengers would be dropped at a research station in the Lima Zulu Theta region with a select few continuing to Lima Zula Alpha which was the closest research station to the Zoa and the site where they would likely drop off the scientists that were in Jamie's presentation since that was where her super flower had been discovered.

"Everyone strap-in and get comfortable. We won't be at our first stop for another eight hours." After his last statement, Law noticed most people had returned to their pads. Not letting an opportunity to rob his friend of peace, Law raised his hand.

"I'm sorry, Captain. Will there be any snacks or in-flight movies for this trip?" Law asked, failing to conceal the shit-eating grin that was plastered on his face.

"Oh, of course, sir, let me just reach up here..." Charlie opened an overhead compartment and started rummaging around. "I know we have some...oh yes!" Charlie pulled his hand back out, revealing his middle finger to Law. "Think I have another one of those with your name on it. Would you like that now or later in the flight?" Charlie put on the best faux customer-service smile he could muster, leaving Law in stitches. He retreated into the flight deck and sat at the main control at the center of the flight instruments and the window.

"Prepare for launch," Charlie announced, and Law settled in his seat as the plane rumbled like it was atop a newly active volcano.

Jamie grabbed his wrist in a way that pinched him. Law groaned. He had forgotten about her fear of flying.

Law looked in her direction. Her eyes clenched so tightly that her glasses were almost level with her eyebrows. If it weren't for the now heavy rumble of the boosters that lifted the jet to a hover leading toward the bay door of Huey Two, he's sure he would have heard the sharp intake and low exhaling of breath she often employed to fend off panic attacks.

This time, however, it appeared she was struggling to gather herself. Law grabbed her hand, primarily to adjust her grip before she broke skin, before holding it to his chest so she could mimic his breathing. After a few iterations, she started to get a rhythm and moved her hand back to the armrest into his and held it for the rest of the takeoff process.

Law alternated between looking through the large panoramic view at the front of the omnijet where the flight deck was and the side window as they cleared the bay doors into the golden morning sunrise.

A gentle fog had rolled in off the river that runs just a few hundred yards from Fort Kelly during pre-flight check. It carried a wispy haze of orange sunlight throughout the atmosphere. Charlie and his crew piloted the omnijet to the launch zone to prepare for its take off while Law looked toward his hill, where he typically watched the sun perform its majesty.

The jet came to rest on its own before the rumbling intensified. What was a manageable vibration turned into a jarring rattle.

The PA sounded with a countdown. "Three, two, one, Launch!"

The omnijet propelled itself straight up into the air, causing Jamie to go back to baring her nails into Law's skin while his seat swallowed him whole. Just as he felt like the chair had fully engulfed him, it spat him into the air allowing him to hover a few centimeters above its base before the jet pushed him against the back of his seat as it sprinted across the sky leaving Fort Kelly in its wake at what felt like the blink of an eye. Their journey for answers had finally begun.

And there was no turning back now.

A sudden jerk in the omnijet woke Law from his sleep. He couldn't remember if this was the third or fourth time he had fallen asleep throughout the trip. Law had stayed awake until the first stop, which emptied most passengers. At that point, the early rise had caught up with him, and he slept through the second stop, which let out all but Jamie, himself, Charlie, Crew member April, and a single skittish scientist sitting toward the back of the jet.

Considering most of the passengers were gone and things felt less formal, Law took it as a good time to join Charlie on the flight deck. Thanks to some sleep aid to help her get through the trip, Jamie was in a deep sleep.

Law took off his seatbelt and walked up onto the flight deck platform behind Charlie. Crew member April wasn't in a seat or on the deck. Law tapped Charlie's shoulder, who was sipping on a steaming mug of coffee. "We getting close to Ops? I guess I slept through our last stop."

Charlie took a long drag from his coffee. "Mm-hm. Yeah, you were knocked out, man. I figured you took some of Jamie's medicine or something."

Law chuckled as he scratched his head. "No, just a late night that turned into an early morning."

"Well, we are. Close to Ops, that is. However, our two remaining passengers will get off prior."

"Wait, what?" Law asked. "I thought you said we were only making two stops prior to Ops." Charlie sipped from his mug again but nodded emphatically to corroborate Law's point.

"I did, but the request came over right after Research Station Alpha that our man Tiberius wanted those two dropped, along with their cargo, at this location." Charlie looked toward the back of the plane, most likely for April. Once satisfied, he placed his hand flat on one of the blank slates on the flight panel and pulled up a holomap.

His other hand shrank it down to a size just small enough to be obscured between the two of them. A lead line blinked, pointing to a location on the bright shining blue orb before them in the region that was still considered the Zoa.

Charlie plucked the lead line, making the orb hologram reform itself into a topographical map. An octagonal icon glowed red, indicating the location of the Zoa's Operations Center. About thirty kilometers from that point, there was a grouping of small green blinking boxes where they would drop off their other passengers.

"What is that? I don't think I've ever seen that area on any of the holomaps." Law said, now taking over control of the holomap as he grabbed and pulled it closer, studying the terrain and surroundings.

"It's not something uncommon that I've seen. The flight division of the exploratory core usually has the latest and greatest topographical information. Around the Zoa, I see things like this move around a lot. We never get a lot of information about them." Charlie took the holomap back from Law so that he could zoom in on the drop-off site. He rested his chin on his fist as he stared at Law. "This site in particular, however, has been on the map for some time now, which is rare." Charlie paused. Law thought it was about to add dramatic effect but noticed that Charlie was looking back again and scanning the passenger area of the jet before turning back.

"Okay?" Law responded with a question. His eyebrow raised, waiting for Charlie to reveal the point that had to be the reason he was staring at him.

"You don't notice anything interesting about this site?" Charlie asked, his eyes widening. Law looked closer, examining the site. "More importantly, where it's located?" Law stopped looking directly at the site and focused on the surrounding area, and there it was. The site was in the valley, directly flanked by the mountain where the incident occurred.

"Excuse me, sir, is he supposed to be seeing that?"

Law and Charlie both spun in their flight deck seats to find Crew member April standing at parade rest behind them. "Is he supposed to be seeing, uh, what April?" Charlie stalled as he waved the holomap away, causing it to dissolve back into the flight panel.

"The details of the drop-off site where we will be unloading?" April clarified while pointing at where the holomap had once hovered.

"Well," Charlie started.

"Well, I would imagine," Law cut in. "If Tiberius were concerned about what I did or didn't know, he probably would have had Charlie drop my sister and me off at Ops first. Don't you think? April, was it?" Law stood, his hands clenched. He was happy to continue where their last conversation ended.

"That is very likely the case, April. Not to mention, I have been giving Law lessons on flight operations and navigation. As you may not be aware, he has recently graduated from primary studies and is trying to figure out what's next." The crew member looked between the two with narrowed eyes.

"Fair enough. How long until we land...sir?" April finally groaned.

"T-minus-" Charlie turned and looked at the flight navigator's projection. "Five minutes until we're on the ground. Prepare accordingly"

"Aye, sir." April extended his hand toward Charlie. "You're one of the more talented pilots I've had the opportunity to fly with. Usually, going through the eternal storm band over the Trekana Expanse is a nightmare. I could have slept like a baby with you at the helm." Charlie took April's hand.

"Well, some operate and some pilot. There's a difference," Charlie said, adding a quick wink to punctuate the statement. They gave a forearm shake before April looked toward Law.

"Mr. Everstorm." He nodded. Law didn't return the courtesy. Something about this man grated on his nerves, and he didn't trust him. April scowled and turned, heading toward the rear of the omnijet. As he walked off, he made way for Jamie, who was drowsily making her way toward the flight deck.

"Good morning, princess. Or, more accurately, evening," Charlie greeted her as she stepped up onto the platform. "How was your slumber?"

Jamie scowled at him before addressing his foolishness. "Unexpectedly peaceful, thanks to your flying, I suppose," she said as she squeezed Law's arm. "And your help too, of course. Have we arrived?" Law got her caught up on the situation at hand.

"Interesting indeed," Jamie said as she eyed the terrain the holomap showed. "It's not far off from what Rell provided me." She lifted her pad and pulled up a holomap near Charlie's. She pinched it between her fingers and dropped it on top of Charlie's projection. The omnijet's computer picked up on Jamie's intentions and highlighted the differences between the two projections. Charlie's featured several more buildings pulsating in red and spread over a wider area.

"Computer, analyze differences and report," Charlie commanded. The jet's computer complied.

"Holomap A contains five additional structures spanning across three additional kilometers. Metadata on original structures: Type – Operational. Active time – 2 years, 47 days, 25 hours, 15 minutes, 37 seconds. Metadata on new structures: Type – Unknown. Active time – 382 days, 1 hour, 20 minutes, 22 seconds."

"Unknown? How does it not know? All structures have to have a purpose identified. Computer, analyze new structures," Charlie demanded. Law and Jamie looked on.

"Unable to analyze. Security protocol Alpha-Alpha-Omega." The computer offered no further explanation. Law, Charlie, and Jamie looked to each other for ideas.

"Well, maybe we'll get a peek when we drop these guys off. Strap in, we've arrived and I've got to get us on the ground. Instructions were to drop them. People will be waiting to unload and then get back in the air to Ops. Directly from the man, the myth, himself," Charlie said as he already sat back in the center chair.

He waved away the holomaps they were examining and pulled up a larger hologram that spread across the front window of the jet, showing vectors and illuminated a landing zone and flight path. Jamie had already strapped herself into one of the deck chairs the moment the instruction mentioned landing. Law took the second-in-command chair beside Charlie.

"Perfect Law! If you're sitting up here, you're going to work. Get my landing gear out while I set all flaps and switch to landing boosters." Law complied, remembering some of their earlier trips together functioning as Charlie's stand-in second-in-command. He switched all the necessary screens and settings, prompting a loud mechanical clacking followed by the mechanical hum that indicated the four skids were extending before each let out a loud clank as they locked into place.

"Alright. Putting her down," Charlie confirmed as he mastered the controls. He made micro-movements to the levers in each of his hands while he bit the tip of his tongue, constantly looking among the holograms, the screens, and the terrain outside the main window. His forearms flexed against the rolled-up sleeves of his flight jacket. Law enjoyed the landing process. He felt the boosters pulsing through the vibrations of the seat as Charlie tried to put them on the ground as gently as possible. Even Jamie looked less concerned than normal as she watched Charlie intently. Just as they were about to touchdown, Law felt the expected power-up of the boosters that guided them the rest of the way to the ground. He flipped a few switches that blasted steam and smoke, obscuring the outside view. A hologram materialized in front of the main window, showing April and the fidgety scientist disembarking.

Crew member April gave a two-fingered salute as he walked down the ramp, followed closely by the scientist before the feed ended.

"Storage compartment stowed and returned to a locked position," the computer chimed at once after the ramp started its way back up to a shut position.

"Geez, that was fast!" Charlie exclaimed. "They get these guys from a desert speeder crew?"

"Guys, look!" Law said, staring through the main window, waiting for the steam and smoke to clear from the boosters shutting down. As the dust settled, the three of them realized exactly what was in front of them. The walls encapsulating the site were enormous. Law and Charlie were stooping as low as they possibly could to see just how high the walls stood. Jamie scanned.

"I could tell they were tall from the air, but not this high!" Charlie said, almost laying his full chest on the flight panel to see the top.

"They're almost three times the size of Fort Kelly. Why would they need walls so high?" Jamie asked. She tapped at the arm of her glasses as her head lifted to the sky.

"One of many ways they are trying to keep things under wraps, I suspect," Law said before looking toward the ground. Almost a dozen people were hauling the contents of the compartment in which Law had found himself earlier that day. April led the group, followed closely by the scientist. Jamie and Charlie looked at the ground. The line of people looked like a string of black ants carrying food and supplies on their backs into their little anthills.

"What is all of that?" Jamie asked. She looked toward Charlie.

"Don't look at me," Charlie responded, throwing up his hands.

"Shouldn't you know the contents of everything on your ship? Isn't that normal protocol?" Jamie asked, her face contorted as it searched Charlie for answers.

"Jamie, what about any of this has been normal?" Charlie was right. The level of secrecy employed thus far was beginning to be frustrating. Why the random stop that was omitted from the original manifest and the contents of these storage containers no one...

"Wait a tick," Law said, holding his wrist up and staring at his CMP. "I think *I* may know what is in all of those containers."

"What?" Charlie and Jamie said in unison. Charlie continued on. "I know you're not going to tell me you and April squashed things and are best buds now and he told you everything that's going on over here?" Charlie faced Law, hands on his hips, while Jamie looked over his shoulder.

"Cosmos no! But when you came up, I had just got out of the storage compartment with all that stuff. That's when you ran into us. And—" Before Law could, the flight panel chimed, followed by a hologram with Tiberius's face.

"Thank you again, Charles, for making the *impromptu* stop. Hurry over to Ops. We are eager for your arrival and the mess hall is preparing dinner. We will expect you in five. Jansen out." As quickly as he appeared, he was gone.

"Well, I guess that is our queue. Since it's just us, you guys may as well stay up here and keep me company. Wonder what we see from overhead," Charlie said with a mischievous grin. They each took their seats and prepared for launch.

"Oh, wait, Law! You were going to tell us what was in the boxes." Jamie said, her hand up.

"Oh yeah! CMP, pull up recently transferred documents," Law said, holding his wrist for the other to see. The CMP gave its normal affirmative chime, but nothing happened. Law tried once more, speaking more clearly. Still, nothing happened. Jamie lifted her blank stare from Law's extended arm, featuring his CMP, to Law himself. Charlie tried looking back and forth between the heads-up displays he manipulated to pilot the ship and his two passengers behind him. Law, noting their confusion, explained as best he could.

"When I was in the compartment, one of the cases had a display on it. It was locked with an encrypted key. When I tried to get it to stop screaming, it connected to my CMP somehow and—" Law looked at Jamie. "It granted me access as if I were Dad." Jamie leaned forward in her seat while Charlie all but turned his head fully around like an owl perched in the captain's chair. Neither of them said anything, signaling Law to continue. "I mean, it didn't give me access to the case, but it mentioned a *'content manifest was transferred'*," Law finished before he turned his hands over and shrugged his shoulders. "Something is on my CMP, that it gave me access to because it acted as if I were Dad. I just—I just don't know how to get into it."

"Well, that makes two of us," Jamie said before collapsing against the back of the seat.

L aw stood at the back of the omnijet with his sister. Charlie was still at the front, securing things on the flight deck. Jamie had just sent her first report to their commander after arriving at Ops.

Law recalled her mentioning the unscheduled stop to drop off two passengers, the drop-off point being larger than the maps originally showed, and the possibility of sharing the contents of the secret cargo that Law now held on his device—not that he could open it. He stared down at his CMP as if it had betrayed him.

Jamie wanted to send the message before they got into the Zoa's Operations Center, just in case its network had capabilities different than those of Sci-Rez. Law felt it was a wise decision.

"We're all set," Charlie said, walking toward them at the same time as the ramp let out a loud hiss before opening up to the hazy light of the dusk air at the Zoa. A sliver of the setting sun's light shot a beam through the initial crack in the ramp's opening, landing perfectly across Law's line of sight.

Law, Jamie, and Charlie stood shoulder to shoulder, awaiting who or what would be on the other side. The metallic bang of the ramp hit the ground and the mechanical gears and pulleys quieted. A familiar voice Law had not heard in a long time carried across the open space.

The group made their way down the ramp and Law continued to scan around the landing site for others who would join the welcoming committee.

"It's just me here, Law." Tiberius stood at the end of the ramp with a weary grin. "I figured you each have had a long enough journey, a large queue of questions, and a well-placed bit of animosity toward me at the moment. I didn't want to add a bunch of unfamiliar strangers to the list. Let's get you in and get you fed. Then there will be ample time to ask all the questions."

Law reached the bottom of the ramp and stood toe-to-toe with Tiberius. His godfather extended an arm on his shoulder before they pulled each other into a hug. Law melted in Tiberius' arms. A hug he had needed since the day their father walked on that omnijet. Though the embrace did not contain nearly as much comfort and reassurance as one from their father, it had just enough affection to bring back some balance that Law felt was lost in his world. Tiberius broke away from the embrace, holding Law for a moment by the arms and studying him over. He watched Tiberius's eyes study every detail of his face. The muted eyes he noticed in the hologram from days earlier were all but sunken. Crevices prepared for the water that began to well in them the longer he stared.

"It's like I'm staring at—" Tiberius shook his head, his eyes slamming shut before releasing his godson. He walked over to Jamie. Their embrace was subdued as he extended his hand to Charlie to shake. "Thanks for getting them here safely and for the unscheduled stop."

"No problem, sir," Charlie acknowledged as he gave a forearm shake. "Always happy to get the hours in. Wouldn't mind captaining one of those omnitransports someday."

"You'll be there sooner than you think, I'm sure." Tiberius smiled at Charlie. "Much like I suspect Jamie will be taking my job before I know it. Senior Scientist, I hear. Congratulations!" He said looking at Jamie with a hand to his chest.

"Thank you, Tiberius," Jamie said with a curt smile. All the niceties were out of the way now and the group was standing in the Zoa. Law looked around. They were in the middle of the desert, flanked by mountains on all sides, as Law spun around in place. The mountains that encapsulated them were massive, jagged, and sprawling. A broken porcelain navy bowl filled with pale blue sand. Law looked toward Ops. It was as if someone had taken a hab setup and increased it in size for all the families on the block. The Ops Center was a beacon in the middle of the sandpit they found themselves in and encircled by a wall similar to the one at Fort Kelly. A fitting research center for their father and Tiberius to do their work. Now, hopefully, Law would figure out exactly what that was.

"So, Ty, this lockbox you've been mysteriously alluding to in your messages," Law said as he continued to survey Ops. "Where is it?" Ty turned to Law, a stunned look on his face.

"Well, um, straight to the point, aren't we," Tiberius said, his hands on his hips, adding a chuckle at the end before stopping as he noticed none of them mirrored his sense of humor. Surveying their faces, he became more serious. "The lockbox is at your father's site office. Where you kindly dropped off April."

Law did not expect that answer. Immediately, he could feel his neck flushing with heat. "What the hell, why didn't we get off there too, Ty?!" Law yelled, advancing on Tiberius.

"Lawrence!" Tiberius said, his hands raised, "Now, listen—"

Law was done with the games, the secrecy. They flew ten hours to get here, they were taken away before they were ready, just to be here and to be running around in circles like dogs who would never get the opportunity to get the bone. Charlie jumped between Tiberius and Law, blocking a clear path to him, and mimicked Law's sidesteps. Even Jamie had widened the blockade with Charlie, not before staring daggers in Tiberius's direction.

"Move!" Law said forcefully. Jamie gasped, then scowled at Law first, but the longer she searched, the quicker her demeanor softened. Charlie squared up, quickly closing the gap between his friend and himself.

"Look, brother, I know you're frustrated," Charlie said, his gaze intense, locking onto his friend's eyes even while Law tried to evade his gaze. Finally, he gave in.

Charlie's deep green eyes were as steady as his heartbeat as he stood chest-to-chest with Law. "We've had a long trip and I would love nothing more than to see you pop Ty right in the jaw. But let's archive it for now. See what he has to say and what a little food and rest can do for you. Worst case, if you need to hit someone, hit me." Charlie ended, protruding his chin downward.

The fire in Law's head retreated to his heart, not fully extinguished but ready to return at a moment's notice. Law raised his clenched fist to Charlie's face, releasing it and allowing the bottleneck of blood to return to its normal flow around his knuckles. He gave Charlie two exaggerated pats on the face.

"And mess up that beautiful jawline? What kind of monster do you think I am?" Law teased with a smile as he squeezed Charlie's arm.

Jamie rounded on Tiberius.

"Listen, everyone. The fact of the matter is, we did not expect you here for another five days." He slapped his hands at his sides. "Then our newly minted commander steps in and starts moving flight schedules, demanding more and more information and correspondence." Tiberius kicked at the dirt as he circled with his fists on his hips. His shoulders raised and dropped as he pushed a deep huff of breath out into the air of the desert's coming night. It swirled into the air before it ascended and dissipated where the aurora had formed. "It was too dangerous for you to be there tonight. There are people—" He paused, his eyes widening. "Things being done right now, that um, that only authorized personnel can be present for. Not just for your safety, but for the safety of everyone on this planet." Law looked at each other. Tiberius offered no opportunity for requests of elaboration.

"Let's get inside. Jamie, I'm aching to show you some of the cool things they let us test out over here before they make their way to Sci-Rez. Charles, you as well. There's a lot of research we're doing on jet and transport upgrades." The two looked at Law in anticipation. He looked at his sister, reading her eyes. Though her stare was subtle, being here would allow her to do what was needed, not only for Rell, but thanks to IQ's tech, for them as well.

"Lawrence, I would love to show you around the command center here. Show you a bit of what your father and I have been up to over here. Then first thing in the morning, should things be...at a reasonable resolution, we'll head out." He finished, as he walked toward the Ops center, beckoning the group to follow. "Come, please. The chefs prepared quite the feast in anticipation of your arrival." Those were magic words for Charlie, who quickly fell into step behind him.

Jamie grabbed Law's hand, giving it a gentle squeeze. She craned her neck, forcing him to stare into her eyes.. She gave a gentle smile of approval before releasing his hand and following behind Charlie. Law took a deep breath and looked in the direction of the encampment. The sun had finally set behind the mountain range, leaving a jagged silhouette sitting softly under the star-freckled night sky. He turned and followed the rest into the Operations Center.

Law had to admit that the Operations Center was impressive, though it was not imposing compared to Sci-Rez. As Tiberius led them through the establishment toward the mess hall, there was plenty to observe.

They entered through the admin entrance, which led to a landing above the main floor of the dome. They had almost fashioned the administrative suite like the bridge of a ship. The entire front wall was transparent so that you could see almost all of Ops. At the center stood a spire that was a smaller replica of the reactor powering all of Fort Kelly. Unlike at Sci-Rez, dozens of computers, holotable stations, and screens encircled the spire worked by scientists around the clock, according to Tiberius.

As they descended the stairs to the main hall, they noticed several workers stop in their tracks and look in their direction. Some pointed and chatted with the person next to them. One worker even waved with a somber look on their face. People who were sitting, stood from their seats and raised a fist to their chest. Tiberius noticed and turned to Law and Jamie.

"As you can see, your father was well respected here," he said, putting a hand on Law's shoulder and squeezed. They all continued through a door on the far side of the main floor.

"The mess hall is just across here. They've made your father's favorite dish, red richeno pasta, made with a roodeno sausage. Though it will never hold a lantern to how your mother used to make it, they've certainly gotten close based on Max's input," Tiberius said through a boisterous laugh. The familiar smell greeted them at the door. Law was transported back to their hab on Tellathia II. Their mother, Autumn, was in the kitchenette, smacking their father with a ladle as he tried to steal a scoop for himself and Tiberius before they set off on the latest expedition. Jamie and Law would chuckle to each other around the table, watching their parent's antics while they did their homework and their stomachs growled.

Law opened his eyes and saw Tiberius do the same, following a long inhale.

"Jamie, don't worry, they have a gobeeno root option for you," Tiberius directed at Jamie. "You are still a vegetarian, I gather?" he said, nodding his head. Jamie confirmed as they walked in.

Once the group had gathered healthy serving sizes of food, Charlie's being the healthiest, they dug in. Law did not realize how hungry he truly was after traveling. The more he thought of it, though, he had not had an actual meal since the night before the Landing Day celebrations. Jamie was prepared enough to pack additional snacks to supplement the lighter MREs that were on the omnijet. The feeling must have been the same because Charlie and Jamie sat across from each other fully focused on their plates. Tiberius stared at Law from across the table, having opted for a purple-colored *juice* that gave off an overwhelming aroma of sweetened dirt. Law paused, chewed and returned Tiberius' stare.

"What?" Law said with a mouth full of pasta. Tiberius chuckled a bit.

"Nothing, nothing, my apologies. I'm just realizing just how long I've been gone," he said, grabbing his dirt juice and taking a large swig. Law pressed a bit.

"Wouldn't have hurt you to maybe come home for a bit. At least for dad's memorial," he said, using the pasta in his mouth to assist the lump in his throat down. This caught Jamie's attention. Charlie had either chosen to ignore them or was blissfully ignorant of everything except what was on his plate. Tiberius slowly lowered his beverage and let out a measured sigh.

"That is fair. I admit it," Tiberius finally said. He slid his cup in small circles on the table as he stared into it. "Frankly, I apologize to both of you." He looked at Jamie as well. "I could never begin to fathom how hard this is for the two of you. You lost Autumn to an awful disease before any child should be without their mother and now your father," Tiberius pushed aside his cup as he tried to emphasize each point, driving his finger into the table with each word.

"You deserved more from me, not just as his friend, but as your god-father," he said, hanging his head. "I think I'd convinced myself staying here and doing the work so that no one else is taken from us was what Max would've wanted."

"Then why not come back to Kelly and explain all of this, Tiberius?" Jamie chimed in. "All you've done aside from abandoning us is make enemies of Admin, especially of Rell, and for what?"

"For the safety of our planet!" Tiberius yelled, slamming his fist on the table. The handful of people scattered throughout the mess hall had all looked up in their direction. Idle chat paused momentarily until people realized who had the outburst. Charlie started to stand before Law grabbed his arm. Jamie stood her ground.

"I'm sorry," he said, running his hand through his salt and peppered locks. "And yes, Jamie, I understand that. But there are forces at work here and now, that are just—" He searched the ceiling for the right words. "Hard to explain at the moment. I am trying so hard to get them under control without causing unnecessary panic. Something I tried to explain to your father." Tiberius' voice trailed off as he let his face fall into his hands. He rubbed at it briefly before he softly uttered his next words. "I just needed a little more time."

Seeing Tiberius this way and hearing the closest thing to an explanation for his absence was eye-opening. Law's empathy resided with his sister. Something about Tiberius' words felt too measured to him. Too pointed. Law thought of his father and his mother. He stood with his tray in hand, looking down at Tiberius.

His godfather wasn't the only person who needed time.

"So did I," Law said in a low tone, shutting down any interest in continuing to hear Tiberius' excuses.

After spending the remainder of the previous evening with Tiberius in a more subdued manner following his outburst, he eventually ushered everyone to their temporary quarters. Before assigning their bunks, he allowed Jamie to mingle with a few scientists on the floor while he showed Law and Charlie around.

Charlie joined Law in his father's old quarters at the base. Though most of it had been stripped of his personal effects at this point. Jamie got an empty bunk a few doors down.

This morning Law woke up and made his way to the mess hall to grab a pastry and some coffee for him and his sister before they would make their way over to the hangar together. Tiberius said they would head to the forward base to finally open their father's lockbox first thing today. Law took a bite of his pastry as he made his way to go get Jamie. As soon as the stale taste of the pastry registered on Law's taste buds he spit it out, about-faced, and threw it in the nearest waste bin. He grabbed two other pastries and resumed his trip to find his sister.

Charlie would pilot one of the Zoa's terrain rovers to get us there as the omnijet underwent mandatory maintenance following the long trip. So, it wasn't a mystery that he was gone before Law woke up. He was likely already at the hangar testing what would be his new temporary addiction.

Tiberius was not very forthcoming after his outburst. After dinner, he was as monotone as a tour guide reciting a rehearsed script from room to room. Law did, however, get to see the office where his father did most of his work in the Zoa. It was at the back of the main level, right beside Tiberius'. Of all the rooms and corridors they had been through, this is where Tiberius said the most.

"He spent more time here than he actually spent in his bunk. Part of his desk can convert into a cot. Our two offices are the most secure rooms in Ops, even more so than the overwatch deck."

Law noticed the hint of a subtle smile Tiberius tried to hide as he talked about it, staring blankly at his desk for a moment before giving two gentle taps to the transparent fiberglass wall. It was the last stop on the impromptu tour before he showed them to their room. He informed them of the meeting time and set off promptly because he was apparently late for a meeting with someone from the forward base. Law couldn't help but notice Tiberius' abrupt change in demeanor between when he showed his father's office and when he got a notification on his CMP and rushed them to their quarters. It was Law's hope that by the fifteen-minute drive to the forward base, Tiberius would have a cooler head and be more forthcoming when he saw him again.

"This pastry is awful." Jamie said, trying to find somewhere to spit out the large bite she had taken before they walked into the hangar.

Law laughed. "They're all awful, sis." He said, handing her his napkin, which she gladly accepted and slapped to her mouth, almost tearing it, wiping her tongue vigorously. Tiberius and Charlie stood next to one of the terrain rovers. Charlie was inspecting one of the airless tires, which were almost twice as tall in diameter as he was. He weaved his hands in and out of the large honeycomb pockets in the wheel.

"Guessing that was one of the pastries?" Tiberius asked with a chuckle as Jamie was crumpling the napkin. "Yeah, we use a lot of bran over here when we run low on ingredients from the Oasis. The chefs are still sorting through everything you brought over. Not nearly as good as your gozooberry muffins though, Jamie," he said with a wink.

Jamie agreed and blushed at Tiberius' compliment. Law took relief in it. Whatever meeting he rushed off to must not have been as negative as his expressions led Law to believe last night. He wasted no time informing them of the current itinerary.

"Again, I just wanted to apologize for my outburst last night. I have been extremely insensitive to the two of you. I lost my friend, but you lost your father. You've lost your mother. And you've probably all but written me off, which I deserve. I need to do better. You deserve that," Tiberius said.

"Ah man, Ty," Charlie said, joining the group. "You big softie. Bring it in, everyone." Charlie grinned wide and outstretched his arms. Jamie groaned, rolling her eyes as she walked past him and tapped him on the head.

Law seized the moment, walked up to Tiberius, and pulled him for a hug. It still lacked the comfort Law had hoped for when they first reunited. But this one felt different. Tiberius relaxed under Law's embrace and his chin rested on Law's shoulder. Once his shoulders had dropped, he exhaled heavily as if to release the worries he clung to. Law held his embrace for just long enough until Tiberius spoke in a hushed tone.

"I'm so, so sorry, *Max*, for everything I've done. I didn't mean for it to be this way," Tiberius said. He broke away from their embrace and grabbed both Law's shoulders and squeezed before he walked toward the rover.

Law looked at him. Did he mean to call him by their father's name? It did not appear that he even knew that he had made the mistake. Law watched Ty walk toward the rover and climb up the embedded ladder to the cockpit. Charlie guided Jamie up after Tiberius, watching her make her way up.

"Isn't she a beauty?" he asked as Law walked up. Law, surprised by the question, had some fun as a much-needed distraction.

"That's my sister, man," Law said, putting on a convincing expression with his raised brow. Charlie snapped his neck to the side.

"Wait, what? No! I mean, well. Damnit. The rover, man." Charlie swung at Law's arm and missed as he jumped away.

"I know, man. Just messing with you," Law said. Though it was a bit of a lie. "You ready to pilot this thing" Law asked as he took a few steps back as he looked up at the large vehicle.

The rover was lowered from its normal height to where its undercarriage almost touched the ground like a sphinx staring majestically out of the hangar's bay door and over the sands of the desert landscape. Charlie walked over and weaved his hand through the combs of the airless tire.

"Oh, hell yeah! Ty was nice enough to let me test this baby out early this morning once he changed its schedule." He turned to Law while hopping up and down like a kid who just found his electribike outside of his hab on Christmas. "It rides like a dream, man. It takes these dunes like a unicorn galloping across clouds. If it wouldn't take us the better part of a year to get back to The Oasis, I'd take this thing back with me." Charlie stopped his child-like bounce and put his hands on his hips and gave it a once over as well. He would have taken it even if it took him a year, Law thought, but unless it could float or transition into a submarine, he'd have to find a way to get it across the Trekana Expanse.

"You ready?" Charlie asked. He leaned on the rear wheel As Law put his foot up. He knew Charlie was asking him much more than that. Not just if he was ready to go, but if he was ready to find out what was at the end of what had been an arduous and roundabout journey.

"Yeah, I think so," Law said, stepping back off the steps embedded in the rover's side. "I think more than anything, I want to know what Dad left. Maybe for closure. Not just for me, but for J." Law looked up toward the cockpit of the rover. He hadn't really thought about what he hoped was in the box. More than anything Law wouldn't mind hearing his voice again. It would be a bit anticlimactic for everything they have been through. But at the end of the day regardless of all the misdirection and secrecy, at the very base of it all, this was about a boy who missed his father.

The ride to the forward base was quick enough to be uneventful. Tiberius pointed out different parts of the desert as they passed, detailing his and Law's father's adventures. It was understandable that he was a bit more upbeat with a cooler head, but Law almost felt like he was jovial, which was not off-putting but was certainly unexpected. Law clung to his every word, letting the stories paint images for Law. It was as if he could almost see his father outside their rover. The blue dunes of the desert rolled like a sandy ocean. In one direction they went on as far as the eye could see. In another they went as far as the mountains that looked more like shadows against the horizon.

After arriving at the forward base, three armed guards emerged from one of the domes. It looked like an oversized hab with over a dozen cubes and channels attached. To Law's surprise, the armed group was led by crew member April.

"Sir, our guests have left, but there's no guarantee..." Tiberius waved April off before he could finish his sentence. April ceased talking at once and looked at Law and Jamie. Tiberius half-turned his head as they stood behind him before giving his command.

"We'll discuss it shortly. For now, I'm going to take Max's son and daughter to his office," he said, continuing to walk. Law and Jamie followed suit as April and the two others stood aside.

"Yes, sir. We'll report to the command center," April said after them. Tiberius did not respond.

"Right this way, guys," Tiberius said as he ushered Law and his sister into the dome.

"Guests?" Law asked.

Tiberius grumbled at the query, looking back at April and sneering. "Yeah, we, uh, are having a predator problem," Tiberius said with a nonchalant wave of his hand. "It's not important."

It wasn't uncommon for exploratory teams to encounter animals of all kinds during their missions within uncharted territory. Their father had shown them pictures of fauna that stood taller than the omnijet hangars when on their hind legs, while animals no bigger than cats spit venom that melted through metal.

They walked into a miniaturized version of the atrium of Sci-Rez that buzzed with people running around in every direction. Drones whizzed overhead, darting across the sky and into the tunnels branching off the dome. The only way Law could think of what it reminded him of was if IQ's hab and the Sci-Rez atrium had merged, and IQ was put in charge.

"What in the name of Helios?" Tiberius muttered as his head swiveled at the chaos. What kind of predator would cause this kind of chaos at a forward station? Law wanted to ask, but Tiberius was now adamant about getting them to their father's office.

"Let's go, guys; I've got to figure out what the hell is going on. This is why you can't change schedules without—" He shook his head and cut off his thoughts. Clearly, the man didn't agree with the way Rell was making decisions. Law followed into the first corridor on the west side of the dome. Law looked at the screen to the right side of the door, Tiberius stopped at. The screen's still-screen read:

Maxwell Augustus Everstorm

Head of Exploration and Discovery

Above it was Law's favorite photo of their father. He stared boldly with his honey-colored eyes. His brownish-black locs were pulled back into a ponytail while his jacket, the jacket Law was now wearing, clinched to his broad shoulders. It gave an authoritative juxtaposition to a man he knew was so loving and gentle.

Bold yet beloved.

Jamie gently placed her hand on the rim of the screen, letting it slide down the side. Tiberius gave them a moment before speaking to the screen.

"Computer, open office," he said just audibly enough not to be harsh.

"Office locked. Please provide authorization," the computer responded. A cursor blinked as it awaited input.

"Override code: Jansen, epsilon, theta, 336." He took a step toward the door.

"Confirmed." The pad let out a two-beeped tone, and the door slid aside almost immediately. Tiberius stepped into the office before moving aside so Law and Jamie could enter and walk toward the center of the room.

It was a mess. Journals lay scattered around on holotables. Mini-data storage drives were stacked on the desk that sat in the center of the room. Law walked toward the desk. A holograph hovered above its base.

It was his family.

His father was behind his mother with his arms wrapped around her waist and chin on her shoulder. A younger version of Law and his sister stood in front on either side of her. Autumn wore a flowing yellow gown. She was the sun around which they all orbited. Law remembered the day. He and Jamie were about ten years old, and his mother demanded that their father postpone his latest expedition so that they could have a proper goodbye. They had a picnic by Tellathia's grand waterfall. There wasn't a cloud in the sky, but the mist from the waterfall was ethereal. Jamie and Law played in the pool at the base. It rose to their hips while the mist covered their skin like a sheer, silk shawl. It was one of the last outings Law remembered with his mother before the electrical storm that ravaged their planet.

They were happy.

They were whole.

Law looked past the photo to the rest of the desk. More journals lay open behind the data drives Law saw stacked when they entered the room. The journals were in his father's handwriting. Law could make it out from a kilometer away. His father preferred writing with pen and paper versus pen and pad.

"Was someone looking for something?" Law asked. He reached over and grabbed the nearest journal, running his fingers over the ink etched into the paper.

Law glanced at Tiberius, who focused on his CMP, then to Jamie, who squatted down in front of the lockbox.

Law replaced his father's journal exactly how he had found it on the desk and walked toward his sister. Tiberius yelled a couple of commands at April before lowering his wrist to end the comm.

"I'm sorry Lawrence. What did you ask me?" Tiberius asked, looking at Law.

"Nothing. Wasn't important," Law lied as he walked up beside his sister.

"Right, look, I've got to get back to figure out what's going on around here. Let's get this thing opened so I can get you guys back to Ops and away from the madness," Tiberius said. He walked up to Jamie's other side and rubbed his hands together.

"Excuse me?" Jamie asked. She stood, facing Tiberius.

"Jamie—" Tiberius' patience must have been running thin based on the harshness of his tone. He faced her and Law stepped beside Jamie, awaiting her next words. Law prayed she chose them wisely.

"*We're* not opening anything. *Our* father left something that he clearly only wanted us, his children, to be privy to. So, I think *we*," she waved her hand between Law and herself, "Could use some privacy." Law inched forward. He was a step closer to Tiberius, slightly placing himself between his godfather and his sister. Tiberius heaved a sigh, dropping his head and pinching the bridge of his nose beneath his glasses.

"I recognize that, Jamie," he said with his eyes closed. "Geez, I don't have time for this. Look, I just need to make sure there is nothing dangerous when you open it, then I can leave you alone with whatever he left for as long as you want."

Jamie made to rebut, but Law fired his query off first.

"Dangerous like what, Ty?" Law asked. "Do you think Dad would leave a case here for his two children with something life-threatening or fatal in it? Besides, I assume we can't just wave our CMPs in front of it to open it or you would have been able to mimic that without using Admin overrides, right?" Law side-stepped between Tiberius and Jamie and waved his right arm over the cases screen.

The case chimed twice while the screen flashed red.

Law shrugged his shoulders and walked back toward Tiberius. "You said something about us *holding the key*? We have no idea what that means. At least I don't, do you, J?" He looked at his sister, who continued staring at Tiberius, but shook her head, no. Law put his hand on Tiberius' shoulder. "Ty, look. You seemed to be preoccupied with whatever is going on here. Why don't you go handle that while we take a moment to figure out what Dad's playing at. It's probably just," Law paused and smirked. "Just one last puzzle he left for us." Tiberius' furrowed brow relaxed, and his shoulders dropped. He drummed his thumb on his side before he looked back toward the office door. Law drove his last point home.

"Look, if there is something more or something that looks off, we will comm you straightaway."

Jamie walked up beside Law and added her reassurance. "Yeah Ty, does this office have the same safety precautions and procedures as all laboratory-based offices?" she asked. Tiberius looked at her with a smile.

"It does," he said, nodding his head, impressed.

"Right. Then, if anything is severe enough, the automated process will kick in and we'll vacate the room immediately before lockdown goes off. I'm sure the recordings come straight to you, anyway."

"Fine. Fine. You two have convinced me enough." Tiberius started walking toward the door hastily. He turned back as it slid open. "I expect you two to find me immediately. Anything that looks off, any objects, no matter how tame they may look." He pointed at them while looking over his spectacles. They both nodded before he ran out the door and it closed. Watching the door, they waited for Tiberius to come back in. When he didn't, they turned and nearly ran back over to the case.

"What is his deal?" Jamie asked. "You think Dad took something, or he's lost something that he thinks is in here?"

Law shrugged his shoulders as he examined the case. It was half the size of the ones Law encountered on the omnijet before almost being caught by April. It sat squarely at the corner of a holotable. It was embedded in the table, almost as if it had been built within it and could not be detached.

"Does it look like someone's been in here looking for something?" He asked as he continued to examine the case. Jamie took a quick scan of the room.

"I had that thought when we walked in as well. I mean, Dad was messy, but never like this. It was always more of an—"

"Organized chaos," they said in unison before sharing a laugh as they reminisced over the number of times their father would justify his penchant for messiness when in the middle of research.

Law finished examining what he was sure was going to turn out to be their father's last puzzle for them. "Any ideas, J?" he asked. "Any *keys* you know about that Dad left us we were supposed to remember somehow?"

"Nothing that I can think of," Jamie said, now taking her turn to examine the case. "At first, I thought he could have left something significant in here for us."

Law looked around the office. There was nothing he could immediately make out that meant anything to him besides the photo on his desk. Law sighed. He felt defeated, thinking about all the times they would come so close to figuring out one of their father's puzzles before he would reveal something hidden in plain sight and staring them directly in the face.

"Yeah, this just looks like one of Dad's offices to me."

Jamie conjured a chair at the head of the holotable after tapping it a few times. She was in her thinking pose. A spitting image of their mother with the mannerisms of their father. Her elbows were on the table, hands in front of her face with her two index fingers pressed together and aligned with her nose. The tips ending at the center of her forehead. Law always found it funny.

"Shut it, Lawrence," she said, trying to force a scowl in place of a smile. Law raised his CMP to his face to give it a command.

"Maybe there was something in Dad's main office back at The Oasis we should have thought of before coming." He arched a brow at his sister before looking down at his wrist. "CMP, show me a rendering of my father's office based on saved images."

"Actually Law, I had thought about that! I stopped by his office before we left, after I met with Commander Rell. I didn't see anything that stood out. No more than I see here." Her eyes clinched while she thought.

"Well, damnit!" Law yelled, slamming his other hand on the case. His father's watch rattled at the contact.

"What the hell?" Law stared at his fist on top of the box.

"What is it?" Jamie jumped up from her chair, causing it to collapse back into the floor.

Law was not sure what was happening. "Dad's watch. It's vibrating? Or pulsating, maybe?" He nodded his head toward the watch to get his sister to confirm.

"What in the…" Jamie held Law's wrist, looking between the watch and her brother. "Has it ever done that before?"

Law shook his head. As far as he was aware, it was an ordinary watch. He lifted his hand and the pulsing stopped as soon as he did. Jamie grabbed his wrist again.

"Weird," Jamie said. She paced the room with crossed arms as she scratched at her chin. "Maybe you're supposed to do something with it? Try laying it on top of the actual screen."

Law complied, placing his fist on the screen. The pulsing restarted, and this time, the case chimed twice. Instead of blinking red, it blinked green once and then back to red.

"Yes!" Law shouted in excitement, pointing to his sister. "That's what I'm talking about, J!"

"It's definitely something," she said with a smile as she bounced from one foot to the other. "What else, though?"

Law already knew, hiding in plain sight as he looked at his sister. Their mother's titanium compass necklace bounced around her neck, glimmering against her brown skin. She stopped jumping around as Law pointed at the talisman.

Jamie slapped her hand to her forehead. "Of course!" she said, dropping her head back. She moved her hair out of the way and grabbed at the clasp at the back of her neck. She dropped the pendant and chain into one hand, kissing it in her palm. Walking around the corner of the table, she dropped the necklace on the other half of the screen while Law put his wrist back in place.

The case chimed twice as it had the prior times, but the tone was higher, and the screen blinked green. The case let out a hiss as the top raised from its shut position until it was completely open.

Both Law and Jamie stood in front of it. The moment they had been waiting for since they received Tiberius' transmission and traversed half of a planet.

They leaned over to look inside the case. Before they could see over the lip of it to view its contents, the holotable the case was on sounded off an ascending electronic whistle that made the hair on the back of Law's neck stand up.

Jamie immediately stuck her fingers in her ears, and when the sound peaked, the table flashed, disorienting Law.

Bang!

A rush of air from the table's base blew over Law's feet. His ears rang as he called for Jamie. He couldn't hear himself until he yelled it so hard he felt his throat get sore. Law slowed his blinking and tried to stretch his eyes as wide as possible to get his vision back to normal. He wiped his eyes when he heard Jamie's muted voice.

She held both of his wrists and tried to bob and weave to stay in his field of vision. Law stopped yelling for her, but he could still feel that his voice was elevated from the vibrations in his ears. Jamie's voice became more apparent, as if someone were turning up the volume on a projection.

"Lawrence! Lawrence, can you hear me now? It's okay. Just keep blinking," Jamie said. As Law steadied, she released his wrists.

"What in the cosmos happened?" Law asked. He intermittently mixed in a hard blink as he looked around. Luckily, the room was dimmer than before, and his hearing had returned to almost normal.

"I think it was an electromagnetic charge of some sort. Our CMPs are down. The tech in my glasses is down. The power in the office is on emergency backup. Or at least some version of it. There are no sirens and some of the normal protocols have not fired. So, whatever that was, was pretty powerful or pretty targeted." Law nodded as he stared at one spot for a moment.

"Did you not get disoriented by that flash?" He asked Jamie.

"No, my glasses respond pretty quickly to drastic changes in external stimuli," Jamie started before Law waved his hand. She cleared her throat. "The lenses dimmed enough to block the flash to where it didn't hurt as much. Couldn't do much for the bang, though; my ears are still ringing a bit." She stuck her finger in one of her ears and winced. "That must have been when the EM charge went off because it took my glasses out and everything went dark."

Law got it. Maybe Tiberius was right. Maybe they should have waited for him. "Why would Dad have us come all this way to hit us with an EM charge?" Law looked at the case to answer that question. Apparently, the case complied. A bright green beam shot from the center of the case's lid before spreading a blanket of neon green light across the room. It started at the top and then panned down, bathing both Law and Jamie in its effervescent glow. Once it had reached their feet, it sprung back together, shooting the single beam of light between them and retracting back to its source.

"Confirmed," the case's robotic voice stated from its permanent place on the holotable. Law and Jamie re-approached the case with caution in their steps. A light turned on this time, just above where the green beam had sprouted on the case's top and shined down to the floor. A 188-centimeter-tall hologram of their father materialized right in front of them, starting from his boots and ending at the crown of his head. Their father appeared to look directly at them before he spoke.

"Lawrence. Jamie. We don't have much time."

L aw and Jamie stared at their father to the point where they barely allowed themselves to blink. He looked flustered. His untied locs cascaded over his shoulders as he spoke. Stubble peppered his typically clean-shaven face. However, his words were measured and concise despite seeming like he was rushing.

"There is so much I wish I could say to the two of you, but that will have to wait. I'm leaving this message for you so that you know it is me. So that Jamie knows I am the man who sang to her for three hours straight until she fell asleep while fighting off Cerulathian fever. She fought like the fighter I've known her to be since the day she looked me in the eye and rubbed my stubble with a hand barely the size of a Tellathian spider." Maxwell smiled and rubbed his stubble but continued. "And Law knows I am the man who taught him how to ride his first hoverboard and took the blame when he rode it in the jutted lands when his mother told him not to."

Jamie turned to Law with her jaw hanging. Law looked out of the side of his eyes, pretending not to see her. Their father went on. As he was recording, Law noticed he was fiddling with things. At one point, he picked up one of the data storage units he had noticed on his desk when he walked in.

"Things have taken an unexpected turn here. I don't want to say too much as I'm not even sure if I'll be able to keep all of this from being compromised," Maxwell paused and looked off into the distance. It seemed like he was looking toward the door. Law did the same out of instinct. "Forces beyond our world have come into play, and Tiberius is compromised. Operations in the Zoa are compromised. I don't know what promises he made to him, but we have been trying to uncover—" Maxwell paused again. He walked in the circle as if he was walking around something. It had to be his desk. Law saw him raise his hand and heard a familiar double chime. The chime of the lockbox this had come from. "Everything you need to know is in here." Maxwell held a thick brown leather-bound journal.

Law remembered seeing his father carry it with him all the time. He opened it once when his father requested that he bring it to him when he had forgotten it at their hab once and seen nothing but symbols and, at the time, the least legible writing he had seen before. Unlike with the pads, these journals did not take what you wrote, make it more readable, and format it for you.

Maxwell's transmission flickered, causing him to stop and look around the room before looking back in their direction. "It is of the utmost importance that these items get to Vice Commander Rell. The fate of our... The fate of Aurornova and of Cerbraxia depend on it." Law's heart raced while his mind swirled. Why would they take this stuff to Rell? He looked at Jamie.

"The fate of where?" he asked. In all his studies, he was almost certain he'd never heard of Cerbraxia.

Jamie waved him off before shushing him. Law complied as Maxwell continued, his transmission flickering again. This time he stopped in his tracks, dropping everything he was holding. His head hung between his massive shoulders. His locs fell around his face like massive stalactites pointing toward the ground. The transmission flickered more frequent-ly now. Whatever was happening was coming to a head.

Maxwell grabbed something from the desk and stood tall. He pulled his majestic main of locs back and unraveled a bold headband from his wrist before wrapping it around the ponytail he made. Law squint-ed to see the band through the interference of the flickering from the transmission. Then he looked at his sister, who was gently caressing her headband, the same headband with tears running down her face. Maxwell zipped his jacket up and walked around the desk. Sitting on it, like he had done so many times before, whenever it was time to have a serious discussion with them.

"I've got to go. I'm worried whatever Ty is doing with them will tear our planet apart." Their father stood in front of them now. Law fought every feeling in his body to hug the holographic man who stood before them. He was trying not to collapse onto this ethereal being that was merely a representation of the rock that would have been otherwise capable of the weight he had.

"I love you both so, so much. I hope with everything in me, you will never see this. But if you do, just know that there has yet to be a planet I've found that compares to the world I've had in my hab," Maxwell said, tears welling in his muted gaze. Though he was solemn, a gentle smile graced his face, forcing his single dimple into his cheek. "I know you're trying so hard to find your place in this world right now and that feels so scary, so uncertain…don't limit yourself. Your light is meant to be among the stars, my son."

Law's chest tightened, and he clenched his fist.

"You bring people together in a way I haven't seen since I met your mother. And like her, you'll unite civilizations someday."

Somehow, Maxwell had found him. It was as though he knew exactly where Law would stand because his projection looked directly at him. His father's eyes had a look in them that was steady, resolute, and stable even though the transmission was not. It was not a hug, but Law took comfort in it.

Maxwell turned to Jamie. "And my baby girl," Jamie choked out a sob and her hand lifted to cover her mouth. "Keep leaning into the leader you're becoming. This side of the universe will find its way through what is to come and will do that while looking to you." Maxwell looked at his shoes. His hands clasped in front of him. "There is no point in time or direction in space you could ever find where your mother and I wouldn't be proud of the two of you. Only one where we would meet again." Maxwell's head continued to hang for a moment before he looked up. The transmission ended and his projection dissolved. They were alone again.

Law and Jamie walked directly toward each other and embraced as their CMPs powered up. Their father's office initiated its restarting sequence.

L aw remained frozen in the middle of his father's office, disregarding how much time had passed. All he cared about now was he had a better idea of what happened to his father and that Tiberius could be at the cusp of it all. His world felt smaller now, and hope was harder to than ever to grasp. Everything he thought he knew about his father, godfather, and the new commander was wrong, and his father's warning set him on edge.

Law's CMP chimed loudly and vibrated violently, pulling him from his sister's embrace. He was getting an urgent comm. Law looked at the screen. It was Tiberius. Jamie waved at him to accept it.

Law wiped his eyes vigorously, needing to hide his devastation. Jamie reached over and straightened his jacket and gently fluffed out his hair. He swatted at her hands, ducking and weaving to get her to stop.

"Cut it out, Lawrence."

He stopped and accepted whatever she was doing as his CMP chime blared louder.

"Okay! Okay! " Law demanded, glaring at his sister. He straightened himself up and patted at the top of his head to make sure everything was even before answering the comm. "Uh, Hey Ty," he said, trying to look as convincingly natural as he could muster.

"Lawrence! What is going on?" Tiberius demanded. "I have commed you at least twice. I was getting ready to send April and his team to check on you two. Did you get the case opened?" Law looked up at his sister. Jamie shook her head. "Uh, yeah, we got it opened."

Tiberius' eyes widened, and he snatched his glasses from his face. "I'm on my way!"

"Wait! It's—"

Tiberius ended the comm before he could finish his sentence. Jamie held her hands up in confusion.

"Why the in the cosmos would you tell him, Lawrence?" she asked.

"If I would have said no, how much more time would that have bought us before he randomly popped up without us knowing or before he sent April and his goons?"

"I don't know, but he's coming now. So, what's your solution to that?" Law looked around in the office.

"How long before the office is back to main power? Before the cameras start recording again?" He remembered she knew the procedures based on what she told Tiberius earlier.

"It usually takes about five minutes at Sci-Rez, but we have so many redundant power arrays over there between all of our different sources of power." She raised her CMP and tapped at it before she pinched it, tugging at it as if it had an imaginary thread at its center.

She threw it straight up into the air as if to discard it, instead her CMP cast what looked like a net over the room, starting from her wrist and shooting toward the ceiling and all four corners of the room. It then burst, sprinkling down on them like translucent blue rain. She looked at her CMP as if she were impressed by the results of whatever it was, she just did.

"It looks like it's still struggling to find its restart routine. We maybe have ten more minutes," she said, looking to Law.

"So that gives us about seven to hide whatever is in there before Ty gets here," Law said, looking back at his sister. She asked no further questions as they leaped toward the case and looked inside.

First thing Law saw was two of the data storage units like the ones on their father's desk. One with a label that read *Family —– Use This*, while the other was blank.

Law raised his eyebrow at the weird label but looked on. The journal that he recognized as his father's was in the center of the case and then a smaller case, similar to the one it was in.

Law reached in and grabbed the smaller case and held it in between him and his sister. He flipped the two latches on the miniature case and slowly opened it. Law lifted the lid and a powerful amber glow erupted from the seams of the opening at its top. Once it was fully opened, Law shielded his eyes from the light and angled his head back.

Jamie smirked and pointed at her tinted glasses. Law lowered the case further from their eyes and squinted to figure out what was giving off the powerful glow. It pulsed and made a high-pitched whistling sound.

In the center of the case was a jagged amber crystal. It wasn't smoothed and faceted, as though it was a gem to be admired or styled into some ornate shape; it was raw. Like someone chiseled it from the side of a mountain. After Law's eyes adjusted, the light emanating from the crystal had dimmed until there was a faint glow at the center. It was like a small fire trapped inside of amber-colored glass. The crystal gave off a warmth that Law felt on his skin, even though the rock was small enough to fit fully in the palm of his hand. He handed the case to his sister.

"My glasses aren't picking anything up from it. There is no information on any known databases about this substance," Jamie said as she gyrated the case in her hand, making sure not to tilt it too harshly or it would fall.

Law grabbed the journal and opened it to a random page. His father's scribbles, ink-lined drawings, and rough sketched maps littered the page. Jamie's CMP chimed.

"Three minutes to main power restoration," the computerized voice said, bringing them back to reality.

"We got to move," Law whispered harshly. He grabbed the case from his sister and slammed it shut. With the journal in hand, he grabbed the data storage unit that was unlabeled. He walked over to the wall across the room where their father's old satchel hung. He stuffed the items in the satchel, then tried to make it look as unbothered as possible.

"Why'd you leave this one?" Jamie asked, holding it up.

"I'm thinking Dad thought ahead," Law said as he returned to Jamie. She handed him the unit. He flipped it over and showed her the inscription. She looked at him as if she did not understand. If Law was being honest with himself, he was not sure he knew what he was doing either, but it was worth a try.

He gave one last look in the case before the main lights in the office came back up. Seconds later, the door to the office slid aside and Tiberius came through.

"So? You got it opened?" he asked before barely passing through the door. Law looked at the unit in his hand.

"We did Ty," Law said. He held up the storage unit so that Ty could see it clearly. "Dad was nice enough to leave us something to remember him by." Law hoped the trickle of sweat that passed the corner of his eye would be mistaken for a stray tear.

"That's it?" Tiberius asked, taken aback. He shuffled. "I mean, uh. That's great. That's really great." Tiberius' voice trailed off.

Law swore he heard him grumble something under his breath as he turned his head. "Would you mind if I—maybe looked?" Jamie advanced to stop Tiberius, but Law added some additional misdirection.

"Sorry, it's just that we haven't had a chance to see what's in it. I'm sure it's okay, J. I mean, Ty is family, right?" Law held the data unit toward Tiberius. He hesitated, looking between Law and Jamie. His sister shared the same stunned look of their godfather.

Law's stare was stone cold. At least, that is what he was going for. But his nerves were shot. Whatever his father meant by, *use this*, on the inscription was about to come to light very shortly and Law's gamble would either pay off or be the exact opposite of what their father wanted. Tiberius accepted the handout.

"Um, thank you, Lawrence," Tiberius said as he took the storage unit toward the holotable. Jamie huddled close to her brother as they followed in Tiberius' wake.

"I hope you know what you're doing," she said under her breath so they could not be heard.

"Me too," Law responded. Tiberius placed the data unit at the corner of the holotable opposite the case before tapping at the table in a sequence until it powered up before he stepped back. They all eagerly awaited the end result. Several moments passed. Law's sweat was unmistakable now while his sister chewed on her cheek. Even Tiberius was scratching at his thumb with his clasped hands at his waist.

After what felt like an eternity to Law, the holotable sprayed a square holographic video out from its center. It was their mother...in labor? With Tiberius by her side? He looked worse for wear, as their mother was sweating and screaming in pain. Tiberius screamed in pain as one of his arms was contorted in what looked like an uncomfortable fashion. He arched his arm around to talk to Maxwell on his CMP.

"Get here now!" the Tiberius in the recording shouted. The recording skipped ahead. Their father was dabbing the sweat away from their mother's head while he hung from the side of the infirmary bed. She was holding two newborn babies in each arm. Tiberius sat in a chair in the background, rotating his right arm at his shoulder. This elicited an audible chuckle from him as they watched.

The recording skipped ahead once more. This time, someone had the drone pointed at their chest. As they backed away, allowing it to hover for the recording, it refocused to show what looked like a younger Commander Rell. She walked backward and threw her arm around Tiberius who stood beside Autumn and Maxwell with an omnijet behind them. Tiberius dropped his head and pressed at the holotable. The transmission dissolved. Law noticed Tiberius lightly tapping his fist at the table several times as his head hung.

"This was all that was in there?" he finally asked, still not looking up. Law answered.

"Yeah. When it opened, there was a comm recording for us. He just said he loved us, and to follow our hearts in life." Law answered softly.

"And that we'll meet again someday," Jamie added.

Tiberius slammed his eyes shut again before tapping at the table once more. The case responded.

"Recording retention set to single view. Recovery options — not available."

Tiberius's hardened expression landed on Law, then flicked to his sister. "And you are sure that is all he mentioned?" Tiberius asked, studying them as he scrutinized every movement of their face. They both nodded. Jamie moved in closer to Law and laid her head on his shoulder.

She was selling it. Hopefully not overselling, Ty believed it.

"Okay...okay," Tiberius relented, grabbing the storage unit from the table, holding it in both hands and giving it a gentle tap before handing it over to Law. "Thank you for allowing me to look at that. It wasn't..." Tiberius cut himself off as he searched for words. "We have to go. I thought we had more time than we did, but apparently, we didn't. I'm going to send you back with Charlie and remain here to smooth things over. Please don't ask me why. It's been a trying morning already."

Law had no intention of asking any follow-up questions. Getting away is exactly what he wanted. He needed to fill Charlie in and find a safe place to discuss exactly what all this meant. Law held his hands up innocently to indicate he would abide. Jamie did the same. All they needed was the last piece to make a swift getaway.

"Hey Ty, would it be okay if I grabbed dad's old satchel? I always been quite fond of it," Law said, motioning over to the wall the bag he had visited moments ago still hung. Tiberius stared at Law, who sat before him in his best friend's jacket. Law suppressed the instinct to run toward and grab it, sling it over his shoulder, and tuck tail.

Instead, he tugged at the shoulder strap a bit and smoothed it against his hip, taking a cue from his sister, this time hoping to sell the innocence of the request. Tiberius had scooted over to the case and peaked inside it. He sighed and stalked back to the door of the office.

"Let's go. I need you two back to Ops post quickly," Ty said, stopping within the door frame ensuring they were following.

Law made toward them. Jamie winked at him as she made toward the door. As Law reached the door, he took one last look into the office and over at the case where he got to see his father one last time. Something he never thought he'd get to do. For that, he is grateful and filled with a new sense of purpose. The door slid closed, and they followed Tiberius back to the rover.

Tiberius had ushered Law and his sister back into the rover and demanded they head straight for Ops, exactly the way they had come. No detours and no stops. Ty demanded they he be notified the moment they arrived. The first ten minutes of the ride were practically filled with Law and Jamie word vomiting everything they learned to Charlie while also showing him their newly acquired parting gifts. After they had both taken turns telling Charlie the minute-by-minute bit of action, he could do nothing but drive and digest. After sitting for a moment of satisfaction getting all of that off his chest, Law realized he'd forgotten all about Charlie while in his dad's office.

"Where have you been? What have you been doing this whole time?"

"Watching," Charlie said slightly over his shoulder as he focused on navigating. "Mostly at least. There wasn't much going on to begin with. Then something happened." Charlie tapped some controls to his side before he released the steering mechanism and rotated to face them. "Auto-pilot should be able to take it from here now that we're through the dunes." He braced his elbows on his knees and swiveled his attention between Law and Jamie. "I chatted with our friend, April, a bit. Tried to really get the nature of his involvement here. He was much less gratuitous with me this go 'round. You'll be happy to know," Charlie directed at Law. "After several additional unsuccessful attempts at small talk, he got some weird alarm on his CMP, and everyone lost their mind. I'm guessing that's when Tiberius must have left you guys in the office." Charlie said. "They kept saying things like, why are *they* coming back? What do *they* want now?" Charlie said as he shook his head.

"That's certainly no coincidence," Jamie added, referring to the ominous group their father kept mentioning in his final comm. Law agreed. There was another party at play here, and that was clear. Whoever or whatever was causing problems was likely who or what cost them their father. Based on the activity today, they or it seemed to be more relentless now and it was keeping Tiberius off his game.

"So, what do we do with what we have now?" Jamie asked in no specific direction. Charlie put his hands up and looked at Law.

"Well, sis. I say you feed Rell a little bit of information. Apparently, Dad trusted her and that was before she was a commander. But…"

"Don't give her a snargolopod before she's shown me, she can milk the fangs," Jamie said with an indulgent nod. Charlie stared between her and Law before he spoke.

"I hope you know what that means because I don't want to know what that is, why it has fangs, or what we need its milk for." Charlie faked a gag and Law smiled, but he was just as confused about those things as his best friend. But he got the gist of what his sister was saying.

"Right...I think," Law said, his eyebrow raised. "Maybe she'll voluntarily clear some of these gray areas we have. From there, I say we take a little tour of Ops while Tiberius is otherwise occupied at the forward base. Maybe people will be a bit more talkative without him around. Maybe we'll be able to find some people loyal to Dad?"

Jamie and Charlie both nodded their acceptance of Law's idea. Charlie raised his hand. Law looked at him, then up at his hand before he pointed at his friend.

"Uh, Charles? How may I help you?" Law asked, tilting his head to the side.

"Uh, yes, thank you, Mr. Everstorm. So happy to be here, by the way. Will we be starting our secret mission before or after dinner? I saw that we're having fresh granger fish tonight." Charlie finished with a hand on his belly.

Law let his face fall to his palm while hearing a groan of annoyance from his sister beside him. Law leaned forward to grab the seat cushion of Charlie's chair and slowly rotated it back to the forward position as they all laughed, and Charlie took back the rover's controls.

21

"So, what have you learned?" Law asked his sister as she handed him a hot cup of coffee. The two stood on an observation balcony looking toward the forward station that they would be traveling to via terrain rover.

"Nothing more worth reporting to Rell so far beyond what I told her yesterday," Jamie answered Law's inquiry, taking a slow sip of coffee from her mug and leaning on the balcony railing. She shook her head as she looked across the horizon. "But there's definitely something going on here, Law. Nothing that I saw yesterday makes any sense."

"How so?" Law asked, turning away from the view and now locking in on what his sister was saying.

"Well, Ops serves as the hub to conduct all sorts of experiments and research similar to what we do at Sci-Rez. The nature of what they normally do is analytics based on findings in the name of terraforming, environmental impact, or things along those lines." Jamie looked behind them, scanning up and down the observation balcony before double-tapping her CMP. "I was able to grab a few shots of what they may be working on over by the site of the accident before the workers dissolved them or switched the screens away." She swiped through a few snapshots. Many of them were blurry, others obscured by an object or doorway. Law's eyebrow was raised as he took over, scanning the walkway for Jamie, waiting for her to show him something identifiable.

"You're not exactly a top-notch investigator with these shots," Law said. He started bouncing on the balls of his feet, waiting for her to get to something.

"Shut it, Lawrence. I wasn't sightseeing. I was trying to spy. It's not like I could just raise my CMP and start tapping away." Jamie glared before lifting her spectacles into her hair to look closer at the images. "Here we go," she said, holding it closer to him. Jamie pinched the image and pulled it away from her pad so that she could 3D render it.

Law had no idea what Jamie was showing him. It looked like a miniature version of an omnijet part Law had seen Charlie working on. Law raised his hands as he waited for an explanation. Jamie mimicked Law, shaking her head.

"It's nothing I've ever seen before. I would have said maybe a part for the omnitransport or something, but they don't have any hueys here to maintain those. Why would they be looking into that?" She expanded it as much as she could after taking an additional scan around the deck. "Hell, Law, it's nearly the size of one of the hueys. I haven't seen anything like this in our databases back at Sci-Rez for anything: geological, biological, terraforming, nothing. If I didn't know better, I would think..." Jamie hesitated as she spun the holographic machine several times, examining it from every angle.

"Think what, J?" Law asked. She was still shaking her head.

"Law, if I didn't know better, I would say this looked more like—like a weapon." She finally got out, though she chewed at the inside of her cheek for a bit.

"A weapon?" Law asked. He grabbed the holographic replica and studied it like Jamie did. Trying to figure out what could have led Jamie to the thought. "Where—how would you come up with such a thing?"

"Shh, Law!" Jamie slapped her hand across Law's mouth as someone walked by, blowing their coffee and offering an enthusiastic wave. The twins waved in unison as Law slapped Jamie's hand from his mouth. The passerby raised an eyebrow but did not break their stride. Law watched them as they opened a door into Ops about twenty meters from where they were. When the door closed, Jamie continued, not before she scowled at Law.

"My bad! It just caught me off guard," Law said in a hushed tone. "I mean, we've got *weapons*. I'm not fuzzing out about that. There are plenty of things Dad encountered on all his exploratory missions he would tell us about that wanted to rip him apart on planets they gave up on. But none that needed to be the size of a building!" Law said through clenched teeth. This time he made sure to scan for more friendly passersby. Jamie finally waved away the holo-image. She took her coffee back off the ledge and took a long draw.

"Everyone I passed by seemed super stressed. The one giving me the tour thought Tiberius brought me here to *help them meet their deadline*," Jamie said, letting out a nervous laugh. "She seemed so relieved. She even hugged me." Jamie stared into Law's eyes. He knew that look of empathy. If Jamie could have, she would have helped that worker shovel Veloceros dung had she asked.

"Helped her with what? What deadline?" he asked. Law grabbed his sister's arm gently, giving it a slight squeeze.

"That's just it, Law. I have no idea. Had Tiberius and Dad been under some sort of deadline to deliver something to Admin, I suspect Rell would have told me." Jamie was back to chewing at the inside of her cheek as she paced side to side. "But Rell acts as if she has no idea of what's going on over here and she's scared if she comes over herself, she'll spook Tiberius or something."

They had been there only one night, and Law felt like he was drinking from the Trekana Expanse. Since they touched down in the Zoa, they had seen Tiberius fuzz out after being only slightly questioned. Law learned his father spent most of what was his last few days in a forward station that they had to wait to visit because it was *too dangerous*. And the most surprising thing was that whatever they were working on over here had to do with something neither he nor Jamie had ever seen before. If his sister's intuition was correct, maybe something dangerous and, more importantly, prohibited by every Interplanetary Coalition he had ever learned about in his primary studies. Even worse was that whatever it was meant for, his father either had something to do with it or it was the reason he wasn't here with them today.

Law prayed it was not the former.

Jamie put her hand on his and, without prompt, said, "I'm sure whatever it is, Dad had nothing to do with it." She gave his hand a couple of reassuring pats before adding one last squeeze. "Where's Charlie?"

Law had almost forgotten Charlie had woken him up before daybreak. He explained to his sister that Tiberius would allow them back to the forward base at midday. Charlie would take Tiberius over ahead of them so that he could *facilitate* things after what happened yesterday.

"I'm sure he did," Jamie said to the last point.

Law nodded. "Well, let's get going. The sooner we get back over there, the sooner we can start piecing together all of this."

Law took one last long drag of his coffee, letting the liquid warm his chest against the crispness of the Zoa's morning breeze. Jamie followed suit, and they set off toward the hangar to find Charlie.

"What do you mean he's not ready for us?" Law's words reverberated through the empty hangar. He, Charlie, and Jamie were the only ones there. Charlie threw his hands up at Law's frustration.

"Look, man, I'm just the messenger at this point. I told Ty, he's starting to walk a thin line. It's one thing when Jamie's patience runs thin with him, but you..." Charlie searched Law's face, likely to see how much heat Law harbored from the night before.

"You're right. Apparently, I was more tired than I thought. Sleep did me some good. Coffee too," Law said before returning to his original inquiry. "How long did he say it would take before we could come?"

"He just said he would comm me when they were ready. Doubled-down on the whole, *we weren't supposed to be here for another week,* business." Charlie said, rolling his eyes. His words were a little less savory, along with the names he had for Commander Rell.

"I'm getting anxious too, Law. The longer we wait, the longer until I can show you two how this baby runs through these blue sand dunes." Charlie growled at the anticipation before turning back to his friends. "I can't, for the life of me, figure out what requires that much safety that we are *forbidden* to come."

The twins looked at each other before looking at Charlie. He examined Law's face first then Jamie's before his eyes widened.

"Wait. What did I miss?" Charlie asked. Law's arms crossed as he rubbed his face with his free hand. Jamie was already pulling up the holo-images.

Law, Charlie, and Jamie climbed into the rover as it rose to its full height. The rover was twenty meters off the ground with the hatch open. Law and Jamie stared at Charlie as he flung through the images at different angles the same way they had that morning. He'd spin it around, squint into the finest details they had overlooked, groan, and move on to the next image.

"What do you think, man? Are we completely off?" Law finally asked after what felt like half an hour of repeating the cycle.

"I don't know, bro. I mean, a lot of these shots show parts that could be used for omnitransports, but I just don't know about them as much as I do about the jets. Fundamentally, they're similar, but the biggest difference is the transports are made for interplanetary travel, not cross-planet travel. They're more powerful on so many levels for that reason alone, as you would imagine," Charlie said. He leaned onto the armrest of the rover pilot's chair. The steering wheel rested directly behind him at its center. Law and Jamie were in similar cushy chairs that felt like they hovered above the rovers' floor panel rather than being bolted down.

"Exactly," Jamie chimed in. "The transports are capable of interstellar travel and have planted our species to the farthest reaches of space, time and time again. The power at the core of their engines can easily be converted to weapons of mass destruction, like any and every power source we've harnessed since the dawn of time." Jamie grabbed the last holoimage from him and expanded it to its largest render point. The bright blue image hovered between them until she moved it to one side of the rover's cabin. She double-tapped her CMP, causing the image to flicker slightly. "Render, an omnitransport's main power manifold." A second holoimage sprung from of Jamie's CMP pad, a similar shaped image displayed next to the unidentified object from Jamie's shots. Jamie was able to take this one and explode it into a million pieces surrounding a pulsating core. It looked like a miniature sun with a thousand satellites orbiting its aura.

"This is our phasic, anti-plasma core that makes interstellar travel possible, but more importantly, powers much of our planet along with the more environmental ways we harness," Jamie said, pointing at the tiny sun. The glow cast an eerie light off her face that matched her tone. She was reverent yet astounded. "The fact we are able to funnel this level of power into an energy we can control is nothing short of a miracle.

There's so much we don't know about it aside from the intergalactic elements used to create it." Jamie collapsed backward in her chair and stared at her companions.

Law opened his arms wide to grab the exploded view before closing them to squeeze it back into its original container. He studied the similarities between the structures. He grasped at an idea, half hoping he could pardon his godfather with it.

"I mean, look at the similarities. Maybe they're working on a new—" Halfway through, Law realized he was way out of his depth. "Container?" He threw out the only word he could think of.

Charlie stepped in to save him. "More of a powerhouse, but we get your point, buddy," Charlie said, smacking his friend on the back.

"Right, a powerhouse! Dad said before he left, they had discovered something that could possibly change things for not only Aurornova but beyond, right?" Law questioned. He was staring at Jamie. She, however, did not seem convinced.

"I don't know, Law, maybe, but looking through some of the other photos and the specs on this thing that my CMP was able to pull out in the short time, nothing points to a flight application." Jamie stood opposite her brother, looking between the two structures now. "And if that was the case, why be so secretive about it?" she asked.

"Because they almost got caught," Charlie said in a solemn tone Law had never heard. Law and Jamie turned in unison.

"Caught with what?" Jamie asked, seemingly perplexed. She waved away the images, causing them to be absorbed back into her pad.

"Caught testing their weapon. And it cost your father his life." Charlie's eyes widened. He looked at Law first, waiting for him before recognizing his mistake and waving him off. He looked at Jamie and decided to tell them what he was thinking. "Jamie, I agree with you. Like you said, the fact that we were able to harness the power of that core is a miracle, but one of the first things we learned about it in flight school is that it is volatile like nothing else that we've discovered in the universe." Law hung onto every word. Any substance they exposed it to later turned it into a deadly bomb capable of destroying a planet.

"Cerosia!" Jamie said, slapping her hand to her forehead.

"Exactly!" Charlie shouted. He clapped his hands, causing it to echo throughout the hangar.

"Cer-where? Charlie, haven't you talked about that planet before?" Law asked.

"Cerosia." Jamie repeated, "It's a planet that we've since deemed a test planet, back when space travelers were a bit less regulated and we discarded uninhabitable planets as if we had dominion over them. It's where some of the first tests using the power source from the transports were done. In its early stages, many space organizations were still trying to figure out all the applications it could be used for. That, of course, included for offensive capabilities."

"I roughly remember something along those lines in our studies," Law mentioned, barely following what they explained. "It was still early then, though, right? Blowing up and not nearly as reliable?" he asked.

"That's the thing, Law! It nearly cratered the entire planet. If there were possibilities of life on that planet in the slightest, it annihilated that possibility for the next several lifetimes. All because they were trying to combine it with other elements. Make it stronger, make it more controllable. It's the reason almost a dozen galactic bi-laws and more exist now."

"Laws that Ty could very well be breaking right now," Charlie said.

"Laws that he and our father could have been breaking?" Jamie asked more to herself than to her brother or Charlie.

Law turned in time to see a solitary tear slide down her cheek. She quickly slid her arm across her face.

"Absolutely not, J. Don't think that for a second," Law said. "Maybe not for Tiberius, but especially not for Dad. There's just too much static here to make any judgment calls." Law grabbed his sister and pulled her in for a hug as her tears flowed more freely. He could not help letting a few tears flow himself. "We'll get to the bottom of this. If Ty is going to keep pushing us off, then we're going to dig worse than we would have if he just let us come over." Still embracing his sister, Law looked at Charlie. "Did he give any idea of a time he would be ready?"

Charlie shook his head before tapping into his CMP on his arm, checking his messages.

Law waited to see if, by some miracle, Charlie would say that he had a new message from Tiberius that they had missed while they were sitting in the rover speculating. Charlie looked up with pursed lips. He shook his head as he dropped his gaze. Law broke his embrace from his sister and looked at her tear-stained face. The embers that remained from the anger Law temporarily quelled had found new kindling.

"He has until this afternoon. Otherwise, tonight, we'll make the trip whether he likes it or not," Law said, his heart picking up the pace.

Charlie looked up at him. "He'll see us coming as soon as I pull this baby out of the hangar. Unless you know how to tap through the encryption and disable...well a couple of things, really."

Law coaxed Jamie to sit down after she gave him a reassuring nod. He did the same.

"Don't you know how?" Law asked Charlie.

"I operate 'em, mate. Hacking wasn't part of the training," Charlie answered. Law chewed at his nails as he thought through their options. He looked at the blank screen of his sister's pad that lay on the tactical table between the three of them. Hoping it had been listening to their conversation and would sprout out a holoimage diagram of how to disable the rovers' trackers and GPS signals.

It did nothing of the sort, but it gave him the idea he was looking for. One that he had to wrestle with in his mind a bit before he would allow himself to say it out loud. Perhaps a better route than the one suggested.

Any other route. He chewed at one extra nail in hopes something would present itself, but it did not. So, he gave in.

"Charlie..." Law let his face fall to his palm. "Does IQ owe you any more favors?"

It took a lot for Law to ask Charlie to call in a favor to IQ, but time was of the essence and Law was getting desperate. If Tiberius had just been straight with him and his sister and quit stalling or *protecting them,* then it would not have had to come to this.

But Law had been in the Zoa for almost twenty hours and the only thing he knew was that he had more questions than when he arrived. Even worse, his questions felt more perilous than what they had before. The most important ones to him right now were what happened to his father, what they recovered from the lockbox, and whether Tiberius was involved in whatever his father warned them about.

Whether what Jamie found was a weapon, an engine, or an energy source made no difference to Law, but unfortunately it was the only thing they could possibly gain more insight on until they got to the forward camp.

Law looked at Jamie sitting with him just outside the hangar. They had vacated the rover to allow Charlie to work whatever magic that he could with IQ. Charlie felt it best that Law and Jamie not be there. He did not want to entice IQ with any additional opportunities or open-ended *favors.* Law agreed and Jamie preferred it. So, for now, they waited outside on a cold metal bench beside the bay door. The Zoa was notably cooler during the day and nothing short of brisk at night. As it sat essentially on the opposite side of the planet as the oasis, these seasons opposed each other. In The Oasis, it was the summer. In the Zoa, it was the winter. Something about the blue sands and faded mountain range in the distance made it feel that much colder were it not for the Sun shining boldly directly above them.

"They've been at it for a while, don't you think?" Jamie asked, looking at her wrist CMP to check the time.

"Yeah, well, I learned IQ can be a bit long-winded." Law rolled his eyes, as he recalled their encounter just a couple of days ago. "I'm sure he's trying to get whatever he can from Charlie to make it worth his while." Law turned to look back into the hangar and up into the rover. The translucent glow within the domed top of the rover had disappeared, signaling the call must have ended.

"I just hate that they're using my pad to do whatever it is they're doing," Jamie said, her leg bouncing rapidly on the ball of her foot as she looked back toward the rover with Law. "Oh good! He's coming out," she said, a hint of relief in her voice.

The hatch at the top slid back as Charlie climbed out of the cockpit and down the embedded ladder that flipped out after the hatch reached its *open* position. As his boot plopped on the cold cement floor of the hangar when he jumped down, Law and his sister jumped up in anticipation. The three met in the middle. Charlie held Jamie's pad toward her as they reached each other. Law was eager to hear the results.

"So? Was he able to get us off the grid?" Law asked.

"Oddly enough, yeah. Whatever they packed into Jamie's tablet makes that a scary little device." Charlie let out an audible groan. Law knew that it meant it must have cost them, just as he feared.

"Okay, out with it. What did it cost us?" Law asked. He heard his sister suck in a breath off to his side.

"Well..." Charlie started. He scratched his head and searched the ground.

"Come on, Charles. Out with it," Jamie demanded, her tone laced in frustration.

"Well, he wants us to leave one of his drones in the forward base whenever we get in."

"Absolutely not!" Jamie shouted. "No, he can't make us do that. Not to mention, I'm still at the behest of the commander. I'm sure she's fine with us bending the rules a bit to get intel for her, but I'm sure she has limits." Law didn't want to admit Jamie was right, especially since it aligned with them doing the commander's dirty work. Not to mention, Law's insides were turning at the battle between respecting Tiberius' wishes and finding out what their father had left behind for them.

"She's right, Charlie. I mean, aside from the commander and whatever she's playing at. I don't feel great about betraying Tiberius to begin with, especially if he really is trying to protect us."

Jamie must have been on board with everything Law said, until the last part, because she immediately went from nodding along to turning on the spot. "Oh, Law again with this betrayal of Tiberius?"

Law rolled his eyes. He had no intention of tapping into this conversation again of where his allegiance lay. And he most certainly did not need Charlie to assist her.

"She's right, man. At this point Ty's way off-world. He should be your last consideration in all this," Charlie added with a reassuring smile at the end, trying to soften his own betrayal as much as he could.

"Okay, whatever. Either way, it's a hard pass on IQ's request. We'll need to find another way. If the drone is uncovered, who's to say it won't immediately be traced back to us?"

Charlie returned to scratching at his messy red locks. "Well, it doesn't quite work like that, mate. Once that can of worgles is opened, they don't go back in," Charlie said. He shoved his hands in his pockets and kicked at the bit of sand that had blown into the hangar. He let out a huff and continued. "Asking him was bad enough because he already knew what we were playing at. How would he not? Anyway, he got one of his guys to tap into the rover through Jamie's pad. Once the deed was done, he said he would expect a connection to a live drone within twelve hours or he would accidentally send the transmission to the commander's office."

"Oh, for fuck's sake!" Law shouted out before he roared into the cavernous hangar, causing his voice to echo. "Why is this whole ordeal becoming so ridiculously convoluted?" Law squatted to the balls of his feet as he pulled at tufts of his high-top. Charlie walked over and squatted directly in front of him.

"He's a snake, man. Useful in pesky situations until they themselves become the pest," Charlie said as he tapped his fist on one of Law's knees. Jamie placed her hand on Law's shoulder, giving it a firm squeeze.

"Well, here's what we'll do," Jamie said. Her voice was steady, and her words were confident. "The rover is untraceable, ready to go, and assigned to you, Charles. What's done is done in that accord. We can't do anything about it now. So, let's see what we can gather from here while Tiberius is gone. I found the workers here are much more at ease when he's not around." She paused. Law noticed a soft smile curling at the edge of her lips. "Even more so, I realized, there are many here that were fiercely loyal to Dad and there is some discourse about how his death came about and was handled by Tiberius."

Law's ears perked up at the revelation. Both he and Charlie stood to their feet and hung onto every word of Jamie's plan.

"We use that to our advantage. Charles, you chat with some of the exploratory core members." Jamie rolled her eyes. "Especially the female ones, since you seem to be so good at that."

Charlie tried to chime in with a rebuttal, only to be rebuffed by a wag of Jamie's finger before she turned to her brother. Law reveled in his friend's reaction, like a sibling who could bear witness to a parent who caught on to their brother's antics. Charlie huffed and crossed his arms, driving the feeling home for Law.

"Lawrence," Jamie said, bringing him back to the seriousness of their situation. "You figure out some people who worked closely with Dad, maybe who were on the team at the forward base with him prior to the accident. See if they'll share anything." Law nodded at his sister. He understood her orders, and Charlie saluted her.

"Understood, commander," Charlie said sarcastically. "May I ask what your mission will be?"

"I'll revisit with my tour guide from last night. Maybe even see if I can help out and gain a little more access to things since they seemed so eager to have more hands. We'll meet back here in a couple of hours?" Jamie asked, as she waited for suggestions. Charlie looked to Law for his input. Law was impressed. It was a solid plan. At the very least, it gave them something to do. Beyond waiting for an invitation from Tiberius that at this point, Law was not sure would ever come.

"We'll meet back here at sunset. If we're going to go uninvited, it's probably best if we have not only tech on our side but also the environment. Charlie, can you manage getting us there at night? It seems to get pretty dark," Law asked his friend.

"I've got the lay of the land locked in from our first visit. I'm pretty confident I got some of it when we flew over, as well. Plus, I'm thinking we can use that nifty pad your sister's got to help us out in a bind." Charlie pointed to Jamie's pad, sitting between her arm and her side.

"Alright. Well, we've got our direction. Let's get to it." They each looked at one another and nodded before turning and going in their separate directions. Charlie headed deeper into the hangar, likely to find the maintenance sheds and breakrooms. Jamie and Law headed back toward Ops, Jamie toward the lower-level science labs, and Law toward the admin entrance they used the prior evening.

Law looked out through one of the Ops' skylights to see the sun steadily making its way closer to the ridgeline of the mountains in the distance. Since he had set off, he had not found a single person who was at the forward station around the time of the event or who was willing to talk about it.

He had gathered from one woman who apparently served on a few off-world missions with their father back on Tellathia II that most of the people who would've been there during the event had been ordered to stay at Ops because things were *too unpredictable*, her included. She was a member of his father's team, but he had ordered her to stay at Ops the entire time she had been in the Zoa for her safety. When Law pressed her, asking why, she told him she didn't ask.

"He was my field commander in the corps. When he gave an order, I didn't ask questions there and I didn't ask them here."

Law appreciated her candor but wished he had found someone a bit more insubordinate. Law found her on "below ground level three." One of the scientists walking the main floor directed him her way.

This level was relatively empty except for a random maintenance worker dropping some things off for storage. The entire level appeared to be dedicated to materials and data storage. Law walked past the server room that serviced Ops and was used as the disaster recovery center for Fort Kelly. He didn't have much time before he was expected to meet up with Jamie and Charlie. Hopefully, they were having better luck than him.

As he walked by, he surveyed the server racks littered throughout the room. It was a city at night of black buildings and twinkling lights quietly in an empty room. Law turned after marveling at it for a moment and hit the elevator button across from the server room. Moments later, the ding of the elevator arriving, followed by the controlled banging of the doors opening, broke the silence. Law walked in and turned, falling against the elevator's back wall. As he took one last glance at the server room, the doors began to close. When almost a sliver remained, a man slid into view, staring Law directly in his eyes.

Law froze in place, the man's silhouette remaining in his retinas as the doors slammed shut. He lunged at the open door button and, by no easy feat, got it to open before the elevator began its ascent. The door groaned open, and Law stared.

The figure was gone, but he couldn't have gotten far, and the only place to go was up, either by stairs or by elevator. Law was certain he had seen the man before. He just was not sure where. Law closed his eyes, hoping the frozen image was still strong enough to jog his memory. Was it one of the people from the floor when they first arrived? Was it someone from Sci-Rez?

He leaped out of the elevator as it tried to close on him once more, walking over to the door to the server room. It was locked and required an authorized CMP to enter. He decided it was too suspect to attempt to wave his and would indeed be logged somewhere as soon as he did. He walked back down the hall, stooping low, taking care not to be seen through the windows of the server room, hoping he would come across the person again. He scanned the room, crouching just high enough for his eyes to see over the barrier between the floor and the window.

The city of servers was in its original state, undisturbed. Save for this time, a single terminal glowed in the middle of the room, like a beacon casting light into the night sky. Had Law not noticed that before? As he replayed his original pass of the room in his head, he heard the familiar ding of the elevator bell. He swung his head around just fast enough to catch the tails of a white coat sweep in the car.

Law clumsily stood to his full height and sprinted toward the elevator, panting in exertion to reach the doors before they shut. Just before he reached them, he slammed his feet to the ground, sliding the last few yards to a stop right in front of the elevator doors. There he was, staring bright-eyed at Law, sweat pouring down the sides of his face just before the doors slammed shut—the fidgety scientist from the omnijet.

Law wasted no time sprinting for the stairs once the elevator doors closed and he kept his pace most of the way up. He would have to thank Charlie for those intense Saturday morning workouts he had been forcing him to do for months on end. But the elevators here were fast and there was no guarantee the scientist actually went to the main level. He could have stopped at any of the below-ground levels or went above that.

Law skipped two stairs at a time, running the entire three levels below-ground, up to the main level. He did not know why at this point or who he was chasing. Only that it was the skittish scientist from the omnijet they had dropped off at the forward base with Crewmen April. Why was he here now? But more importantly, Law stopped to breathe and brushed the sweat beading on his brow. Why was he trying so hard to avoid him? One more level to go and he should be able to catch him.

Law slung himself around to the last flight of stairs and cleared the landing in four leaps, throwing himself through the door to the level. He stood in the middle of a sea of people, panting and sweating. They stared at Law, who tried to straighten up and wipe himself off.

"Sheesh, those stairs are steep. Got to get back in the gym," Law said, not directed at any one person. He got a laugh and a nod from one individual. A few others raised their eyebrows and rolled their eyes, but he didn't care as long as no one asked any questions or slowed him down. He waded through the white coats and tactical gear adorned drones of people, checking every direction, trying to lay his eyes on the elevator's floor.

It was here.

It was open.

It was empty.

He had missed him. For all he knew, in the sea of people that had passed him on the way over. Law spun around and scanned side-to-side, trying to see if he could make the scientist amongst the crowd. There was no chance. He had a better shot at finding a bolt in an omnijet engine. Law would have to add him to the list of oddities that were growing by the hour the longer they found themselves on this side of the planet. He postponed his hunt to regroup with Jamie and Charlie. Perhaps they had better luck with their missions than he had.

Apparently, Law had returned from his endeavor last, only moments before they agreed upon meeting time. As he walked into the hangar, he saw Charlie and Jamie talking inaudibly by the terrain rover. The hangar was as empty as they had found it that morning, so as soon as Law came in through the main bay door, they both turned. His sister greeted him first as he approached.

"Hey, are you okay? I overheard a group talking about how you busted out of the stairwell looking panicked or something?"

"I wasn't panicked," Law said with a scoff, then filled Jamie and Charlie in on what had happened.

"He seemed dodgy on the omnijet for sure," Charlie agreed after hearing about Law's chase.

"Croacherson. I looked him up when I got on. I only saw him at Sci-Rez briefly. I was curious as to why he was on the jet with us. He's assigned to the experimental science division and has been essentially Tiberius' go-between for what is going on at Sci-Rez," Jamie said, sneering as she said it. "He's more like a little roach, though. He comes in, demands a bunch of data and samples with no explanation as to why or for what and then brings it back here, I guess, to do who knows what with it."

Law scratched his cheek making note of the stubble starting to come in. That could explain why he was in the server room, but not why he was so set on evading him.

"So, you said Dad was adamant about this woman not to be at the forward base?" Jamie asked Law as she recapped his points.

Law nodded, remembering his conversation before his cardio workout.

"Interesting," Jamie said under her breath. "Charlie and I were just talking about that. Several of Dad's closest workers, or at least ones he has a history with, said something similar."

Charlie was beside Jamie, nodding before he added. "Yeah, mate. Same with the mechanics and pilots. That was roughly when Ty started relying on people fresh off the transport, people new to the exploratory corps like your friend, April. They were rolling with your father at first and then he just started ordering them to stop. Made Ty bring in new people. Apparently, they had some big blowout about it up in the overwatch. They ordered everyone out."

Jamie nodded, adding, "Said Dad stormed out after a few minutes. Apparently..." She hesitated, "Apparently, this was a few days before the incident." Jamie's hands were on her hips, and she paced. Charlie looked at her and then at Law.

"You thinking what I'm thinking?" Charlie asked with an eyebrow raised.

"Dad knew something was about to happen and he was trying to protect those closest to him," Law said.

"My thoughts exactly," Charlie said. "Leave it to Mr. E. A top-notch guy through and through," He added, shaking his head with a reverent smile. Law appreciated the admiration and could not help but take a bit of pride in it.

"Thanks Charlie," Jamie said with a smile. The sweet moment was just that, a moment. Jamie brought things back to reality. "It's time for me to send a comm to the Commander while Tiberius is away. How much of our hand do I reveal? We have logs and maps from Dad's notebook, some crystal that feels like the sun, schematics for some machine, and a rogue group of scavs that Tiberius may be working with," Jamie summed up.

Law chewed at his lip. There was no harm in sharing the schematics and the crystal they had found. However, he wanted to hold off on the logs and the map, as it seemed to line up with the additional catacombs in the map Rell provided. The logs stopped abruptly. Their father was investigating something or someone. Could it have been the scavs that Tiberius was meeting with in secret and were causing so much trouble at the forward base?

"Let her see the crystal and the schematics. That's what Dad asked of us. Whatever they're building seems pretty serious, and I don't want our safety to be compromised because we took too long with it. Maybe they can make some sense of it," Law said as he pulled the crystal's case from the satchel and handed it to Jamie. He pulled the journal from the bag and flipped it open, thinking about what to do with the information inside. Jamie started walking toward the rover to make her comm before she stopped.

"Law, why don't you come with me to make the comm?" Jamie asked.

"Why would I do that, J? Clearly, Commander Rell and I haven't quite seen eye-to-eye," Law said.

Charlie let out a definitively audible laugh at the statement.

"Maybe this is an opportunity to gain her trust. She already knows that you know what she's asked me to do. This will show her you're willing to help more than protect Tiberius, which she already thinks," Jamie said, waiting for his response.

Law couldn't care less about what Rell thought. She was being just as sneaky as Tiberius, as far as he was concerned. What made her any better?

"Jamie, I don't care if—" Law started, but Jamie talked over him.

"And! You can see for yourself how she takes the information. See if she's cooperative, maybe even collaborative. Or if she continues to keep us in the dark. Decide for yourself if she's truly to be trusted," Jamie said with an eyebrow raised, waiting for his rebuttal to that.

Law looked at Charlie, who merely shrugged as he leaned against the back wheel of the rover, confirming it was a good idea.

Law saw the potential for Jamie's reasons and relented. "Fine. Let's go." He climbed into the rover's cockpit behind his sister. Charlie followed behind.

"I'll hang just outside of the cockpit," he said, stopping at the top run of the ladder.

"Ready?" Jamie asked. Law nodded. She sat her pad on the tactical desk and took her seat from that morning. Law took his seat and looked over to where Charlie had hidden. His friend was just out of sight on the rover's ladder with folded arms and resting his head slightly out of view over the cockpit's rim. Jamie tapped at her CMP, which controlled the pad.

"Authorization?" the pad requested.

"Everstorm-Epsilon-Theta-1-0-7."

"Voice and Code accepted. Connection initiated," the pad confirmed, and Rell was on-screen within seconds.

"Good evening, Ms. Everstorm." She looked in Law's direction. "And good evening to you, Mr. Everstorm. I assume the two of you have news, considering it's 0300 here."

"My apologies, commander. I did not consider the time difference," Jamie said. Neither did Law. It was 1800 where they were, putting them fifteen hours behind, just over half a day.

"No apologies needed, Ms. Everstorm. I made it clear there were no time frames for you to contact me, whatever you needed." Now that the niceties were out of the way, Rell remained true to form. "What have you got for me?"

"Well Commander, we were able to get in my father's case and he has a drive that he left behind with the instructions to get it to you." Jamie held the drive up so that Rell could examine it.

"That's great! Lay it on your pad. We should be able to transfer everything on it to admin. That's good work," Rell said, beaming through the transmission.

Jamie complied, placing the drive on her pad. Several lights on the sides lit up and a gentle whirring sound could be heard as Rell turned toward something off to the side. They could hear someone in the background.

"Ma'am, are you seeing this?" Rell held her hand up, reprimanding the person and returning to the transmission.

Jamie turned to Law. It was his turn. Law held up the case that held the crystal, raising the lid to it. Rell and one of her assistants in the background squinted and threw their hands up to shield their eyes.

"He also left this and said to get it to you as well. We're not sure what it is. Maybe amongst the stuff from the drive, you'll be able to tell us." The transmission must have adjusted on Rell's side because she and her assistant were leaning in, trying to make out the details of what was in the case. Rell had seen what she needed. Her jaw clenched. She turned and, without speaking, cleared the room behind her. Law and Jamie watched Rell as almost half a dozen people headed toward the back of her office and out the door. She turned back to the screen.

"Your father contacted me in private several months ago before his accident. He told me they had found something. Something that could be big. Something powerful. At the time they had found it, they had tried several methods of extracting it, but everything they had used to that point had proven insufficient."

Rell paced within view of the transmission, one arm firmly behind her back as she fiddled with something in her other hand. She watched it twirl in her hand as she spoke. Law hung on to her every word, leaning forward, placing his elbows on his knees. Out of his periphery, Charlie hid a few inches higher than he originally was over the lip of the cockpit, with his ear pointing toward the table.

"After endless trial and error, they could finally extract this minuscule bit of mineral that held within it *the power of the sun.* I believe Maxwell coined it." Rell stopped pacing and stood squarely in the center of the screen. "It was only after your father had suspected Tiberius had found a greater source of this mineral after seeing anomalies in the search area logs, undocumented travel, and gear use. He had inconsistencies in his team being dispatched without his knowledge and unexcused absences by Tiberius. That was when he saw fit to share their discovery with me. Together, we attempted to pin down his movements. Mr. Jansen kept them concealed in ways we could not figure out." Rell stopped as if to let them digest what she told them before giving her next command.

"Keep that safe, Mr. Everstorm. It appears Mr. Jansen has gone rogue, and it is my belief that the last time we got too close to learning about his dealings...it cost a great *friend* his life." Rell dropped her head in reverence. It felt as though they all gave their father a moment of silence. Rell spoke first.

"We will analyze what we can from here. I feel it's premature to lead the constable division there now and risk spooking Tiberius before we understand what could be a potential threat under my watch." Rell's stare was steadfast.

Law maintained his, although his head was swirling. His godfather was a potential threat, and his father was a great friend of Commander Rell. The commander had analyzed Law's reaction enough.

"Anything that the three of you have found—" Law and Jamie both looked over at Charlie with wide eyes. He tried to lower himself slowly back down the ladder. "It's okay, Mr. Sloane. If Maxwell or I did not trust you, I wouldn't have signed off on it."

Charlie hesitated for a moment and then finished climbing the rest of the way into the cabin of the rover. He walked around them to the pilot's seat.

"Anything you discover from here forward is vital to the security of Aurornova."

Charlie fired off a question he had likely held onto since they started the comm. "Uh, commander. Do we know who Tiberius may be working with? Is it scavs?" Charlie asked. Law was grateful to have his best friend here with him. He was still stuck on his godfather being rogue.

"A great question, Mr. Sloane. One of the final transmissions I received from Max before he went dark, he alluded to an off-world entity. My assumptions were scavs," Rell said, scratching at her tightly curled hair. "But none had been reported within fifty AUs of our system by any space agency's watch databases."

"Well, they wouldn't be good scavs if they could be detected, now would they?" Charlie said, more under his breath than directed at the commander.

"You are correct, Mr. Sloane," Rell answered. Charlie looked like he had just been caught by a teacher sending a secret comm in class. "However, the detection systems for scavs-based transports have become very extensive over time. Largely thanks to both Maxwell's and my best efforts. That said. If it is scavs, they are ones we have never encountered before with technology far advanced beyond ours." Rell's shoulders dropped a bit at her last point as if she were grasping the full weight of her own words. Law had seen enough. At least enough to reconsider his stance on Rell.

"Well, Commander, you have my word. If we come across anything else, we'll send it to you straightaway," Law said, before looking to his companions for reassurance. They each nodded in agreement. Rell, who was staring in his direction, lifted her shoulders and shuffled her stance, though Law could make out just a bit of surprise in her gaze.

"Thank you, Mr. Everstorm. Rell out." The commander reached toward the screen before she stopped. "Oh, and all of you," Rell paused, looking in each of their directions before speaking again. "Be careful. You have done a great duty to our planet." The transmission cut and the projection dissolved.

"The commander has been briefed," Jamie said, falling back in her seat.

"And she was working with Mr. E. the whole time," Charlie added.

"Now," Law said, standing from his seat and walking toward the front of the rover's cabin to lookout the main window and the bay door. Law scanned the sky. The sun was setting. This time of year, they should see the moon somewhere in the sky. He searched a little further away from where the sun was setting and there it was. A half-moon amongst a decent amount of cloud cover. "These things got night vision?" Law asked.

Charlie swiveled his chair and tapped around the controls. "Yup. We're good to go," Charlie said, pointing at a screen that showed *Stealth and Discretion*. "I'm sure they use it for approaching unknown animals and such," Charlie shrugged.

"Good! We'll need that tonight. I think it's time to see who has made Tiberius their errand boy," Law said, gently tapping his fist on Charlie's shoulder.

Jamie jumped up. "Wait a minute, Law, we don't have to do that now. Rell already knows we're looking around for her. We can call IQ's bluff," Jamie said.

She had a point, but it was no longer about preserving their secrets while they were there. At this point, for Law, it was not about getting all the answers to all the loose ends. The fact was that Tiberius got mixed up with someone who got their father killed. And Law would do whatever it took to make him, and especially *them*, pay.

Though an argument could be made for Law, Jamie, and Charlie not making the trip to the forward base in the middle of the night, the group settled it. The stakes were too high and their planet had lost enough. No one could attest to that more than Lawrence and Jamie Everstorm. Initially, Jamie was hesitant on the trip, mostly because she was not keen on IQ's involvement, but she came around after considering the commander's openness and, more importantly, Law's determination.

She mentioned she noticed a distinct look in his eye as they were loading the rover's cabin. Charlie asked if he was alright almost half a dozen times prior to their departure. The truth was, Law was not sure if he was okay or not. He spent so much energy trying to figure out the commander's angle only to find her on their side, at least as far as he knew. Law spent almost as much time anticipating his reunion with his godfather that he did not think Ty could ever be at the center of this. Law felt betrayed and childish. This mission was just as much about finding one of the final missing pieces of this mystery as it was an opportunity for him to confront the man his father trusted, he trusted, with all the facts for him to choke on.

As Law chewed at his fingernails in anticipation, Charlie expertly and carefully navigated them to the forward base. The difference this time was they were not only navigating at night by the dim light of the half-moon and the night vision on the rover, but they also used a path Charlie had come up with as he was waiting for them the previous morning.

The current route was way off the beaten path, taking cover within the desert's dunes. The trip took twice as long because Charlie drove slower to avoid kicking up too much sand and dust. He also had to reroute several times out of fear of getting the rover stuck.

Additionally, they had not received any comms from Charlie or anyone pinging the rover. The people likely assumed Tiberius had requested the rover, so the worry of being caught had been even lower than they expected.

Jamie calibrated the drone with her pad and extended their control to Law's CMP so that he could control one.

Law's drone would be the primary and serve the purpose of getting the intel they needed for themselves. Chiefly, he would seek Tiberius' location and see if they could decipher whom he was working with and if they could gather anything from him. Jamie would control the secondary drone. She would gather anything additional that may be useful for the commander and admin, while also using it as a decoy to send garbage data back to IQ for giving them the ultimatum.

"We should be smooth sailing from here on out, guys. Sorry for a few of those detours," Charlie called out over his shoulder. He kept his eyes ahead of them. Law thought nothing of it. If nothing else, he admired Charlie more for it. There was no reason for Charlie to be all the way out here with them. His parents were safely on the other side of the planet, going about their days while he was escorting them in the dead of night for what could very well be a dangerous endeavor. When Charlie revealed his concealed route back to the forward base, Jamie jumped into his arms and praised him for having the foresight.

"Thanks, Chuck! For everything," Law said. It was not the full tome of praise he deserved, but it was at the same time. Charlie looked over his shoulder as he continued his drive.

"Anytime, buddy," he said with a smile before turning back around to focus on the path ahead. Law scanned the surroundings. The cabin dome of the rover was fully transparent and the night vision extended around the entire dome, giving them a 360 degree view of the landscape. The prior trip to the forward base allowed for a much more visibility. For this trip they only saw tall hills of sand on either side of them displaying in the subdued shades of green of the night vision.

"Alright! We should be within visual range of the forward base just over this last hill."

Jamie put the drone and pad on the table and stood beside Charlie. Law stood on his left side as they both looked ahead in anticipation. Just as the rover crawled its way over the sand hill, the forward base came into sight. Its lights were almost overbearing them just before the night vision deactivated on the cabin's dome. Everything around them went black except for the base directly ahead, roughly ten kilometers ahead and below them. Charlie navigated them to the foothill of one of the mountains surrounding the base. He tapped at the control panel of the rover so that the overhead projection on the dome zoomed into a spot halfway between them and the base.

"When I was preparing the rover for the return trip yesterday, I imagined this would be a good place to set up if we wanted to sightsee around here. You know, really take in all the secrecy and such," Charlie said with a mischievous smile.

"Good idea. Let's go!" Law whispered and turned to walk back toward his seat as Charlie started the rover's descent down to the lookout spot before he slammed on the brakes. Law gripped the seat to keep from being slung to the floor. Behind him, Charlie holds onto the control panel to keep from flying through the windshield.

"What the heck?" Law asked, reaching out to check on Jamie before spinning around to look at Charlie and then out the window. Charlie pointed at something moving across the dome. He tapped at the control panel and it zoomed in, showing three other rovers moving at high speed away from the forward base and toward the mountains.

"Who is that?" Charlie asked. The zoomed-in tracker was following the movement of the caravan across the desert. He switched views to a heat signature view into the cabins of each rover. The readout showed almost a dozen persons within the vehicles. Occupants were listed as unknown. Charlie looked up at Law, who looked at the caravan and then back at the forward base.

"Those are our rovers, right?" he asked, unsure how to understand the screen.

"Yeah, that's the model number these go by." Charlie pointed at a combination of letters and numbers that were displayed on the readout.

"I bet one of those people is Tiberius," Jamie said from over his shoulder. She pointed at the lead rover in the caravan.

Law hummed in agreement. Where were they going and what was Tiberius leading so many of his team to do?

"What's the move, Law?" Charlie asked. Revving the engine of the rover as they sat idly on the slant of the hill. This was their chance to clear some of the gray area with Tiberius' disappearances. Could he possibly be going to meet with this unknown group or were they the others already in the rovers crossing the desert?

"If we're going to follow them, now's the time. I assume once they cross that ridgeline, we'll lose track of them. It looks like they have their tracking capabilities off too," Jamie said, swiping at the zoomed in view before tapping at her CMP.

"Absolutely," Charlie yelled this time as he was revving the engine even louder.

The spur-of-the-moment change in plans had Law reeling. He looked between the caravan of rovers mysteriously driving off into the night and an unguarded forward station. Which would provide more answers, Law thought. He didn't have time to consider the options. He made his choice.

"Gun it, Charlie! Go! Go! Go!" Law shouted. The tires spun in the sand under them, throwing a cloud in the sky behind them as the rover raced down the hill in pursuit.

"We still have to stay out of view!" Law shouted against the high whistle of the rover's electric engine. Law gripped the handrail as if his life depended on it. Though he was thankful for the rail's existence. He was sure they were there for this specific application.

"Yeah! No, I got it," Charlie said. With gritted teeth, he grunted, trying to whip the rover to run across the hill. He pressed several controls with his right hand before masterfully switching to his other and taking the wheel. All the while keeping his eyes locked on their subjects. The rover lowered closer to the ground as they picked up speed. Law noticed the wheels changed shape too. They expanded in width in front of them. He looked back and saw less dust and dirt was being kicked up.

"Crap, we're not sitting as high now. I'm losing visual," Charlie yelled. "Hold on!" The rover hit a pit at top speed and threw Law and Jamie into the air. Law was able get a good enough grip on Charlie's seat and the handrail to keep him from being completely thrown. Charlie grabbed Jamie by the waist, wrapping his arm around her as he got the rover back in control.

"Didn't even think about the night vision," Charlie said, with his head on a swivel.

"I got it," said Jamie as she tapped at the control panel, working to get it back up. "Let's see if I can lock back on them, too. You just worry about driving, Charlie."

"I've got it," Law said, finding the space in the panel where Charlie initially turned on the zoom and tapped at it. The square on the heads-up display projecting on the dome window moved around until it encapsulated the other roves in the distance and enlarged them on the screen.

"Computer, project concealed route from current location to subject," Charlie commanded. A red line appeared on the window, showing the way. Charlie slowly turned the steering wheel toward the direction of the arrow and picked up speed. The projected distance to the target decreased almost immediately.

They pursued Tiberius' caravan for about twenty-five kilometers before it finally stopped at the mouth of what looked like a mine. Charlie redirected to a hilltop off to the west to avoid detection. There, they could set up, send in the drones, and gather intel. Charlie began the power-down sequence and, to their benefit, found a stealth mode that concealed the rover as they made their way to exit it.

"Couldn't we have used that while pursuing Tiberius? Rather than trying to stay back and out of sight?" Jamie asked as she descended the rover's embedded ladder.

"No, I don't think so. The option didn't exist while we were driving. The shielding of the rover essentially mirrors the environment around it with the thousands of tiny cameras built in like the jets do." Charlie said. Once he reached the bottom of the ladder and hopped off into the spongy landing of the meadow's grass and dirt. The rover began to disappear against the background of the hilltop's trees as if it was dissolving from top to bottom.

Charlie ran his hand over what looked like an invisible vehicle. "My guess is it can't render things fast enough when in motion as it can when parked. Jets, though, are in the sky. Not a lot to render up there," Charlie finished while pointing at the sky.

They stood in the middle of a meadow area at the foothill of the mountain. The terrain was drastically different from the rest of the Zoa's blue desert landscape. Up here, it was green grass littered with colored weeds and flowers similar to the Oasis. A few snakelike trees forced their way from the ground sparsely around the meadow, while large, jagged rocks jutted from the ground. The line between sand and grass was visible about halfway down between where they were and Tiberius' caravan. Law squinted, looking toward the caravan. It was hard to make out, but it appeared the inhabitants of the rovers were getting out and making their way into the mine.

Charlie walked up beside Law and handed him some binoculars.

"Found them and a few other supplies in the back of the rover," Charlie said. He lifted a bag that dangled from his hand and pulled out another pair that he handed Jamie and then a set for himself.

"Let's set up over there." Law pointed to three rocks that rose almost five meters from the ground. They were the perfect cover. The three hurried over to the rocks, looking down toward the caravan through the spaces between. Through the binoculars, Law saw most of the individuals from the rovers had disappeared, likely into the mine. There were five that remained. Tiberius, April, April's two cronies, and the last two made Law bring the binoculars down and blink his eyes heavily several times.

"Who are these giants with Ty?" Charlie asked. He was still looking through his binoculars at them, his mouth hanging open. Jamie sized them up.

"They both have to have at least twenty centimeters of height on him," Jamie said. She, like Law, had dropped her binoculars and was looking at him. Tiberius was by no means tall, but he was certainly above average. He was about eye-to-eye with Law at 175 centimeters. Charlie's chin was about at his eye level. These two had to be at least two meters and then some. Law lifted his binoculars again but did not need them to see they were making their way toward the mine's entry.

"Sis?" Law said as a question after he put his binoculars to his eyes, watching the group approach the mine.

"Yup, it's definitely time," Jamie said. Law looked over. Her binoculars were on the ground beside one of IQ's drones. "I think we can suffice with one for now. We'll double back and grab some footage from the forward base to quell IQ's request later."

They huddled behind the rocks that shielded them. Jamie set her pad at the center of the group while she tapped at her CMP on her arm. The drone's propellers fired up, blasting air in all directions. Jamie's and Charlie's hair thrashed at the wind, released as the drone leaped into the sky. As it hovered over their heads, the sound it gave off dissipated.

"To be so small, those babies really have some power!" Charlie said, looking to the sky.

Jamie tapped a couple more times at her wrist before her pad projected the video. Jamie had control and tilted the drone down so the camera pointed directly at them. Charlie waved as he watched himself from the pad's projection. Jamie nodded as a smile spread across her face. She looked to Law as she sat cross-legged in the grass. Her forearm was parallel with the ground, ready to send the next commands to the drone. Law adjusted his place on the ground, scooting closer to the pad.

"Let's go in," Law said, nodding at Jamie. She looked up at the drone before swiping her finger across her CMP. The drone darted off toward the mine without a sound. As the drone zipped off, the figures disappeared into the side of the mountain one by one.

The moments of anticipation stretched into what felt like hours. By the time the drone made it to the valley, which only really took seconds thanks to its speed, Jamie had slowed it down. The drone hugged the face of the cliff while they watched the feed from her pad. She synced her glasses to the drone so that she could get a better view to pilot it.

"I'm trying to find where they went in. Keep an eye out for any distortions or anything weird," Jamie said. She moved her head around as if she was down there, scanning the cliffside herself. Apparently, this controlled where the camera pointed. Law and Charlie leaned in, focusing on the feed more intently.

"They kind of walked in a little more toward the right, almost where that crack is over there," Charlie said, pointing at the edge of the feed from her pad. Jamie turned her head slowly to the right. "Yeah! There!" Charlie said, tapping at the ground.

It was like he was watching a nidio match. He knew Jamie's piloting skills excited Charlie. Anything that could be driven or flown was a sport to Charlie. In his defense, Law had to admit Jamie was doing a phenomenal job. The way she learned how to pilot the drone, how she integrated it with everything and took it a step further to make sure the data got saved to her encrypted pad was one of the first steps where they finally felt like they were getting the upper hand.

"I think I got something, guys," Jamie said, looking just slightly up toward the sky. They looked at the pad. The drone was pointed at the rock face at the base of the mountain. The drone focused and refocused on the wall in front of it as it bobbed up and down. "Wait for it," Jamie said. Law's eyes watered as he strained to open them, trying not to blink. Just when he thought he could not hold them open anymore, the projection flickered. Or was it the wall? "You see that?" Jamie said.

"What? The transmission flicker?" Charlie asked. "Yeah, I'm sure it's just because of the range or something." Jamie shook her head.

"Oops sorry," Jamie said. She straightened her focus back on the spot on which she wanted them to focus. "No. That wasn't the transmission. It's the entrance." Jamie smiled, studying the entrance.

"But how?" Charlie asked. His nose almost passed through the projection from the pad.

"The moment I saw them disappear, I started thinking. It's like the projection that you're even looking at there. But so much grander in scale and in power," Jamie said. She placed her spectacles at the crown of her head and waved her hand through the projection. "Imagine this same thing, times ten and with a power source so far beyond the energy cells we currently have that powers things like our CMPs for nearly a lifetime in and of themselves."

"So, it's just a big false projection that's been doubling as a rock face for who knows how long?" Law asked. "What would there be to hide on the side of a mountain? Not that Tiberius should hide anything at all, but here we are." Law said, partially answering his own question.

"Well, let's find out," Jamie answered. She grabbed the glasses at the top of her head and put them back on as she raised her arm back in front of her. Jamie eased back into the controls on her CMP and the drone slowly moved toward the rock face. Law clenched at the grass under him.

He trusted his sister's instinct, but based on the technology they had seen to this point, to expect anything less than the unexpected would be foolish. Jamie's chest rose and fell slowly, her gaze steady. Jamie counted down as the drone was at the point of a collision.

"Three...two...one...impact," she said as she inhaled, holding her breath with her shoulders at their peak. The wall was steadfast until the last minute and then it phased out as the drone hit the zero barrier. It was as if it had passed through a waterfall and revealed a secret cave behind it. The camera refocused, revealing a dozen people more than had arrived in the rovers. The drone was just barely out of arm's reach of two people who had their backs turned to the entrance.

"Oh, crap!" Jamie screeched. She threw her hand through the projection in her CMP, launching the drone to the cave ceiling. To their luck, the ceilings in the cave were nearly as high as the atrium at Sci-Rez. Jamie weaved between the azure stalactites that hung from the cave ceiling like earthen icicles frozen in time. As Law watched the projection from Jamie's pad, he looked toward the concealed rover. The breeze picked up as the temperature dropped, making the ripples in the waving grass look like the end of the tide rolling in on the sands of the beach. His eyes were steady at the back of where the rover should be. The longer he stared, the more it looked like he could see airy white wisps of smoke riding the breeze as it caught the subtle moonlight between the clouds.

"There he is," Jamie whispered. Law squinted for a second longer before turning back to the projection.

"What the..." Law said. He could not believe his eyes. There was Tiberius flanked by the tall, hooded figure standing on the terrace of what looked like a canyon. "J, you're recording this, right?" Law asked. Jamie merely nodded as she scanned what was in front of them from end to end. Law felt like his jaw had detached from his face. The amber glow illuminated a similar look on Charlie's face as his emerald-colored irises danced with the iridescent glow, like fire mingling with water. It was a bottomless pit of the gem their father had smuggled, a mere piece of.

"Is there audio? Are we too far away to hear what they're talking about, J?" Law asked as he turned his ear toward the screen. His eyes were pointed back toward the rover again.

"Yeah, the mic is strong but tiny. Let me see if I can get a bit closer. There is a large stalactite just over their heads. Maybe if I use that..." Her voice trailed off as she chewed at her cheek, trying to navigate the drone to her target while remaining concealed. The audio crackled a bit before coming in. The hooded figure on Ty's left spoke, but it was gibberish.

"Is there something wrong with the transmission?" Charlie asked, his eyebrow raised. Jamie shook her head.

"Everything I can see seems fine. Oddly enough, though," she adjusted her glasses on her face. "Well, that can't be right," she said.

"What is it?" Law asked.

"Well, the energy cell on the drone. Once I got closer to the pit, the power surged back to 100%," she said. Law looked toward the projection and saw both the camera and drone battery levels indicating 100%. "Not to mention, it's getting harder to control this thing since we got in." Jamie's hand was steadily moving, tapping at her CMP.

"Just hang in there, Jamie. You're doing great compensating," Charlie said from the side.

The gibberish ceased between the two figures. Tiberius turned and was talking to the one standing in front.

"I hope the work done to this point has been satisfactory toward our agreement," Tiberius said. He waved his hand over the pit of gems glowing in the distance. "There should be more than enough here for our two worlds to share amicably."

The hooded figure stared at him but said nothing. Law felt the shakiness in his breaths. He wasn't sure if the breeze was settling on his skin or his nerves, but the longer the figure stared, the colder it felt. After what seemed to be a few more tense moments, the figure nodded, eliciting a mirrored nod from Tiberius. He then held his hand out to April, who handed him what looked like a pad similar to Jamie's. Tiberius handed it to the figure. April immediately put on some type of goggles and was followed by Tiberius and most of those standing around witnessing the meeting who did not already have them on. The figure tapped at the pad several times and lowered it, looking over the pit. The crystals' brightness slowly increased, causing Law and Charlie to back away from the projection they were watching.

"Cut feed to glasses," Jamie said after wincing at the brightness likely coming through the drone's feed and looked toward the projection from her pad.

"Uh, guys, do you feel that?" Charlie asked. He beat Law by a second. Underneath them, the ground gave off a soft, pulsing vibration. The longer they sat, the stronger the shaking became. "Is it an earthquake?" Charlie asked. Looking around, he ran toward Jamie and threw his arms over her head.

Law looked at the satchel he was carrying. The amber glow that came from the projection was blasting out of the opening. He pulled the satchel's strap and flung back the flap, sticking his hand in. The case with the crystal vibrated violently. He took it out and sat it in front of him. Charlie and Jamie came closer. Law flipped the latches, letting the cover get thrown backward from the force coming off of the crystal before it jumped out of the case as it was thrashing back and force violently. Without thinking, Law grabbed the crystal before he howled into the night. His voice echoed off the mountainside.

"Fuck! My hand!" He looked at his hand and the skin looked as though it was bubbling from where the crystal had made contact. Law smelled the flesh searing as it hissed at his impulsiveness. Jamie slid beside Law, grabbing his hand. Charlie rummaged furiously in the pack he had before throwing her a first aid kit. While Jamie flung it open and grabbed the medical supplies to address his hand, Charlie squatted near the crystal.

"Don't touch it!" Law said, as he still winced in pain. Jamie doused his hand with antibiotic agents before pulling a medipen to close the open wounds from the burns. "It's scorching," Law said through gritted teeth.

Charlie hovered his hand over it like someone trying to gather warmth from a campfire. After a few seconds, he shook it to cool it. Charlie stood and grabbed Law by his other arm, helping him to his feet as they backed away. Jamie held the other hand as she had wrapped it in a mesh-skin graft.

"That thing's going to give away our location," Jamie said, whipping her head from side to side before turning her attention back to Law's wounds. The crystal was a beacon in the darkness at this point. They could barely distinguish what was happening on the transmission from Jamie's pad beside it. It was getting harder to walk, especially backward, as the terrain shook under them. And then it stopped.

The crystal suddenly dimmed, and the shaking ceased. The three of them froze in place as they scanned the area. Law looked at his hand. The pain was more subdued, partially due to the adrenaline but mostly thanks to Jamie's first-aid abilities.

"Uh, those are probably second-degree burns, Law. It's a good thing they had a medipen on board. It should ease the pain and help you avoid any serious scarring," she said as she let go of his hand after being reassured the mesh was taking hold.

"Thanks, J." Law smiled at his sister and flexed his hand a bit to force the mesh to give a bit. They all walked back toward her pad to see what was going on with the transmission. The light had died down from within the cave as it did with their small piece of crystal. Law looked at it as he kneeled beside it and held his bandaged hand over it.

"If you burn yourself again, so help me," Jamie admonished him, forcing her voice to remain low. But Law didn't feel any heat. He cautiously put the tip of his forefinger on it and to his surprise, it was ice cold.

Law grabbed it and held it toward Charlie, who shared his surprise as he engulfed it in his hand. Jamie took it from Charlie before staring at the both of them, putting it back in its case, and slammed it shut. Each of them looked toward the pad's transmission. It appeared that whatever had happened kicked up some dust within the cave. As the dust swirled within the transmission, slowly dissipating from view.

The tall, hooded figure came into view first, standing at the precipice of the canyon, unphased and unmoved. Tiberius was crouched down with his hands over his head, like everyone else, even the other hooded figure. The pit of crystals returned to their initial dim glow like the shard Jamie put back in the case. All the workers within the cave were back on their feet and slowly returning to what they were doing. The hooded figure returned the pad to Tiberius, who turned and handed it to April. And off to his side was the fidgety scientist who gave Law the slip.

"Look who it is," Law said, pointing at the transmission.

Tiberius looked to give him a few commands before the scientist nodded and stalked off. Tiberius walked back to the rail terrace, looking over the crystals, pointing as he looked to yell orders to some workers around the cave. The tall-hooded figure looked on for a moment. And then the figure turned. His companion walked back toward the entrance of the cave. He followed, but after a few steps, the figure stopped abruptly and slowly lifted its head toward the sky. Slowly, the figure's head tilted back until it looked like it was looking in the direction of the drone.

"Uh, guys!" Charlie yelled, smacking Law's shoulder. "What's going on?"

Law's fight or flight kicked in just as he could see directly into the opening of the figure's hood, where he found what looked like two deep amber-colored eyes glowing and looking directly at him.

"Jamie!" Law shouted.

"Resume transmission!" she screamed. The soft glow around the rim of her glasses ignited as the controls from her CMP sprung from her wrist. The transmission spun from the figure and darted toward the cave opening, weaving between the cave structures like a snake fleeing a predator. "Crap!" Jamie shouted.

The transmission spun around as a small plum of dust and pebbles rained in front of the it. The drone rose back toward the darkness of the cave's ceiling. The stalactites thinned as she retreated, allowing Jamie to beeline for the opening before she brought it to a complete stop almost a meter away.

"What are you doing, Jamie? Get out of there," Charlie said. His head was on a swivel between Jamie and the transmission.

"Just wait for it," she said. She began looking toward her feet. Law looked at the projection. Under the drone was the tall-hooded figure's companion walking toward the entrance. Just as he reached the barrier, the projection phased out and Jamie sent it. The drone flew out into the night sky, showing them the moon-lined clouds that hung over their heads as it raced back toward them.

"That's how you fly!" Charlie shouted, howling in excitement. He grabbed Jamie's face and kissed her on the cheek, causing a smile to trickle across her face.

Law looked to the sky. The drone slid across the cloud before it got bigger as it descended upon them. It slowly lowered beside the pad, its force pushing the grass next to it down forcibly before Jamie cut the engines, and it bounced harmlessly on the ground.

Law let out the breath he held trapped in his chest since seeing those harsh amber eyes staring through him. Jamie collapsed beside him. Charlie was between them as he slung his arms around their shoulders.

"I don't know about the two of you, but all this excitement has left me famished," Charlie said, smiling a full-toothed grin. The last bit of tension melted away as they all laughed before grabbing their things.

Law was relieved that they were able to get out before getting caught. Whatever was going on here was way beyond anything they should be involved in, to the point they were putting themselves in mortal danger. All he could think about were the ominous eyes staring at him. He didn't know who or what that was at this point. All he knew was he wanted to put as much distance between him and this place as possible. Law picked up the satchel after he put the crystal's case back in and secured the flap.

"Ok. Let's get out—" Law's words were cut short before everything went dark. He felt a smooth, silken Fabric cover his face before an arm wrapped around the top of his chest and dragged him away.

L aw's heart raced as he thrashed his head back and forth and clawed at the arm around his neck, trying to pry himself free. Faster and faster, he slid across the grass as his captor overtook him. He tried to think, strained to hear his surroundings. Where was Charlie? Jamie? That's when he heard Jamie scream.

"There are six of them. They're huge. Get off me!" she shouted through grunts and more screams. Whatever they had covered Jamie's face with, her glasses must have seen through it.

He patted at his pockets, the satchel, anything that could shift the balance of power of whatever was pulling him away against his will. He reached up above his head and felt some sort of tube. Wriggling his fingers in as much as he could, he ripped through the tube, hearing a soft hiss of pressure let out. His captor released him, dropping him to the ground. Law grabbed at the bottom of the fabric that covered his face. He tore it off, catching his breath. The figure grabbed at its face as the *tube* Law disconnected, flailed about like it was alive. Law blinked, trying to get his eyes to adjust. He couldn't tell who or what was trying to capture him. It was shaped like a person, but bright white tubes dangled and thrashed from its head.

Charlie roared, his voice not as distant as Jamie's. "Get the fuck off her!"

Law turned toward his best friend's voice only to see a body flying. One of Charlie's three captors. It appeared they were having a much harder time with him than everyone else. Law finally spotted Jamie about twenty yards further past Charlie with a person on each of her arms.

Law jumped to his feet and tore off toward them, sprinting toward Charlie, who was closest to him. The captor Charlie had thrown made their way back to their feet and charged at him.

Law yelled to alert him to the danger just out of his line of vision. Charlie was quick, spinning to his right and launching a knee toward his attacker's face. The blow sent the attacker's head skyward and lifted them off their feet and on to their back. Law ran up behind Charlie's second attacker while the third had his arms round Charlie's back, trying to wrestle him into submission. Law placed his boot squarely in the back of the figure that was facing Charlie, sending them off balance in his direction. Charlie stuck his tree trunk of an arm out and clotheslined them, sending their body crumbling to the ground.

"Go!" Charlie roared. But Law was already gone. Jamie had flipped one of her captors over her back and onto the ground. She straddled them and squeezed her hands on their throat. The other captor quickly came up behind her, trying to rip her off their comrade.

The two that were fighting her were getting the full weight of Maxwell Everstorm's training and each of Jamie's black belts. Law reached his sister as the captor standing over Jamie reached both arms in the air with their hands joined in a balled fist. With every bit of speed Law had picked up in the one-hundred-meter dash toward his sister, he sent it directly into the attacker's flank.

The captor howled as Law tackled them, sending them both flying several yards. Law rolled up to a knee in time to see Charlie racing toward them like a bull unleashed, leaving his three attackers scattered in his wake. Law threw a hook at the assailant he had just tackled with his good hand. He heard a crack at the side of the face covering. It threw the combatant off balance enough for Law to get to his feet.

The three of them had the numbers now, even though these *things* had the size and strength. He looked at Charlie, who was about ten yards away, barreling toward them, when suddenly his body went rigid. His best friend's arms clasped by his sides and his legs snapped together, sending him flying in their direction before he collapsed to the ground, sliding a few additional meters.

Charlie was fully unconscious on the ground. Looking up to see what had immobilized his friend, Law saw it. His abductor he had left grasping at their face mask was now holding a glowing weapon. As soon as he saw it, he did not think, he just ran to put himself in front of Jamie as her two attackers jumped out of way and stood at attention to the side.

But it was too late.

The creature shot a stream of lightning in Jamie's direction and hit her dead in the chest. Tears immediately flooded Law's eyes as rage filled his heart. Law caught her before she fell backward. He let her gently continue to the ground before launching himself at the nearest attacker and grabbing it by the neck. He looked into its cold, mechanical eyes just as he was hit in the side with a burning, searing pain.

Law's captive scratched at his forearms as they tensed from the shot. He could feel his vision blurring, but he blinked furiously, refusing to let the world slip away from him. Law was not sure he could let go if he wanted. Whatever had hit him felt like it turned his body to stone. He screamed inside his head as loud as he could until he forced the sound from his mouth, shaking his head. He had to stay alive, at least long enough to take someone with him for what they had done. But the next shot came, which was more than Law could take. His body went rigid once more, but not before his victim was able to wriggle free from his grasp. He looked to his left and barely made out his original attacker being within arm's reach before he hit the ground. The moon slipped behind a cloud just as the world slipped away and Law was out.

As Law regained consciousness, a searing headache awaited him. His blurry vision forced him to blink repeatedly until he could see directly in front of him, much less his surroundings.

He was lying face down. But where?

He slowly regained control over his limbs and dragged his arms to his sides, pushing off the ground. A single thread of drool tried to keep him tethered before he closed his mouth and hoisted himself to his knees. Law pressed at his temples and contemplated laying back down. The headache felt much worse when he was upright. He massaged for a moment before he looked around.

"Good morning, sunshine," Charlie said from behind Law. He turned to see his friend leaning against the rock face of the cave they were in. It looked like they were sitting at the dead end of a tunnel. Torches were at his back and ahead of him on either side of the cave, almost twenty yards forward before they stopped, giving way to darkness past that. Law welcomed the slight breeze that brushed over his face in the humidity of their environment.

"Are you hurt? Can you move?" Law asked Charlie. He slid side to side, trying to see past the winding of the tunnel, before he looked toward his friend. Charlie nodded, though he remained sitting.

"I'm good. Little bruised up. Nothing a medipen and an ale couldn't fix."

"Good, let's get out of here."

"Can't," Charlie said, pointing up toward the opposite cave wall. Law turned, trying to see where Charlie was pointing. Just a meter over their heads a small device was attached to the cave wall. It looked like a miniature spotlight that was turned off. As he traced the cave's wall, there was another directly under it. Charlie was propped near the one on his wall and one more hung across from him on the opposite wall.

"Some kind of invisible barrier," Charlie said. He picked up a stray pebble and threw it toward the tunnel. A loud pop reverberated down the tunnel before a golden projection rippled from the rocks impact outward, like a rock being thrown in a pond.

"Good eye," Law said, looking into the open space in awe.

"My eye didn't discover it as much as my ass did when I got thrown over here after trying to walk out," Charlie said. He arched off the wall and massaged his lower back as he recollected his experience. Law grimaced at the thought of him running headfirst into it.

"How long was I out?" Law asked. He looked at his wrist before panicking. "Where's our CMPs?" He spun, searching the ground. Then Law's heart dropped. He looked at Charlie, his heart racing and his eyes wide.

"I don't know, mate. It was my first thought when I came to." Charlie answered the question he read on Law's face. Jamie was nowhere to be found in whatever dead-end cave corner they found themselves in. "Why do you think I learned the hard way with the barrier?" Charlie reiterated. Law's breath escaped him, and tears flowed. He collapsed to his knees, trying to catch his breath. After another moment, Law laughed. This was enough to get Charlie to hoist himself from the ground and crawl toward his friend. He put his hand on his shoulder.

"Uh, you alright, Law?" Charlie asked cautiously. It had just occurred to Law. Before everything went black, he thought his sister was dead. He thought Charlie was dead. Even though Jamie was not with them, she got hit with the same thing they got hit with, and they were still alive. That would have to be comforting enough until they could figure out where she was and where they were.

"Yeah, I'm good. Just finding some silver linings," Law said. He wiped his face with his sleeve and took a deep breath. He needed to focus on the problem in front of him, one at a time, before he could get to his end goal. At least that's what Jamie would say. This time, she was the end goal, and then from there, they could worry about what these things were that took them and why they did it.

Law raised himself to a single knee before standing up. He paused as he saw a sliver of light spreading at the tunnel's far end. Charlie noticed Law's face and looked in the same direction. The light wasn't only spreading. It was coming toward them. Law sprung to his feet. Charlie did the same as they stood side by side, unsure if they would fight once again or try to break their way out. Either way, they wanted to be ready.

Two of their kidnappers approached. Law noticed the one on the left had a cracked helmet. He was the one he tackled off Jamie. The other was much worse for wear. He must have been one of Charlie's.

"Aww, you missed me? How sweet of you to visit," Charlie said, stepping closer to where the barrier had materialized. His attacker balled its fist by its side. The torch it held shook just a bit as its gloved hand wrapped around it tighter. The other attacker had something in its hand. In one, it held what looked like a plate.

As Law stepped closer, he noticed a spread of flat-dried bread, berries, and what looked like dried meats. The attacker placed the plate on the ground and slid it across the barrier line without issue, causing Law to test its presence. Though he saw nothing, his hand felt like it hit a plexiglass wall, followed by a zap that made his fingertips to his elbow tingle. He flexed his hand, trying to make the tingling stop as he rubbed at his forearm.

The attackers were unphased. The one offering the food merely stood up.

Law took this moment and stared at the *thing* in front of him. It had arms, legs, and hands with fingers like him. Aside from its size, he felt like he was standing among three juggernauts when he included Charlie. The masks they wore were less intimidating when he wasn't fighting for his life.

The things that Law confused for cables coming from the masks in the heat of the moment looked like locs. The two attackers before them had brownish-black hair, but a few of the locs intermingled throughout were a deep green. The color was so bold and vivid; it was as though it grew in that color. Buried within the vines of locs were their masks. A rectangular amber band crossed the mask where the eyes would be. Beyond that, the mask was smooth. It outlined their face down toward a point where a normal chin would be. But there was an ornate design on them in white.

This is where the two attackers differed.

The designs on the mask were stylistically similar and in the same vibrant white color. But the one on the left was more circular, thinner in lines. The one on the right was more jagged and angular. Where one was vines, the other was intermingled staircases. Their attackers delivered food and now stood sentry in front of Law and Charlie, guarding them. Law continued to study them. Everything about their physiology said they were people, but every detail contrasted with what he knew as normal. The different color locs sprouting from their heads were only the initial indicator, but they were both large, having almost a quarter of a meter on him. Charlie squared up with them, and what he lacked in height, he made up in size, having at least a couple more kilograms in muscle than the one on the left. He probably went toe to toe with the one on the right. Charlie paced between the two, staring them down.

"You come back for round two?" Charlie sneered. "Because that's what you'll get unless you tell us where our friend is now!" His muscles flexed as his fists balled as he stopped in front of the larger one.

"Charlie, we don't know who—" Law paused, looking between their two captors, "Or what these things are. They probably don't even understand a word you're saying," Law said as he grabbed his friend's arm.

"Save your strength, man. We may need it." Law tried to coax him away from the force field, which he was likely only centimeters away from.

"Then maybe it can sense this," Charlie said, drawing himself to his full height. His chest puffed upward. The figure before him shifted as it was face-to-face with its captive. "Every moment that passes without us laying eyes on her is another I'll take tearing it the fuck apart." Charlie's broad shoulders rose and fell with each breath. He tried to impose every bit of his presence through the thin layer of protection their captors had from him. His adversary had stepped as close to the barrier as Charlie was, matching his stance. Law squeezed at his friend's arm.

"Don't antagonize them, Chuck. Not until we know Jamie's okay. Taking them isn't our problem. We're still behind this force field," Law said. He looked at the captor that stood in front of him. He had not noticed it mirrored his actions with their partner, leaned in, and mumbled something inaudible to them. Their partner backed down first while Charlie remained steadfast. The pair snapped their arms to their sides before they leaped to the sides of the tunnel. Both Charlie and Law's heads swiveled at the sudden movement.

"Uh, what are we doing here, guys?" Charlie put his hands out as if they would offer an explanation. But Law already knew the answer. Walking slowly up the tunnel was another one of their attackers. Judging by how quickly the other two jumped out of the way, this one must have been important.

As the glow of the torches hanging on the cave walls found its mark, Law saw a group of white and purple cable braids dangling down around the leader's waist. One braid looked as though it was torn, only coming three quarters of the way down like the others around it.

It was Law's abductor, and it appeared to be the leader.

This one was as tall as its subordinates but had a wirier frame. As it approached, its eyes locked on Law. Charlie slid in front of Law, picking up on its intent, but Law stopped him, gently pushing him on his side and giving him a reassuring nod. The leader stopped right before the barrier as if they could see it as clearly as a cage, a zookeeper observing their subjects.

The leader began raising their hands at their sides, sliding them past what looked to Law like two curved sabers. They almost looked like lassos dangling from their hips. Law heard Charlie's feet shift in the dirt as he prepared for whatever came next. The leader bypassed the weapons at its side and instead grabbed the sides of its mask and pulled it from their face.

They dipped their head slightly to avoid interfering with the dangling braids revealing the face of a *woman*. This woman, though, was like none Law had ever seen. No human, Law had ever seen.

Her features were striking, but her skin almost glowed in the firelight. At first, it looked brown, no different than his or Jamie's, but the closer he looked at *her* face, the more it almost looked metallic or a copper color. Law looked up at her eyes. Around one was a tribal-like marking in white, the exact same that was engraved around her left eye on her mask, Law noticed. The other sported a long gash that lined right through the middle of her eye.

Law felt his veins go cold as her eyes glowed a bright amber. He thought of the feed from the cavern with Tiberius, but this time felt different. It looked different. Law could not tell if it was because the eyes felt like they spotted him through the drone or if it was something else. This time, though, there was a fire in them that raged on a face that accommodated them in kind. Then, as he was sure the fire in her eyes had melted the ice in his veins before attempting to boil the blood in his chest, she spoke. The accent was heavy, the words sure, and the rage definite.

"Wur ees, Maxwell?"

"What did she just say?" Charlie asked, his mouth hanging open. He was alternating his stares between Law and the leader. All Law could do was shake his already spinning head. The accent was thick, but Law was sure he heard his father's name at the end. From what he could tell, it was English. He asked for clarification, hoping it was indeed English that he had heard.

"I'm sorry. Did you say, Maxwell?" Law asked. He turned his head slightly, presenting his ear to her, determined to confirm what he thought he heard. The leader seemed in no mood to be misunderstood again. Law saw the bottom of the barrier blink its translucent amber glow twice and dissolved upwards between them. Charlie bounced on the balls of his feet, ready for a fight. Charlie's adversary squared up with him, ready for his command. Law looked back into the fiery eyes across from him. This time, her accent was as clear as her impatience.

"Where ees, Maxwell?" she demanded. The smug look on her face and the fact the barrier was gone made Law think she would not ask a third time. This time, Law understood fully and, rather than an answer, the first question that came to his mind escaped without the least bit of resistance.

"How do you know my father?" Law asked. The leader took a step back as she drew a breath. The soldier in front of him gasped audibly, just as its leader did before tearing off their mask. It appeared to be another female. She looked at her leader. Her face softened. She stepped toward Law and pressed her fist to her chest. Charlie's opponent's stance had softened, having taken his mask off also. His fist also pressed to his chest. Law looked to the leader for some sort of explanation. He became impatient as well.

"My father is dead. Who are you?" Law demanded. He had not noticed the look on the leader's face. Her stern demeanor had softened. The bonfire that had blazed in her eyes only moments prior had dimmed to a candle flame, flickering as she searched Law's face. She spun on the spot and walked away

"Hey, get back here. I said, who are you?" Law demanded once more. The leader's soldiers had already followed in her wake without being commanded.

"Come!" She commanded Law and Charlie without slowing to confirm they were actually behind her. Law growled in frustration.

"Come on, let's go," he said to Charlie. Charlie reached his hand in front of him before taking a step, waving it in circles for a second. They looked at each other and jogged to catch up to their captors, once again with more questions than answers.

"Charlie! Lawrence!" Jamie shouted.

The men pushed past the leader and her soldiers as they entered the cavern, running toward the corner where they held Jamie. Hearing her call when they rounded into the cave's opening, Law ignored the fact that they were in a cavern with half a dozen more soldiers. Two that were closest to Jamie sprung from where they sat. He saw the leader wave her hand out of the corner of Law's eye. It immediately caused the soldiers to stand aside. The same force field that had imprisoned them lit up before Jamie and dissolved. She sprung out and into Law's arms as soon as it passed above her head. Law squeezed as hard as he could before he felt the air rush from his lungs. Charlie had lifted the two of them in their embrace, burying his face in between her shoulder blades.

"Okay, Chuck!" Law strained to get out. Charlie gave an additional squeeze before putting them down. Law grabbed his sister by the shoulders, searching for her.

"Are you okay? Are you hurt?" he asked.

"I'm fine, Law. I'm fine." She waved him off with a smile. "They didn't do anything to me. I think they realized my glasses and my CMP had a connection for what it was they were looking for. I realized pretty quickly they weren't the same people we saw with Tiberius." Jamie spoke in hushed tones. She paused and looked over Law's shoulders. "I think they're hunting the two that we saw. Maybe two of their own. The one you followed back here is the one in charge, I believe."

Law smiled. If they were trying to be secretive, they picked the wrong one to put at their center of operations. Where Charlie and Law would have been concerned with the best way to get out, Jamie was the one to analyze every movement, every action.

"Uh, guys." Charlie tapped Law's shoulder. Law looked over, finding him turned and staring in the opposite direction. At the center of the cavern stood the leader. Her fist pressed to her chest. The rest of the soldiers around her throughout the cavern also had their hands pressed to their chest. Those standing close enough to each other spoke in hushed tones. The rest looked toward Law, Jamie, and Charlie with their heads slightly bowed. Law spoke out of the side of his mouth, trying not to turn away.

"The leader asked me where Dad was. They've been doing this since I told him he was gone," Law said.

Jamie gasped. "What? They speak English?"

"Apparently," Law answered. "They haven't said anything to you since you've been up here?"

"No, they just stared, pretty angrily, I might add," Jamie said with a quizzical look on her face. Law decided they would get nowhere unless they started trying to meet their captives in the middle. Something about their father triggered this subdued response, and he planned to find out. Law began walking toward the leader.

"You good, man?" Charlie asked, advancing with him, but Jamie gripped his arm. He put his hand on hers as he searched her face before letting Law go.

Law continued his advance toward the leader. None of her soldiers moved. They were frozen sentries in place. From what he's observed, they only move on her command, and Law noticed whenever she gave a command, she only gave it once and did so without much effort.

Once he was within arm's reach of the leader, he decided that this time, there would be no words, no questions. The situation was reverent. They had the numbers, the advantage, and if Law had not known this was a cave already, they were standing at the center of a command center that rivaled Sci-Rez's. He decided instead to put his fist to his heart and gently bow his head.

Immediately, an ominous hum filled the cavern and then his eardrums. He looked around and realized it was the soldiers that were humming. Law looked back at his companions and noticed they were looking around in awe. He tried to signal to them to do what he was doing. Jamie caught on and lifted her fist to her chest. Charlie took an elbow to his side before doing the same, using the other hand to massage his rib cage. As Law turned, he gasped, trying not to jump backward.

The leader was almost nose-to-nose with him. He looked into her eyes. They were more subdued, more sincere than he had found them to this point, though he had never intended to be this close to them. He was quickly getting close to the edge of discomfort as he thought she was actually going to press her nose to his nose...or kiss him. The leader finally reached out her hand and placed it on Law's chest, next to his fist. Her thumb and forefinger encircled his fist.

Law sat for a moment, wondering what to do next. He looked up slightly at the leader, who was just a bit taller than him. She must have sensed the uncertainty in his eyes because she grabbed his free hand and placed it on her chest, similar to how she had his, even shaping his fingers around her own fist, before returning her hand back to where she had it. Whatever comfort level Law had was certainly gone now. They had no concept of personal space where she was from, he thought. She then put her forehead to Law's and continued her humming. Law decided copying her had gotten him this far. He may as well take it the rest of the way. He hummed, trying to match her tone and hold the note for as long as he could. Luckily, that was the last part the leader must have expected. Because the humming stopped, not just by the leader, but from everywhere around him, and she dropped her hands. Law did the same as she stepped back and looked at him. Charlie and Jamie had made their way to either side of him now that it appeared their moment of reverence had ended.

"My apologies, Lawrence, son of Maxwell. I am Ru Xian-duwan. We share sadness. Your father was…" She paused as she looked to be searching for the words. "Was a great ally."

Law looked at Jamie, who was just as shocked as he was. Law did not know where to begin.

"Um, thank you, Ruzi-I mean, Ru. I'm sorry?" Law decided to stop butchering her name and gave her a chance to say it again. The leader chuckled as she folded her arms and shook her head.

"Zee-An-Du-Won." She mouthed as she sounded out syllables for them, though her thick accent still made it difficult to be sure exactly what a few of them were. "Ru is my family name. Your father struggled like you, so he call me Xia," she said. Her words were stilted, each carefully chosen as if she were piecing together a puzzle with unfamiliar parts of the common language.

She looked around at others in the cavern who had apparently joined her in having what appeared to be a reminiscent laugh. Law thought about his father finding a way to elicit the level of respect from these people and from his colleagues at ops. He felt a lump rise in his chest.

"Right. Xia. Thank you. Thank you all. I take it you know my sister, Jamie." Law held his left arm before her. "And this is my best friend,

Charlie." He did the same on the other side. Charlie scratched his head before he interjected.

"Sorry about everything, everyone," he said. Law continued.

"I think we can all apologize for the altercation. Xia, this is a lot to take in. We have been trying to catch up to what is happening here and what truly happened to our father. I'm thinking, hell, I'm hoping you can help us with that." Law paused and took a fortifying breath. "Who are you? How do you know our father? What is going on here?" His arms fell to his sides. Law felt like he had run a marathon just asking those questions. The reality was he had been running on adrenaline since long before they had made it to this point. The moment of reverence that they had, feeling Xia's hand on his chest, his hand on hers, and pressing their foreheads together, had been the first thing that centered him since they chased Tiberius' caravan.

Honestly, it was the first thing that had centered him since he found out about his father. More than seeing Tiberius had.

"Was it one of your people in the cave in the mountainside with my godfather?" Law finally asked. This question elicited whispers throughout the cave. Xia, let out a sound that echoed in the cavern for seconds. Almost a battle cry. Whatever it was, all of her people ceased their whispering and snapped to attention. She walked back in closer to Law and looked at the three of them. The glow in her eyes grew as it did when he had first looked into them in their cell.

"The male that is with Tiberius is not of my people. He is very dangerous, son of Maxwell. And he will destroy your world," Xia said.

Law, Charlie, and Jamie looked at each other in dread.

"Xia, where are our things?" Law asked. She turned and snapped her finger before muttering what sounded like words that Law couldn't understand. A soldier toward the back of the cavern grabbed the satchel, Jamie's glasses, and the drone off what looked like one of their holotables. The soldier carried the small case separately as he brought their things to them. Charlie reached over and grabbed Jamie's glasses, which he rubbed on her jacket before she put them back on.

"In attempts to...access this, we were unsuccessful," Xia said while holding the case. Law slung his satchel over his head and took the case. He touched his thumbs to the latches, and immediately, they flung open, allowing him to open the case. The crystal's light shot out into the cavern as it had done every time it had been opened. Once he opened the case fully, everything went haywire.

Multiple devices blared different alarms, beeps, and dings. The two curved daggers at Xia's side glowed, as did her eyes. The ornate etchings in her armor and mask, which hung off her belt, glowed, too. The activity sent everyone in the cave into a frenzy. They ran to the various devices, trying to turn off alarms and recalibrate flickering holograms. Even Jamie's former holding cell's force field was activating and deactivating. As the crystal glow tamed its initial stretch of power, as it typically did, the surrounding devices ceased one by one. Xia's eyes remained locked on the crystal.

"What is this, Xia?" Law asked, his voice raised over the few remaining sirens and beeps going off.

"To us, it is xenolis. Your father called it Petra Vivi Solis," Xia said.

"Rock of the living sun," Law said, translating his father's Latin nickname for it. Xia nodded as she pointed at Law. She must have recognized the translation.

"Long ago, on our world, it provided great power, ran our cities, our technologies, until a great war." Xia clasped her hands behind her back and walked toward the back of the cavern. Law walked beside her as Jamie and Charlie followed closely. "Our people learned over many rotations that when used for energy when used for good, xenolis can last lifetimes. Build empires!" Xia and Law came to a stop around a large table that was solid. It looked much like their holotables, but instead of having legs or a mount, it floated. Law crouched, trying to see if he was missing it, going so far as to wave his hands under. Charlie and Jamie did a similar fashion.

"Yeah, I swear I wondered the same thing, Law, while I was in my cell," Jamie said as she giggled in excitement.

Xia merely looked down at him, a subtle smile curling on her lips, but her eyes remained focused, urgent. Law stood up. She looked behind him to his sister and friend with hands still clasped behind her back before she released one and waved it over the table. A golden hologram exploded from the table. The vividness astounded Law. It was as if golden sand had materialized in front of them. Where the projections he was used to were more like ghosts hovering above the table; these were like sculptures that he could reach out and touch.

Around the tables, massive spires manifested as if someone were reversing the destruction of a sandcastle. Dozens of miniature vehicles weaved their way around buildings and bridges. Double waterfalls were like a sash draped over the mountainous shoulders hunched ominously behind the castle she showed.

"Is this your home?" Jamie asked, looking at Xia. Charlie had put his hands in the way of one of the flying projections. The miniature jet broke apart within his hand and materialized on the other side of it.

"Yes. This is Cerbraxia," Xia said. She looked fondly over the projection. It was the softest Law had seen her face since she had taken off the mask. Though it was only for a moment.

"But our people learned soon that great power often breeds--" Xia started to say, but Law and Jamie finished the quote.

"Idealistic opportunity," they said in unison. Xia smiled as she looked at them both before her eyes gave way to sadness.

"As your father often said." Xia pursed her lips into a tight smile before she waved her hands over the vibrant city. The buildings began falling apart as all-out war broke out on the tables. What air vehicles remained were in dogfights throughout their flight. Some were protecting the castle, the ones that made it through fired upon it relentlessly. Bridges fell and a dam had stymied even one side of the waterfalls. What looked like a lush landscape of rolling hills and forests had been trenched and cut. Craters littered the fields while fire scorched the terrain.

"Xenolis was scarce on our planet. Many on our council of leadership demanded strict rule over it. Others wanted to stretch its limits, build empires across our lands. Our people were split the same," Xia said. She hovered her hand over the top of the projections and pushed her hand toward the table as if she was flattening the entire scene. It disappeared.

"The male you encountered with your Tiberius is Ro Jacen'zo," Xia said. Law stepped backward as an imposing figure materialized in front of them. This projection was in full color, three-dimensional, and nearly to scale as he remembered the hooded figure in the cave with Tiberius.

The *man* in front of them was massive. The cloak he wore hung from his broad shoulders like a coat of bandages, refusing to fully tear, but under it, his armor was immaculate. The sheen of the silver of his chest plate glistened in the projection. At the center was a round-cut piece of xenolis. Cables sprouted from it like a grappling spider's legs from its body, leading to other pieces of the armor. Law looked into his eyes. He could tell. He could feel it somehow. These were the eyes that had seared through the drone's projection. The hair on the back of his neck stood. Law scratched at the area as Xia continued.

"He is a...a war criminal from our world and responsible for many atrocities for more rotations than I have seen in my lifetime against my people," she said and paused, looking toward the figure before them. "Our people," Xia turned to the trio as Jacen'zo disappeared from the table. "And now your Tiberius has led him to an endless supply of xenolis and provided him with tech to turn the tide of the war."

Jamie walked forward. "Excuse me, Xia? This is all terrible and I apologize for what your world has been through and likely what you have been through," Jamie said. Her tone was sincere as she approached Xia. "How does our father play into all of this?" she asked.

"*Play into?*" Xia responded. Her face twisted in confusion.

"How did you come to meet our father?" Law said, trying to help clarify. "I assume he was working with you in some way?" It was more a hope than an assumption. His dad would never be on the side of Tiberius.

"Your father was an ally," Xia said, bowing her head in reverence. "We came across your father not too different from how we encountered you. Your father grew suspicious of your Tiberius' actions. Your father bested me and my paxteek..." Xia seemed to get lost in thought. "Apologies, my lieutenant, Loxaria, I think is how you say it. He was a very skilled fighter, your father. Much like my own. But he too was scouting as Jacen'zo and your Tiberius were searching for the xenolis cache."

Xia turned back to the table and tapped at its side. A grouping of symbols and shapes took form. She tapped at several and turned a spherical symbol. A map of the Zoa showed several pulsing points across its landscape. All but two were marked with what looked like X's. One of them was the site where they just were. Law was unsure about the other one, but it looked like it sat squarely between the cave and Ops. "You were able to track them far better than we were capable. Jacen'zo has somehow evaded our tracking technology. Your father tracked Tiberius through a gift he had given him. He gave us this and ensured us we were um," Xia turned to Loxaria. They looked to the cave's ceiling, scratching at their scalp before moving a loc from their face.

"Fishing from the same pond, Maheda," Loxaria said with a slight bow. Law was curious as to what Loxaria had called Xia. He settled for assuming it was some kind of word for leader or captain. Though Xia, shot her a look of reproach at this title. Loxaria bowed like a child who had been scolded, clasping her hands in front of her. Xia turned back to them and pointed toward the satchel where Law had returned the crystal.

"He was able to secure that piece and conceal it from your Tiberius, but not before they used it to lead them to the xenolis cave you found. He taught us your language, about your world, about your ways." She looked Law over, her gaze lingering. "He told us about you."

Law's cheeks flushed for a moment. Charlie looked between Xia and Law. He smiled before his face looked as though a light bulb had lit up somewhere.

"Well then, why the hell did you attack us?" Charlie said. Law could not help but laugh at his tone, though the question was valid. Xia apparently found humor in his demeanor as well.

"We were told stories, but we never saw you!" she said as she now looked past Law and examined Charlie and Jamie. "The trust we built with Maxwell was strong. But he was still very protective of you. Of you all." They all stood in the moment. Law had felt his father's impact and how wide-ranging it was when he interviewed some workers at Sci-Rez but had never contemplated its crossed planets. He pulled the strap to the satchel just a little tighter and felt Charlie's hand slap him on the shoulder and squeeze.

One of the more decorated soldiers inched their way in and whispered in her ear. Xia's eyes went wide, her shoulders rising with the quick intake of breath. She muttered something in her language, looking at her soldier in shock. Loxaria handed Law's CMP back to him.

"Were they able to decode whatever it was?" he asked—fitting his CMP back to his wrist.

"They have, Law. And it is much worse than we feared," Xia said. She pulled up a flurry of schematics with the machine they had sent to command at the center.

"What are we looking at?" Jamie asked.

"They are weapons of mass devastation," Loxaria chimed in. "But on a scale we have never known. Jacen'zo is the ancestor of our former security and intelligence leader. He wanted to use the xenolis to make our armies more powerful before our great chief forbade him and the council pursued the matter further when we saw the toll it took on our xenolis supplies." Loxaria waved their hand around all the shapes that floated before them. "What you found was the main hub of the massive weapon. What was on your CMP, Lawrence, were the remaining pieces needed to make the weapons operational. This coincides with the intel provided by one of our spies who remains deeply undercover on Cerbraxia within Jacen'zo's camps."

Loxaria's articulate explanation and grasp of English impressed Law. Xia appeared to praise Loxaria with a curt head bow.

"My paxteek is an academic at heart. Able to absorb the language as your father spoke it much faster than most of us. It makes them an invaluable member of my team," she said, giving them another bow.

"I'm sorry, absorb the language?" Law asked, convinced that was not the word she meant to use. Loxaria elaborated.

"Yes, we process the stimuli around us in a much more permanent way than it appears your species can. Hence the masks that you encountered us in. As we hear things, see things, and feel things, we are able to process them and often mimic or understand them almost instantly. The masks we where, help us, uh, *quiet the noise* I believe your father mentioned." Loxaria nodded as she examined their faces. Law couldn't help, but to think how much easier Mrs. Sloane's classes would have been.

"With the supply of xenolis that Jacen'zo now has access to on your world, Law, this weapon has the ability to destroy both your world and mine," Xia said.

Loxaria jumped in, doubling down on the starkness of the warning. "Not only that, Maheda, with the technology that the scientists of this world have developed, it appears, thanks to Maxwell's journal, they have found the way to consume half the xenolis at two times the power. Or at least they are coming close. It appears the tests they have run at this point have been inconclusive. The last test resulted in the loss of Maxwell, Zilli, and Zulo."

"I'm sorry, who?" Law asked, not recognizing the names from any of the reports or logs they had studied following the incident.

"Zilli and Zulo were two of our operatives that were assigned to your father to help gather intel," Loxaria answered.

"That's right!" Jamie said, snapping her fingers. "They were two unidentified people that were listed as being with Dad in the incident reports. No one at command could figure out who they were based on the people who had come in directly to the Zoa and those had transferred back to the Oasis," Jamie said. She tapped into her pad that she pulled from her hip, pulling up several reports to validate her memory. "They just chalked it up to clerical error. That it was two workers who made it on the new world and had not been registered yet when Tiberius was actually taking his pick," Jamie said, guiding her way through the report lines.

"Yes. Your father requested two of our operatives accompany him in place of his own people, but also refused to allow our Maheda to accompany him, to which earned him my respect," Loxaria said, placing his hand on his chest and bowing.

"So, it was an accident that took our father out?" Law asked. He tried to follow. Was it just a case of his father being in the wrong place at the wrong time while gathering intel?

"We do not think so. As you are aware, the body of your father was never found, though we were able to recover Zilli and Zulo before any of your investigators got to the site. Hence our attack against you, hoping you were a surveillance scout that detached from the rest of the caravan. The hope was that you may have known something of whether Maxwell was taken or..." Loxaria hesitated, glancing at their leader before continuing. "Or worse."

"Worse?" Charlie dared ask.

"That he was unrecoverable," Loxaria whispered. "The power of the blast was immense. You may have felt it on your side of this world. So much so that we questioned whether a breach of that magnitude could be that severe or..."

"If it was sabotage," Xia cut in. Her tone was definitive, as the fire had rekindled in her eyes. "There was only one difference from this test. One difference from the others." Xia's fists clenched at her sides. "Jacen'zo was not there."

That was it. Had Law been of Xia's world, he was sure his eyes would burn like the bonfire he had seen in Xia's. A fire ignited by the fact that she had lost an ally like he had lost a father.

"What do we do now?" Law asked. His question was an invitation to more strategic ways of letting his vigilant desires take hold. If it was up to him, he would leave the cave he was in right then and find Tiberius and punch him squarely in the jaw, repeatedly until he told him where this Jacen'zo was hiding. Then do everything in his power, even if it cost him his dying breath, to be the person who was nose to nose with him as he extinguished the flame in his eyes.

But there was a reason he had made it here. There was a reason he was able to continuously wage war on their planet. This Jacen'zo was smart and deadly. A combination that had kept him alive and apparently a step ahead of Xia and her soldiers. Something, it appeared, Xia was determined not to let continue.

"We stop Jacen'zo once and for all. Sho qua, nu zah!" Xia shouted, thrusting her fist into the air. Each solider around her repeated her chant in unison, their fist thrown above their heads in solidarity. Law looked at Charlie and Jamie, who surveyed the cave of soldiers dotted around servers and projections. Their armor of the ones in the shadows gleamed in the firelight each time they pumped their fist.

Law was unsure of what they had found themselves involved in, but it was so much bigger than them now. Their father chose a side and so had

Tiberius. Law looked at Xia who turned to survey each of her soldiers chanting with her, before rounding back on Law. She nodded her head as she looked into his eyes. Law lifted his fist to the sky.

"Sho qua, nu zah!" he shouted. Law had chosen his side, too.

The previous night ended on a much higher note than the one they were captured. Once everyone had digested the starkness of the current situation and it was decided they would need to strike sooner rather than later. Xia ordered everyone, including Law, Jamie, and Charlie, to eat and get some rest. Loxaria secured the three of them cots for the night after two of their scouts returned from tracking Tiberius. His caravan had set up camp at the cave for the night. Based on their report, Jacen'zo had made his exit shortly after the test that they had witnessed before Xia and her team brought them to the cave. They followed him deep into the mountain range before they lost his trail, something that was not uncommon since they had traced him to the planet.

Jamie and Charlie joined the rest of the soldiers for morning rations in a small, enclosed grove at the end of one of the cave's many tunnels. It was obvious to Law why they'd taken up camp here.

The cave had tunnels that exited to almost every side of the mountain range. As well as tunnels that led to nowhere. Unless you had the tech to navigate through the caves, you could easily walk into one entrance and get lost forever. They kept a map projected to one of the cave walls to help the soldiers navigate it, as well as to monitor anyone coming in or out.

Law watched everyone indulging themselves in the grove at the center of the cave system. It was likely a place where the caves had collapsed, Law thought, as he spotted half a dozen tunnel entrances directly across from where he stood. The grove would have been a postage stamp completely enveloped by the Sci-Rez atrium. To Xia's soldiers, Law noticed, it was a refuge in a foreign land.

The morning was much warmer, with the sun at full strength even in the season's colder breeze. Charlie had apparently come to terms with the soldier he had gone one on one with. They were sharing combat moves as they both held some kind of jerky in their mouths as they tussled. Jamie initially wanted to send a communication to command with all the information they had learned, but Xia had implored her to hold off. Aside from being very protective of their position and not wanting any outgoing transmissions outside of their own tech, she told them Maxwell never actually alluded to who they were or where they were from. He had been leading command to believe they were ordinary scavs from the off-world, as they had hoped not to alert anyone to their existence.

Their father had respected Xia's wishes of allowing them to try to capture Jacen'zo and his followers and leave their planet undetected until they could connect on better diplomatic circumstances. Jamie agreed, after much consideration, to do the same earlier and had now turned her attention to what looked like a large projector in the center of the grove with one of Xia's tech people. The device portrayed a holographic net into the sky and, from what Law had gathered from overhearing some of their conversations, was projecting a false canopy of the grove that made it look like the continuance of the mountain range that surrounded it. Where he and the rest of Xia's soldiers had an unabated view of The Zoa's sky, anyone flying over it would only see the tops of the blue-leafed Kamoa trees that shaded their location.

The trees' leaves rustled in the dry desert breeze that rushed through the grove and passed over Law's upturned face like sandpaper dragging across his cheek as it looked to return to its open desert playground.

It was the first time he was not on high alert since they landed. He was unsure if it was because he felt he was finally shedding the weight of the unknown while he was within Xia's camp or if it was something else. As he leaned against the cave's opening wall, he continued to watch his companions intermingle with their Cerbraxian counterparts. Law took a bite of the strange jerky they had given him, ripping a much larger piece than he wanted. The more Law chewed, the more the tough, leathery texture gave way to be a tender and hearty snack. Law held it out before him, his face twisted in astonishment. It was like he bit into jerky, but he may as well be chewing on steak. He took another bite before raising his arm and speaking to his CMP.

He swiped through to his saved files and recordings and pulled up a screencap of the video with Tiberius, Rell, and his parents. All intertwined and young with an idealistic twinkle in their eyes. His last bite of the jerky had a harder time getting down his throat.

"Autumn... Your mother," Xia said from over Law's shoulder.

"Geez!" Law said with a start. "How long have you been standing there?"

"My apologies. I have just arrived." Xia held her hands up. She bent her knees and was slowly backing away. Law raised his own hands.

"No, no. No need to apologize. I was just startled," he said. Law turned to face Xia but leaned back against the cave's opening. "Yes. That was our mother before we lost her too." Law swiped away the still frame and crossed his arms.

"Was she a warrior? Like Maxwell?" Xia asked. Her eyebrow raised as she shifted her stance. She walked toward Law and took a spot against the cave-opening wall beside him. Her arm brushed his as she made contact with the wall, sending a tingle up Law's spine. Xia and her people were not big on personal space, Law thought. He scratched the back of his neck.

"Uh, yeah." Law laughed. "Well, no! My father joked she may as well have been."

Xia craned her neck to the side. Her eyebrow was still raised, contorting the long dark brown scar that ran through her right eye, stopping just above her cheek. The person across from him differed from the last time she was this close. The pearled white braids that Law had grown used to seeing in a military-grade bun that was almost as big as her helmet, now draped from her head over her shoulders and down to her waist. The sun's rays wove their way through the trees in the grove and reflected off her face. The jewel at the top of her forehead pulsed as it absorbed the sun.

"Speaking of warriors," Law said after blinking and shaking his head. "How does someone like you become the leader of an operation like this?"

"Someone like me?" Xia asked. She folded her arms this time. The muscles in her shoulders threatened to tear the seams of her jacket.

"No, I mean." Law rubbed feverishly at his face. "I'm sorry. I mean, you don't seem that much older than me or even Charlie." He looked back toward the grove, scanning the soldiers eating on top of rocks around several fires. They laughed, raising their canteens to each other. "There are people here that seem older than you. In some cases, significantly older." He pointed at the soldier Jamie was conversing with beside the concealment beam. "How did you become the one in charge?"

Xia dropped her arms instantly, tugging at the bottom of her jacket and straightening it. Her gaze fell to the ground as Law noticed she seemed to fidget.

"It is, uh, complicated? I believe is what you say," Xia said without lifting her gaze.

Law gritted his teeth. He overreached and there was nothing he understood more than having a complicated path, now more than ever. So much so that it did not take him very long to figure out what to say to recover the moment.

"Well, you're doing great. Given the circumstances, morale is high," he said, knowing that is what he would've wanted to hear in her case. Law gestured toward the grove, hoping to draw her gaze. It worked. Xia looked up at Law before scanning her troops for herself. A subtle crack of a smile appeared in the corner of her mouth. "And they seem to have great respect for you." This brought Xia's gaze back to Law. Her eyes were warm as they searched his before she dropped her head again.

"Well, Law. They are required," Xia said. She shoved her hands into the pockets of her jacket.

Law's head jerked. He had no idea what that meant. Perhaps because of her rank and the customs of their military. He decided not to press with too many questions. He was already on a thin line, but added one last thing before he would let the matter rest.

"Well, I'm not. And I do," Law said. "Not to mention, I'm pretty sure I just got the feeling back in my arm." He rotated the arm that Xia had twisted when she first captured him. This elicited a laugh with a cute little snort at the end. She brushed away a few braids that had made their way in front of her face and grabbed his shoulder and arm, assisting him with the rotation.

"In defense of me, you are a capable fighter." Xia massaged his shoulder firmly, digging her strong fingers in, driving him between pain and relief. As she did, she pulled him closer, bringing back the chills that never really left his spine. The massaging got deeper and slower. Law groaned. The pain had subsided, leaving only relief as she circled his joints. Pleased with his reaction, she smiled, staring into his eyes. The two amber orbs, he had realized, looked like they were spinning as they glowed in the sun's light.

"Your eyes…"

"Excuse me Maheda," Loxaria cut Law off before he could finish.

Xia's hands stopped immediately and dropped to her side. Law heard a growl under her breath before a sneer spread across her face. She turned on the spot facing her lieutenant and causing her to immediately go into an apologetic bow. Loxaria wasted little time after the gesture before they spoke quickly in their own language, alarm lining their face.

Law heard a couple of words he recognized from before when they were referring to Jacen'zo, and he clearly understood Tiberius' name. He kept looking between the two of them, wondering when they would bring him into the conversation. Loxaria stopped abruptly, leaving Xia's wide eyes darting from side to side as if she were tracing a mouse on the ground. She looked to Law.

"There's been developments. You must get back to your Operations structure," Xia said. She grabbed Law's hand and pulled him off toward her command center, ordering Loxaria to rally the others as she whisked him away.

Law sat with his arms folded, leaning against one of Xia's holotables watching her pace from side to side in front of him. The two soldiers that were the scouts that stayed behind after Xia's team took them stood across from him.

After a few more moments of watching Xia pace while some of her soldiers scrambled around, Loxaria and all who were in the grove came into the atrium. Charlie and Jamie jogged up to Law once they had spotted him.

"What's going on, Law?" Jamie asked. "Loxaria told us we have to get back to Ops as soon as possible."

"No idea. Xia said the same thing, before bringing me back here to talk to those two scouts I think," Law said, pointing at the two soldiers who had been talking to Xia and showing her footage since they got back. Now that everyone had returned from their morning rations, Xia clapped her hands together twice, demanding everyone's attention.

"All. Our scouts have honored themselves by getting intel about Rue Jacen'zo's camp that is troubling." She looked directly at Law and then threw an image from the pad. She held her hand to the table they had gotten a Cerbraxian history lesson on the night before. The image before them caused the soldiers to gasp and look up in awe.

"Holy shit!" Charlie exclaimed, throwing his hands to the sides of his head. Law scanned the image at what looked like dozens of ships that appeared to dwarf even their omnitransports.

"Xia, what is going on?" Law asked.

"It appears Jacen'zo's forces are much larger than we thought. It is likely that these commamauds, what we call our jump ships, were camping on Aurornova's moon until last night, dropping in under cover of night and clouds following the meeting with your Tiberius."

"Jamie, wouldn't Admin get an alert about ships that big dropping into our atmosphere?" Law asked, pointing at the screen. "How could they miss those?"

Jamie shook her head. "Well, theoretically, yes, if we were dealing with normal circumstances. First, Aurornova is a vast planet, dwarfing every other planet our species has inhabited at this point and then some, with the exception of maybe Jupiter? Outside of the Zoa and the Oasis, we have mapped so little at this point. With the right conditions, depending where and when they dropped in and the fact that both Xia's and this Jacen'zo technology are leagues ahead of ours, it's easy to believe they've been here all this time without us knowing. They could come and go as they please and we would be none the wiser."

"Those things are massive," Charlie said as he started walking closer to the image to get a better look. "And I'm no expert in Cerbraxian aviation, but these don't look like flight necessary machinery." He added, pointing at what looked to be turrets hanging off the wing of one of the closer ships.

"You are correct, Charlie," Xia affirmed his fear. "These are war ships on our world. Capable of great speeds, transporting massive cargo, and causing maximum destruction. It does not bode well that he has secured that many and brought them to your planet." Xia's fists were on her hips as she chewed on her lips.

"This next part may be difficult to watch," Xia said, but she wasted no time bringing it up on the table. There was Tiberius, standing with Jacen'zo and his lieutenant, overlooking the fleet of commamauds.

Law's heart plummeted. *What was he doing*? This was the final nail in Tiberius' coffin. It was hard enough trying to defend him to this point, but this was reprehensible, Law thought.

Law walked to where Charlie stood. Tiberius was emoting in a frenzy, pulling at his hair and it looked as though he was yelling at Jacen'zo, jerking his hands in the fleet's direction. Tiberius paced in a circle with his arms crossed and one hand to his mouth as though he were biting at his fingernail.

He turned back to Jacen'zo as though he was going to volley another tirade at him until his Lieutenant stepped in between them and grabbed Tiberius by his collar and lifted him with one hand. He used his other hand to grab a blade from his hilt and rested the tip at Tiberius' Adam's apple.

Jamie gasped as she slapped her hand to her mouth. Charlie threw his arm around her and grabbed Law's shoulder. Law continued to watch, not allowing himself to blink out of fear he would miss the slightest detail. Jacen'zo's henchman continued to hold Tiberius suspended in the air with the blade to his throat, long enough for him to stop kicking his feet before his boss reacted.

Jacen'zo clasped his hands behind his back as he continued to look over the fleet. Law watched his shoulders rise and fall, as if he was taking the time to inhale the sea breeze while his thug held Law's *godfather* at knife point.

Finally, after what probably felt like a lifetime for Tiberius, he turned his head just slightly and looked as though he was speaking. Law could not be sure as the henchmen made no movements, holding his stance and his blade as though Tiberius was merely a weightless rag doll being abused by a petulant child. Tiberius spoke and whatever he said must have been crossing a line, Jacen'zo's lieutenant hiked him higher in the air causing Tiberius to grab the arm holding him up to keep from choking himself on the collar of his jacket. He desperately waved a hand toward Jacen'zo and looked as though he was screaming.

Law watched him nod and turn his head back toward the sea. Jacen'zo's man dropped Tiberius, who sputtered and coughed in the grass. Jacen'zo and his soldier went back to monitoring their fleet and what seemed to be hundreds of soldiers crawling around the beach around the ships. At no point did they acknowledge the man they just assaulted, as he struggled to pick himself up, rubbing at his neck and walking out of frame.

"After this, activity all around the beach picked up very heavily, Maheda," one of the scouts spoke up. "We had to retreat, very carefully. There were soldiers beginning to explore the surrounding area. If we didn't get out while we did, it is likely we would have been captured or worse, they could have traced us back to you, Maheda.".

"Xia, we must alert our leadership. The circumstances have changed drastically," Jamie chimed in. "If Jacen'zo is angling for some kind of attack or invasion, I don't know. We need to protect our people."

"You are right, Jamie. We can no longer avoid making our presence known," Xia agreed, nodding toward Loxaria

"Right this way." He led her toward the opposite end of the cave as she started powering up her pad.

The second scout continued his recount of the mission. "As we made our way back here, we trailed Tiberius' movement for as long as we could before changing course. He mounted his caravan rather quickly to return to their Operational base."

"Which is why we need to get back before he notices," Law said, picking up on what was happening.

"Right, I need to get to the rover," Charlie directed at Xia.

"Brooxton is standing by to take you to it."

"I'll be back in two shakes of a legyupod." Charlie nodded at Law before darting to the cave layout map, then toward the tunnel that led to the main entrance.

Xia walked over to what looked like a row of lockers against the side of the cave. She opened a double door and grabbed three small cases before returning to Law. She laid them on the table and popped one open. At first glance, it did not look like there was anything in the case, causing Law to lean in and squint. Xia reached in and pinched the air as Law looked on, confused. He continued to watch as she pulled the invisible item from the case as if she was pulling a strand of hair that the cave's firelight could not catch. Once her hand reached eye level, a curved instrument appeared. It materialized between her thumb and forefinger before looking past it at the smirk on her face. Seeing it, Law had not realized his jaw hung open.

"These will keep you in contact. Give these to Jamie and Charlie." Xia walked up to Law and softly ran her hand around the back of his ear before attaching the earpiece. Law heard a quick, high-pitched whistle that balanced out after a second. He winced as it felt like something had gently pinched his skin. She grabbed the second one in the case and placed it behind her ear. Law watched it disappear. He caressed the back of his ear after he saw hers disappear, not expecting to hear a tone follow.

"When you run your finger down the spine, it allows privacy for you," Xia said. She took a few paces away from him and pointed toward the earpiece, signaling to run his hand over it once more. Law complied and heard her voice. A familiar tingle ran up his spine as it felt like she was right behind him, speaking directly into his ear.

"I will be with you the entire time. You just have to turn it on." Law felt his shoulders sink a little and nodded.

"What do you need from me?" Law asked.

"You need to find out what your Tiberius has agreed to with Jacen'zo. What has he built for him? What is he planning with all the xenolis?" Xia said, tapping out each point with her finger on the palm of her hand. Law bit his lip and searched the floor. Xia walked up to him and lifted his chin, bringing his eyes to hers. She did not speak immediately. Instead, Law felt as though she searched his soul, trying to determine his allegiance. He had yet to figure out the significance of her eyes, but he took refuge in them. She remained silent, allowing him to be the first to speak.

"I can't help but think—perhaps hope—he's gotten himself in too deep. Like, all of this was just one bad decision that spiraled out of control," he finally spoke.

"I do not envy you, Law Everstorm. I do not envy anyone who must put the needs of their people over the needs of their peace." Though she lifted his head, she lowered hers for a moment as she squeezed her eyes and gritted her teeth. "More than you know." Xia's eyes were glazed until she blinked them away. "But I must ask the most of you, just as I did your father. If Tiberius stands between you and the fate of our worlds, you must let him go. Whatever deal he thinks he made with Jacen'zo, he will not honor it. He will annihilate anyone between him and his end goal. I've seen it time after time." She removed her hand from propping up his chin and placed her hand on his heart, just as she had when they honored his father.

Law wrestled the lump in his throat down and forced the sound of his voice past the blockage. "I will do everything in my power to help you bring down Jacen'zo. For Aurornova," Law said.

"And if you have to take down Tiberius with him?" this question did not come from Xia but from behind him. There Jamie stood, her eyebrows raised. Charlie was at her shoulder. Xia's hand remained on his chest. He looked around, realizing it was not just Charlie and Jamie that had returned, but many of the soldiers that were in the grove. All of them were in their gear and helmets in hand. Law thought of his father. He thought of how he must have considered the same two paths before him. Does he try to save his best friend from himself or does he do what is needed to protect his world? The choice his father made was clear, and Law would make the same choice.

"If it comes to it, Tiberius will go down too... For Aurornova," Law said, barely above a whisper. Xia grabbed a fistful of Law's jacket, the fire in her eyes emblazoned brighter than he had ever seen them. She responded just as he did, loud enough for just him to hear.

"For Aurornova!"

Charlie got them back to Ops as fast as he could. Law knew he took joy in drifting in and out of the desert's dunes as he tried to get them back before Tiberius. His face was stoic with concentration. They all knew this trip back to Ops would differ from their last.

Before they left, Law outfitted Charlie and Jamie with the communication device that Xia had given him while she briefed them on their tactical plan. She had sent a communication to her Loxaria. That was a meeting she had to take alone, ordering all of them and her soldiers out of the cave.

She had requested reinforcements, given the size of Jacen'zo's fleet. A detail that was news to her intelligence. They did, however, mention that Jacen'zo's commamauds were wrecks that were salvaged and enhanced. A spy that Xia's group embedded in Jacen'zo's base back on Cerbraxia could not explain the technology being used to make them fast and the weapons more powerful. They now had their answer.

It was Aurornovan technology and science coupled with Cerbraxian mechanics.

Reinforcements would take seven hours to arrive. Until then, Xia's orders were clear. Law, Jamie, and Charlie would handle recon, while Xia dispatched a team led by Loxaria to covertly disable as many ships as they could. Xia and a few soldiers would follow them and stand by to see what they could learn from their reconnaissance mission. More importantly, given the tension of the last meeting between Tiberius and Jacen'zo, she suspected the latter was not done imposing his point.

Commander Rell and the rest of admin were informed of the severity of the situation and would take almost as long as Xia's reinforcements to get to this side of the planet, bringing the bulk of the planet's constables with her along with some of the colony's able-bodied men and women. The commander only allowed a moment's shock when Xia presented herself before declaring if Xia had Maxwell's trust, she had hers.

"Ten kilometers out," Charlie announced. It prompted a sharp intake of breath from Law, pushing his lungs against a steady, beating heart.

"Acknowledged. Good luck to you all," Xia responded over their communicators. "Lawrence, be careful." Her words lingered for a moment in Law's ear. Jamie turned, her dimple sinking in. Charlie's head jerked before he thought better and kept his eyes on the path ahead.

"You too, Xia. Sho qua, nu zah," Law responded. Jamie smiled and averted her gaze.

"Sho qua, nu zah! Going silent. Eyes open," Xia said.

Law turned. The speeders, Xia and her small team of soldiers, had cloaks like the rovers and followed in their tracks closely to mask their trail. As they peeled off to conceal themselves at the end of the mountain chain, just before it was all desert leading to Ops, Law noticed five dust clouds pull themselves from the rover's collection.

With them went a slight sense of security that Law had not felt in months. He also felt a little more went with it. Almost leaving him a bit empty again.

"Oh, Charlie! You need to turn off IQ's signal jammer!" Jamie said. They had completely forgotten the technology IQ had given them to conceal the rover from the tracking systems at Ops.

"Good call, J," Charlie replied. He swiped one of the projections on his display and tapped furiously. Once he got to the screen he needed, he slid several toggles to the off position.

When he flipped the last one, a chime sounded from the rover's display. Charlie looked over his shoulder at Law. Jamie did the same. It was Tiberius. They all knew it. He must have beaten them back to Ops and noticed the three of them and one of his rovers were missing.

"What do we do, Law?" Charlie asked. The chime sounded ominously within the rover. Law chewed at the inside of his cheek as he looked at Jamie. He quickly thought through possible explanations to give for their absence. None felt strong enough to debunk what he could quickly query from a vehicle maintenance tech who noticed them taking the rover or one of his workers who had not seen them in days. Regardless, none of it would matter if they did not answer his communication.

Law nodded at Charlie as he chewed at his thumbnail. Charlie acknowledged and turned, his shoulders rising while he drew in a deep breath, just as they all did. Once his lungs were filled with what felt like enough air, Tiberius' face materialized to Charlie's right.

Law immediately noticed Tiberius' appearance. Charlie's eyes widened as he looked at Law. It was as if Tiberius had rolled directly out of bed. His beard had overgrown. The gray was on the borderline of being white. Where it was usually peppered within his walnut-colored scruff, it now overtook it. When he finally spoke, he was stiff as a board. It felt unnatural. Jamie leaned in, resting her chin on her hand and squinting her eyes, likely honing in on his weird demeanor.

"Charlie, Jamie, Lawrence," Tiberius said. It sounded as if he were a professor reading names off a list for roll call. Law saw Tiberius' eyes dart to the side, then back to them. "Uh, good to see you returning from the outing I sent you on."

"Excuse me?" Jamie said. Her voice trailed off before she finished as she tried to catch the words.

"Uh, yeah! We're five kilometers out. We should be in view. Is everything okay?" Law said, trying to pry answers from more than Tiberius' facial expressions.

"No," Tiberius whispered. His shoulders sank with the realization of Law's words. Tiberius' eyes darted back to the side once more with a fear in them, this time that was hard to miss. He drew a deep breath and just as he looked like he was going to say something, the communication ended.

"Wait, what happened?" Law asked. He stood from the chair and tapped at the comms terminal.

"It had to end from his side. Signal looks fine from the rover," Charlie said, looking at the collection of indicators on his heads-up display.

"Perhaps IQs tech re-engaged?" Jamie offered as Law continued to get it back up.

"That was my first thought. But, no, still disabled," Charlie said, pointing to the same toggles they saw moments ago. "Maybe they had visual on us and decided to cut the comms?" Charlie pointed toward Ops as it quickly approached. Law leaned against the console, all but pressing his nose to the rover's windshield to see a group standing in front of the rover's hangar.

"Computer, magnify forward view. Focus on the group of people at one o'clock," Jamie said. She stepped between Law and Charlie's pilot chair. Law stood back now that he got a better view.

"It's your favorite person," Charlie said. Standing in the middle of almost a dozen of the black-uniformed men they had transported there when they first arrived at The Zoa stood Crew member April, waiting for them. "Should we book it out of here? I'm sure they weren't waiting to throw us a welcome-back party." Charlie was already throwing up multiple routes and calculations to return to the cave.

"No, we can't risk leading them back Xia's team," Law said, waving off the route options Charlie had laid out. "Not to mention, the moment

Xia senses trouble, there's no telling what she'll do. We can't ruin her chances of catching this guy prematurely. Bring us in slowly."

Charlie acknowledged, revving down the power on the rover and making a roundabout entry toward the hangar.

Law swiped his finger behind his ear. "Xia, breaking comms. We have a problem." They all waited for a response but got nothing.

"I'm running out of real estate here!" Charlie yelled back as they were almost right in front of the hangar. Law cupped his hand over his ear, hoping he missed her initial response. "Xia, come in. This is Law. Jacen'zo may be at Ops already." Law tried once more. This time, a short burst of static followed by a high-pitched whine followed. Law winced in pain, jamming his finger into his ear. Catching Charlie off guard, it jerked the rover off the path before correcting and groaning in pain. Jamie screeched as she tried to claw the communicator from behind her ear. The rover stopped right in front of Crew member April and his men. April led them around to the side of the rover, over Charlie's back as he doubled over the rover's steering wheel, still in pain from the screech of the communicator.

Then it was gone. The communicators went silent. Instead of hearing Xia's voice in his ear, Law heard April off to his side, standing at the top of the ladder with the rover's hatch open.

"You three will vacate this rover immediately," April demanded.

"I'm sorry. Is there a problem?" Law asked. His look of agony dulled his attempt at defiance. His eyes were shut tight while he dug in his ear, trying to remove what remained of the whistle in his ear.

"There will be unless you vacate this vehicle in the next five seconds," April said. He stepped up an additional rung on the ladder up into the rover's cockpit.

"There sure will," Charlie's burly voice answered on Law's left as he advanced in front of Law. Jamie grabbed his hand and placed an aspirin in it. Her eyes fixed on April, who had regressed back down to the rung he started.

"Easy there, big guy," April said as if he were trying to calm a tonnis-bear he stumbled across in the woods. "We don't want things to get messy." He pointed down toward the men who had accompanied him. Law counted six, all pointing suppressant weapons at them. Jamie grabbed Law's sleeve as she looked down.

"What is the meaning of this? Does command know about this? Only constables are authorized to carry those and only in the most severe of situations!" Jamie shouted loud enough for each of them to hear her.

"Times have changed, honey," April said with a snide smile across his face. "And we don't answer to command anymore."

Jamie drew in a breath in shock. "What the hell is that supposed to mean?" she said under her breath, looking toward Charlie and Law.

Law looked between April and his men before staring across the desert's horizon, directly under the setting sun. He looked toward the edge of the blue mountain groves where Xia should have been standing by.

"I'm guessing it means they answer to Jacen'zo now," Law said. He looked at April. "Take us to Tiberius."

"Well, I thought you'd never ask," April said, going the rest of the way down the ladder and sweeping his hand down in invitation. "That is why we are here, to escort the guests of honor in." April's armed guard lowered their weapons and stood aside.

"Do you think Xia got the message? What's up with the communicators?" Charlie whispered before turning and starting his way down the ladder.

"No idea," Law answered. "Something tells me the advantage isn't in our favor, though." Law followed Charlie down the ladder, and Jamie followed him.

"Right this way, they've been waiting for you." April started his walk toward Ops. The armed guards remained behind them. "Let's not keep them waiting." April swung his hand, beckoning them forward. The guards at their back raised their weapons again to reinforce April's demand. Law, Charlie, and Jamie exchanged looks. They then started their walk toward Ops.

The trip through the hangar felt like a day with each step they took as the shade receded ahead of them. The sun had started its descent as they began theirs down toward the observation deck. Law had yet to contemplate what the three of them were walking into, but the delta between his confidence in the cave and what he had left now had deflated significantly. So, it was up to him to find the confidence or the gall to pretend because the one thing he would not do is give Jacen'zo the satisfaction of turning their world, his world, upside down.

Then there was Tiberius. Law wavered on his innocence. He could not help but think about the call to the rover. Before the communication ended, Law believed, or at least he wanted to believe, he was trying to tell them something, but he refused to let that dull his vigilance.

"Have fun." April and his men stopped beside the door to Ops' Observation Deck. It took everything in Law not to punch him in his smug face. Charlie decided to present April with his middle finger before walking past. Had it come from Law, April would have likely kept his smug look, but from Charlie, it stung a bit more.

Law was the last to cross the threshold of the Observation Deck. The thickness of the anticipation washed over him as if he were passing through a portal to another world. The door slid shut behind them, beeping to signify no one could enter or likely exit, Law thought. As he stepped up beside Charlie and Jamie, he was instantly paralyzed.

Standing side by side in the center of the observation deck were Tiberius, Jacen'zo, and his lieutenant. Like Law, the workers that generally operated on the deck were frozen like mannequins on display. Some ventured to act as though they were working, glancing up repeatedly in Jacen'zo's direction.

"Lawrence," Tiberius uttered in a whisper. It sounded as though he were choking on heavy air that weighed heavily on them all. "Where have you all been?"

The question felt frivolous to Law. Almost enough to anger him. Even though Tiberius had no idea, they had contacted Xia and her team. To ask where they were was pedantic. For all he knew, this was the first time Law, Jamie and Charlie had ever encountered being like the two that stood before them. Jamie, however, must have anticipated Tiberius' reaction.

"Well, first of all, Charlie was itching to get us out on these rovers you have over here. He may have taken us dune-jumping," Jamie said, a sheepishness in her voice to sell an idea that they were up to no good. She even slapped his arm to add emphasis. Charlie chuckled as he scratched his head.

"Yeah, sorry, Ty. We didn't really get a chance when we came over to the forward base. You know me."

"Hmm, I do," Tiberius said. He acknowledged Charlie, but his eyes remained on Law. Noticing the attention, Law laughed half-heartedly as his glare toward Jacen'zo and his lieutenant persisted.

"Second," Law continued his sister's line of questioning. "Who are they?" Law pointed to the two figures he knew all too well by now, wanted to see how Tiberius would talk his way out of this one. Jacen'zo, however, made himself known.

Jacen'zo gave a lingering growl as he reached up and grabbed the sides of his hood. He pulled his shroud back slowly, revealing the head and face that held the glowing amber eyes within. However, menacing those eyes were before was only a prelude to the being he now examined. Tiberius averted his gaze the moment Jacen'zo released the hood onto his shoulders. Charlie cursed under his breath.

Law was not sure what exactly he expected within the cloak. But it was not as imposing of a character. Jacen'zo was certainly Cerbraxian, or at least Law assumed he was. His face was mangled and scarred, as though he was lucky to have a face at all. The scars were rail tracks that ran in all directions all the way up to his half-shaved head. Scars congregated as rail tracks would at a central station mangled one side of his head while shortened, unkempt tufts of deep purple locs like Xia's were on the other.

He was the only other with that royal purple hue. Everyone else, Law remembered, had greens and reds, and he noticed a few navy blues. No one had purple locs. Unlike Xia, however, he did not have them intermingled with black, brown, or white locs.

"I forget your kind enjoy certain...pleasantries," Jacen'zo said. The words dripped off his tongue like blood off a predator's fangs. "Though my identity is inconsequential, I'll oblige you just this once, Mr. Everstorm."

There it was. His first warning shot was to let them know he was not to be trifled with. Law's eyes were as wide as saucers. It did not matter how he knew who Law was. It could have simply been a passing conversation with Tiberius. What mattered was that Jacen'zo was intent on making it known as articulately as possible.

"You know who I am?" Law asked as Charlie and Jamie looked on in shock.

"I do."

"Well then, you have me at a disadvantage."

"Do I?" A smirk crept across Jacen'zo's face. He spoke before Law could return his volley. "I am Ro Jacen'zo, true Mah-hed of a free Cerbraxia, last of my name. Jacen'zo began to pace around Law. The low growl continued to emanate from him, through his mangled lips and up Law's spine.

"Jacen'zo!" Tiberius called out. "Enough of this." Tiberius' scowl shattered as Jacen'zo's bodyguard took a step in his direction, sweeping away his cloak and placing his hand on the hilt of the blade that he used on Tiberius earlier. It looked much more prominent in person than it did in the recording. The curved blade rounded from his waist to the middle of his leg. The glyphs inscribed on the blade pulsed in the amber glow. From what Law could tell, it originated from the xenolis at the end of his blade, which looked more like a climbing hook.

"You are right, Tiberius. We have wasted enough time. Why don't you bring the progeny of the great Maxwell Everstorm up to speed," Jacen'zo said. The heat that was rising in Law's chest since he had laid eyes on Jacen'zo had finally risen to his head. The audacity of this being to utter his father's name in front of him was the final straw. Law grabbed Jacen'zo's cloak as he rounded back in front of him. Pulling him in closer and staring into the eyes that had haunted him since they sent the drone into the mine.

"Keep my father's name out of your mouth," Law demanded through gritted teeth. He infused as much venom into his voice as he could muster. He didn't hesitate at Jacen'zo's man rushing to his leader's side. Charlie and Jamie flanked Law. Jacen'zo gently lifted his hand, stopping his lieutenant in his tracks while wearing a smirk that only enraged Law further.

"Lawrence!" Tiberius grabbed at his hands as he tried to place himself between the two of them. "What is the meaning of this?"

Law released Jacen'zo and faced his betraying godfather. "Enough of this, Ty. This man killed our father!" Law screamed. His voice was somewhere between resentment and rage. "And what's worse is you standing beside him. For what? A chance to outshine Dad? Some weak promises from him to get you recognized on Earth?"

Tiberius gasped and took a step back, grabbing his chest. "I—I don't understand. Where is this coming—. Lawrence, after everything I have ever done, everything that *I am* is thanks to your father. I would never..." Tiberius'' voice cracked. His startled expression morphed into something else the longer he looked at Law.

"Wait, what do you mean *he* killed your father? What would..." His eyes darted 'To Jacen'zo, then back to Law. The Cerbraxian's fanged teeth protruded over his bottom lip as he watched the discourse. "Your father left something more in his lockbox, didn't he?"

"He did Tiberius," Jamie chimed in. "He told us everything that's going on. Everything you're trying to do with *him*." She jabbed a finger in Jacen'zo's direction. "Admin has been alerted, and they are on their way. It's over, Ty," Jamie said softly. Law stared at Tiberius, watching the tears start to slide down his cheeks. "I loved your father. I just wish he could see what we were trying to accomplish. What we could build if he would have just..." Tiberius tapped his fist on his thigh. "Your father's death truly was an accident. We were testing the power of the xenolis and the calculations were...off." He palmed the back of his neck.

"I've seen them, Ty. They're still off. I don't know what this machine or..." Jamie hesitated, looking at her brother before she said it. "Weapon is you're trying to build, but I've seen the schematics, the formulae, the calculations. I've also seen what the xenolis can do. There are so many variables that you aren't considering. So many dangerous assumptions."

"Weapon?" Tiberius asked. He shook his head. "It's meant to be a tool, a source of sustainable and powerful energy and so much more. That's why I needed you here, Jamie. You must be the greatest scientific mind on this planet. Neither Mina nor I hold a candle to the potential that you've exhibited since you were in middle grades. You made discoveries scientists three no four times your age have dreamed of making in the best of circumstances."

This was the first time since Tiberius and their father had left for the Zoa that Law saw Jamie look at Tiberius in the same way she looked at Dr. Mina. He went from being the bane of her existence to the mentor that he was supposed to be. That Tiberius *used* to be.

"Is that so?" Tiberius said, looking toward Jamie. He did not seem to direct the question toward anyone. He then exchanged a glance with his lieutenant.

"We've answered for most of the co-variables of supercharging the xenolis with neutron particles, unlocking the elemental power within." He pulled up a projection from his CMP and threw it to the panoramic viewing screen against the long-curved wall of the observation deck. The schematics Jamie had discovered piece themselves together.

"The largest project thus far is this lasered drilling apparatus. Jacen'zo and his people will use it to harvest minerals like the xenoliths—metals stronger than steel, stronger than diamonds. It will open an opportunity for trade between our worlds and people."

"What made you so certain those were his intentions, Ty?" Law demanded an answer. "What guarantees has he given you?"

"You sound like your father."

"You mean he's making too much sense?" Jamie chimed in.

"I mean, he's acting as though I'm driven by ambition. How do you think we built the rovers? Charlie, you've piloted enough of our vehicles. I know you looked under the hood. Do you think we made those solely with Aurornovan tech? The cloaking system?" Tiberius pleaded.

"Mumbled what?" Charlie mumbled, rubbing the back of his neck.

"It's not enough!" Law shouted. "He killed our father!"

"I told you, Law, it was an accident! He wasn't supposed to be there! The xenolis was too volatile; the trials were too unpredictable. You don't know this man. What did your father leave behind in his lockbox? I'm sure you're misunderstanding. My apologies Jacen'zo—" Tiberius cut off his words as he looked at Law's adversary.

Jacen'zo's sinister laugh cut through the silence and bounced around the observation deck's walls, casting an eerie feeling despite the brightly white and translucent 3D-printed walls. The glow of the holograms and surrounding computer screens reflected off them.

"I told you to take care of him before I did, Tiberius," Jacen'zo said, walking toward the door they entered. He put his hand on the pad next to the door. It slid open, allowing several more cloaked soldiers to enter. "Now, thanks to the young Everstorm. I can take care of one of my most persistent annoyances. Ru Xianduwan."

Law felt like he had just been gut-punched. He clenched his right fist to hide the shaking and fought the impulse to touch behind his ear.

Where was Xia?

"Jacen'zo, what is the meaning of this?" Tiberius demanded. His head swiveled as the guards posted themselves on every side of the Law, his sister, and his best friend.

"It appears the Everstorms have found a way to be more mettlesome than I originally thought," Jacen'zo said. He pressed the pad next to the door again, returning it to its shut and locked status. "Even after removing Maxwell from the equation, he found a way to transfer his..." He rubbed at his scarred chin as he looked at the ceiling. Law watched as he paced around them all. "His investigation, to his offspring."

"It was you?" Tiberius asked. His tone was airy with realization but tinged with pain. "You sabotaged the tests? How did you even know he would be there?"

"Dad was tracking him. He was tracking you." Jamie stated.

"The more you and Jacen'zo ran off having your secret meetings, taking you away from your responsibilities," Law added before pausing. He could not help but think the last part subconsciously meant more as a godfather than a chief scientist and explorer. "The more suspicious Dad got."

"Leading him right into the path of my most tiresome vexation," Jacen'zo said. Baring his fanged teeth. His lieutenant sneered.

"Xia," Law said.

"Precisely!"

"You know she's here?" Jamie asked. Jacen'zo stopped next to his lieutenant and grabbed the curved blade under his cloak, removing it from its sheath. He walked toward Law, Charlie, Jamie, and Tiberius.

"I suspected," he said, as he placed the blade on his cheek and slowly scraped it down his face. "You see, in recent rotations, everywhere I've gone, every world on which I've taken refuge, Ru Xianduwan has stayed within my wake." Stopping in front of Law, he tapped the blade against his chin. The muscles in his square jaw tightened and relaxed as he grounded his teeth. "Admittedly, she evaded me this time even after forging an alliance with your father. Once I took him out of the equation. I waited for any sign of the female. Any attempt to apprehend me, but nothing."

"I told you I would take care of him! You didn't have the right!" Tiberius shouted. His hands pulled at his hair as he fell to his kn.

"And you did not have the gall!" Jacen'zo roared back. Jabbing the blade in Tiberius' direction. He slid toward Law's godfather and squatted in front of him. "I told you time was of the essence. I gave you every opportunity."

"So, you killed him? What kind of mad-man are you? You said you wanted to bring our worlds together! We shared technology, knowledge, raw materials," Tiberius pleaded.

Distracted by the sight of Ty on his knees with Jacen'zo towering over him, an arm snaked around his neck and squeezed around his throat. Law fought to break free, but the Cerbraxian was too strong.

Jamie cried out, and in Law's periphery, she was apprehended the same way.

"Let go of her!" he croaked out, the arm tightening until he couldn't breathe.

Charlie roared until it turned into a whimper. A Cerbraxian approached Law and placed a small circular device on his neck, no bigger than the tip of a finger. He crashed to his knees with a crack against the stone floor

He groaned as he clawed at the disc, trying to peel it from his skin before hearing Jamie scream in agony. It felt like the disc injected lava directly into his veins.

Law turned his head slightly, straining against the soldier at his back. Charlie was on the ground on his knees, writhing, his eyes full of pain as he stared at Jamie.

"What are you doing to them? Stop! Stop this at once!" Tiberius pleaded. "You spoke of an alliance of grandeur. An alliance of knowledge, of growth! Of peace!" Tiberius pleaded.

Jacen'zo rose as his lieutenant came to his side. He handed the blade back to him, turning his back on Tiberius.

"Peace is for peasants." Jacen'zo dropped his head and stepped aside as his lieutenant belted out a battle cry. He swung his arms wide, firmly holding his blade.

There was nothing Law could do.

With every movement, electricity was shot into his body.

He was powerless.

As the blade reached its peak, he looked into his godfather's eyes. He heard nothing, not the screams of his sister and his best friend. Not the battle cry of Jacen'zo's lieutenant as he drove the blade down. Law wasn't even sure he heard his godfather say, as he watched his lips form the words.

I'm sorry.

The blade tore through the air before swiftly slicing through his neck with such ease that the moments it took for his head to fall to the floor felt frozen in time. It landed with a crack as if a cue ball had fallen from a pool table before rolling to an ear. Tiberius' muted blue eyes stared at Law, void of life, as his final tear fell to the floor.

Law's rage pushed him to tears. He was either so numb from the pain that the paralysis wore off or the voltage was no match for the hole punched through his chest. Charlie writhed on the ground, foaming at the mouth as he continued to fight the surrounding soldiers, working to subdue him. Jamie's cries echoed his own.

Law willed one of his arms to move, slapping his hand on the cold laminate floor. He grunted and yelled at his own body to comply as he pushed his dead weight off the floor. His eyes honed in on Jacen'zo, whose back remained to Ty's body. The lieutenant muttered something to his leader, who turned his head, his brow raised.

Law's face was wet with tears, sweat, and snot as he forced himself onto a knee.

"You are truly your father's son, young Everstorm," Jacen'zo said. He growled with his face twisted in disgust. Law looked up at his tormentor and spat in his direction. His neck muscles jolted with the zap of pain and it nearly had him collapsing back tothe floor.

Jacen'zo raised his hand just before his lieutenant started in Law's direction. His lieutenant stopped in his tracks and the tasing ceased simultaneously. Instant relief flooded over Law's body, like plunging into an oasis in the middle of the desert.

Charlie stopped writhing as he was pulled to his feet. Jamie jerked away from Ty's body as he was hauled off the ground.

Law shakily made his way to his feet. The soldier behind him grabbed at his arm, but Law jerked it away. If he was his father's son, he would drive the point home.

"He fought too, that day in the cave," Jacen'zo said as he got within arm's length of Law. He held his hand out in front of his lieutenant, who placed his blade in his hand. It wasn't glowing the bright amber like when it was used to murder his godfather. Instead, it was back to its glossy black state. But just on the edge, inside of the curve, a thin layer of blood ran from its tip to its hilt. A few drops fell to the floor as Jacen'zo balanced it in his hand. He laid the blade on Law's shoulder, letting the length of it round his neck so that the tip all but punctured the skin just above his spine.

"Don't you fucking dare!" Charlie yelled before they turned his destabilizer back on, forcing him back to his knees. Law held his hand up, shaking his head, but he kept his eyes on Jacen'zo. Charlie stopped grunting. Law hoped he wouldn't antagonize the soldiers further.

Law took another step closer to Jacen'zo. A calm came over him and his life. He needed his sister and best friend safe. He wouldn't let what happened to his father happen to anyone else he loved.

Not even those he just started to care about.

"If you're going to kill me like you did, Tiberius, like you did my father...get on with it. They're here because of me. Xia was able to find you because of me. Let them go, spare them. Clearly, I'm the one that has ruined everything for you." It was a last-ditch effort. Jacen'zo had no real reason to keep any of them alive and only hoped Xia could retreat and get her soldiers to safety.

Jacen'zo searched Law's eyes, his face. His head leaned side to side as if he were considering Law's words. He said nothing at first before sliding the blade down Law's shoulder and cleansing it of Ty's blood. He handed the cleaned blade back to his lieutenant, who inspected it and then sheathed it.

"A noble effort, young Everstorm. Even as you stare death in its face, you wish to plead for the lives of others. I once held to hope like you." Jacen'zo turned, clasping his hands at his back. He looked to the ceiling, drawing in a deep breath. Without turning, he continued. "I offer you a moment's pause for reflection on the life you've led. Relish in your nobility and know it merely bought your people more time in several nights than your godfather's selfishness would have brought any longer."

He turned back to Law, running his fingers through his locs, sweeping them back to the side and over his shoulder. Jacen'zo stopped in front of Law, almost nose to nose before he grabbed the back of his neck and yanked it to the side.

Law fought for a grip around Jacen'zo's neck, but he couldn't. Jacen'zo was solid.

He may as well have been trying to wring his hand around a jenoboo tree. Law desperately clawed at the Cerbraxian's arm to get free, but Jacen'zo ran his hand up the back of Law's head and buried his fingers in his hair. He clenched a tuft of his hair, all but ripping it from Law's scalp. Jacen'zo jerked Law closer. The solid armor that adorned Jacen'zo's chest pressed against his body. His sweeping cloak almost fully encapsulated them both as it swept around Law from Jacen'zo's force.

The scarred Cerbraxian looked down at him as Law grunted, trying to claw at Jacen'zo's face while also trying not to have the top of his head ripped off. His eyes were bulging, sinister as if he reveled in the weakness of the species he held in his hands.

He turned his head to his lieutenant and jerked it backward. Without a word, His soldier walked up to Jamie, grabbed her by the hair, and dragged her off.

"Get off me! No!" she screamed as she jerked side to side. "Let me go!"

"What are you doing?!" Law yelled.

"Jamie!" Charlie shouted and struggled against the shocks attacking his system.

"She will prove much more useful and compliant than your Tiberius was." Jacen'zo looked at the body on the floor. "His ambition was his demise." He scoffed before his lieutenant dragged Jamie away. Law focused as much force as he could muster into his legs and sent a knee flying into Jacen'zo's torso. He could have sworn his leg broke against the contact, but it gave him enough wiggle room to free himself from Jacen'zo's grip and run toward his sister.

"Jamie!" he yelled. The lieutenant and one of the soldiers carried her by her legs and arms.

"Law, help me! Let me go!"

Charlie cried in pain, sending a chill up Law's spine and forcing him to spin on the spot.

His best friend was on his knees. Two of the three were on the ground around him. The third stood beside him with a blade dripping with blood, pointing dangling over Charlie's severed hand.

Law froze, looking between his friend and his sister—an impossible decision. Jamie's screams faded as she was taken further from him, one step at a time. There wasn't a memory in his life that his sister wasn't a part of. Their relationship was much like Tiberius and Maxwell's.

Charlie's red hair plastered to his forehead, the veins in his neck strained. His jaw clenched, and he fought to keep his eyes open against the pain. He knew his best friend well enough to know what he would tell Law to do.

They'd both do whatever it took to save Jamie. That just meant he would have to turn his back on his best friend.

Charlie nodded as if he knew the debate Law was having. A lump formed in Law's throat. He had to cling to the hope that Charlie would escape this. That they all would.

Law gave one solemn nod, but before he could act on his choice, Jacen'zo grabbed him by his neck, nearly lifting him off his feet and dragged him several steps before stopping his stride.

"No!" Law and Charlie shouted in unison. He was just able to turn his neck and watch the sliding door close behind the soldier who was wrestling Jamie's legs out the door.

"Enough!" Jacen'zo shouted. His booming voice stopped the soldier with his fist drawn back, towering over Charlie. "My grace has run its course. The only mercy that remains is the fact that you will not live to witness the devastation I will inflict on your world. Your people will serve my cause." Jacen'zo ran his finger behind Law's ear and ripped the communicator out.

Law screamed. It felt like his ear was ripped off instead of just the earpiece Xia had given him.

Jacen'zo held the communicator before Law's wide eyes before it uncloaked itself. He crushed it in between his thumb and index finger and let it sprinkle onto the floor.

"Thanks to you, I now have a replacement for your short-minded Tiberius, whom I intend to use as a motivator for your defiant father," Jacen'zo said with a sneer. Law was already struggling to breathe. This revelation all but left his lungs void of air.

"You have my father?" Law croaked out.

"I do. He is back on Cerbraxia. I realized very quickly your father was the more brilliant but the more unyielding male. Tiberius, however, was weak. Anxious to reveal himself from your father's shadow and would have more to gain, thereby offering me less to lose." Jacen'zo's low guttural growl made it feel like he was standing before a lion that had finally caught its prey. The Cerbraxian released him, dropping Law to the floor. He gasped for air, pulling at his collar, looking across the room, finding his friend on his side, still clutching his arm. There wasn't the amount of blood like with Tiberius. But his best friend wasn't moving.

"But it did not take long for your father to catch on. Tiberius was, er—sloppy. Through my insistence on dealing with him, your father was persistent. At first, I could not figure out how he could track us, how Tiberius was leaving a trail until I suspected he had found Ru Xianduwan. Or she found him."

"So why take him?" Law forced out. His voice continued to struggle with his nearly crushed larynx.

"Because Tiberius became hyperfocused by opportunity, unpredictable. To the point where he forgot his place. But he also had less to lose. Whereas your father, as defiant as he is, has two leverage points

I can utilize to my advantage. Information Tiberius gave more freely than he knew. Almost like you did when you broke radio silence with Xia." Jacen'zo tapped his foot on the floor next to the dust that was once the communicator. He kneeled in front of Law, gripping his chin and forcing his head back. Law jerked away.

"Goodbye, Lawrence Everstorm of Aurornova. You shall be the greatest martyr to my cause." Jacen'zo rose and turned to the soldiers. The one that cut off Charlie's hand stood at attention, awaiting his next orders. One of the two that was originally down had gathered himself enough to stand, though he appeared to struggle.

Jacen'zo ran his thumb across his throat as he looked at them before stepping around Law and making his way to the door Jamie disappeared through.

The tasing sensation ignited in his body once again. It hit him threefold and forced him to double over. The soldier standing over Charlie threw his dagger above his head and started the plunge down toward Charlie just as the door to the side revealed crew member April, who fell forward, lifeless.

Xia leaped through the door, throwing a bright glowing purple dagger at the man above Charlie. The force threw him back against the back wall of the room. Loxaria emerged from behind her with some sort of rifle in one arm and her other in a sling. Bright orange hot streams like the crystalized suns shoot rapidly above Law at Jacen'zo. Before they could hit their target, a glowing amber-colored shield materialized from his raised arm, protecting him from the projectiles that crashed against it. He staggered and slammed his hand on the door's pad before launching himself out of it.

The door slammed shut, and he was gone.

And so was Law's sister.

33

"Law! Are you hurt?" Xia was on her knees at his side. She pulled one of the blades he had seen her throw and used it to cut the immobilizer from his neck. Law looked at her, she had a bandage wrapped around her forehead. Her forearm was also bandaged, and her clothing was ragged.

"I'm so sorry. They must have tracked you when I broke radio silence." Law said. His voice cracked as it continued to return despite how much he had gone through. Xia held her hand in front of his face.

"They had us long before you called. They were waiting." Xia said in a calm voice, shaking her head. She was helping Law to his feet.

"Cosmos, Charlie!" Law panicked. He ran around to his friend who was sitting up, drinking from a canteen Loxaria had given him. His arm was bandaged at the end. "Your hand!" Law gasped. "How are you even alive? You had to lose so much blood."

"I'm good brother. They did me a favor and saved me my flying hand," Charlie said. Waving at Law with his left hand. Law let out a cross between a whimper and a laugh. "Plus, those blades run hot when they do that bright, glowy thing they do. It must cauterize as it cuts. Otherwise, " Charlie cut off his sentence as he half-heartedly pointed in Tiberius' direction. Law and Xia looked at the eerie scene. At this point, it was not just Tiberius' body that lay across from them, but those of the soldiers that remained behind that Xia and her team made short work of.

"I told you Jacen'zo is ruthless. He does not care who he must walk through or walk on to achieve his means." Xia explained. "This is why you must remain here. We will pursue him."

"The hell we will!" Charlie said, jumping to his feet with a delayed groan. He only beat Law to it by a second.

"He has Dad and now he has my sister!" Law said as he stepped over to steady Charlie. "We're going after him too," Law said. His tone was definitive. Enough to make Xia drawback a moment before she aimed to clarify her stance.

"This is not a discussion, Lawrence. You and your people are not able to handle this man. He has already torn your world apart, and he will not stop until each and every one of you suffers the same fate as your Tiberius! I cannot allow that." Xia said. Her tone ended more as a plea than it started. Law caught it as he held her gaze. He sensed the sincerity in her eyes as much as in her voice.

"Xia, it is not up to you." Law walked toward her after he was assured Charlie had his balance. "I'm not one of your soldiers, so you can't order me and you can't say this isn't our fight anymore. He has more than brought us into the fold. The longer we sit here and argue, the further he gets away with my sister and with that, there isn't enough of you, space, or time to keep me from finding him. He's taken too much." Law grabbed her hand and placed it on his chest. Xia hesitated before grabbing his and doing the same.

"Okay, Law. We must go." Xia said, nodding her head. She reached behind her ear and tapped. "Report." As soon as she saidit , the door behind them slid open. Two of Xia's soldiers stepped over crew member April's body. It was Law and Charlie's guards from Xia's cave base.

"We have located them, Maheda. They have a smaller group of com-mamauds just on the other edge of the mountains where we were am-bushed. We could not stop them." The soldier paused and looked at his companion before continuing. "We lost Xenotoo."

"No!" Xia whimpered. Law could not help the look of dread that came over each of them.

"Who is Xenotoo?" Law asked.

"He was our chief pilot."

"Do you not have anyone else to fly your ships?"

"I lost many in the ambush, Lawrence. They were expecting my team at the beach as well. We took out many of Jacen'zo's ships, but many remain. Other than those of us here in this room. I have five others." Xia pointed at Loxaria and the two soldiers who had just entered the door.

"Nine?" Law asked. "Only nine of you remain?"

Xia could do nothing more but nod.

"Well, if it can fly. I can fly it." Charlie said. Law looked at him.

"You sure, Chuck?" Law asked wearily.

"You know I am. We need to go get Jamie. Now!" Charlie said. He was holding the wrist that once supported his right hand. Loxaria had wrapped it with the same black bandages that she had wrapped Xia in. "I doubt they could get into the rover we came in. I had it locked down to only me. Another gift from IQ?" Charlie added with a wry smile.

Law found himself questioning every impression he had ever had about people. IQ was sleazy, but he had helped them more than he helped himself throughout the entire trip, even if it wasn't to his knowledge. Law told himself he would thank him the next time he saw him—if there was a next time.

"Let's go!" Law said. Charlie took the lead toward the hangar.

The rover tore through the desert. Xia and her team sat in the main cabin, bobbing around as Charlie pushed them through dunes, making for the most direct bee-line toward the wooded mountains they passed on their trip to Ops. Law programmed his original seat to move into a co-pilot position. He would be Charlie's right hand. But he didn't need it. He was locked in. Somehow, he was able to move all the physical controls to the left side and put most of the holographic controls on the right to accommodate the loss of his hand.

The sun peaked over their destination, threatening to plunge them into the darkness of night as it disappeared behind the desert's hills. Law knew it would only make this rescue more difficult.

"I've got a lock on them." Charlie said he swiped at one of the projections in front Law that displayed a map overhead. "They've got about thirty kilometers on us, but we're closing." Law looked at the blinking red dot that, from what he could see, was about five kilometers from their destination. Their blue blinking dot was closing in on it, but there was no way Law could think they would get to them on time.

"You've got to punch it, Chuck!" Law said, still staring up at the map.

"I know, I know. Our only hope is whatever idiot Jacen'zo's got piloting that thing is moments away from tearing the transmission out of it." He swiped the map away and threw a hologram full of gauges toward Law. "They're red-lining everything on it. If they're not careful, they won't even get close. Shit! Hold on!" Charlie yelled over his head. The sand disappeared ahead of the rover. Law began to hover in his seat before being pushed back into it. Xia's hand was on Law's shoulder, securing him with her other arm against the rover's dome. The rover launched itself to the center of the dune. As Law anticipated the heavy landing, he spun his chair and pulled Xia to his lap, wrapping his arms around her and burying his face in her locs.

The rover slammed to the ground, causing a few of Xia's injured soldiers to groan in pain before it regained its speed and scaled the other side of the dune.

"Sorry, folks. Clearly, I prefer the air. This would be a good time to check your tray tables and seatbelts." Charlie laughed nervously. Law took his face out of Xia's locs, meeting her eyes.

"Are you okay?" Law asked. His chest throbbed. He could not decide if that was due to Xia's shoulder pad digging itself into his jacket or if it was because it was the closest he had ever been to her. He stared as the final rays of sunlight ignited her eyes. Law felt her steady breath against his lips.

"Yes, Law, you ensured it," Xia said. She did not attempt to get up.

"They did it!" Charlie shouted. He looked over at Law and Xia and took in the sight. "Well, not you two. Or did you?" Charlie joked, an assuming grin on his face.

"Chuck!" Law yelled.

"They red-lined it. It stopped maybe a kilometer or two from where we think their commamauds are. They must be on foot. We're closing!" Charlie had the map back on display.

Xia ran her thumb down the middle of his nose and over Law's lips, stopping at the bottom of his chin. She lifted herself off Law gently.

"Cerbraxians. Ready yourselves." Xia said. She waved her hands over the blades at her hilt, lighting the rover's cabin with a bold purple glow.

"I've been ready since I left Cerbraxia, Maheda!" Loxaria answered. She pulled back at the top of their energy rifle and stood. She walked up to the front of the cabin and laid it beside Charlie. "I brought two, so two should be used." They tapped Charlie's shoulder as they returned to their seat and grabbed an identical rifle beside it.

Xia pulled one of the two blades from the sheaths on her back and handed it to Law. When he closed his fingers around it, it ignited in the purple glow like Xia's daggers, but twice as bright. He could feel a rhythmic pulsing from the hilt. It felt like the sword hummed.

Xia stared in awe at her blade's reaction. Law noticed her face but thought nothing of it. He had seen all of their blades, their armor, even their tech emits a different glow of some kind. Loxaria lifted her head from charging her rifle and shared the same look of astonishment. Just as his curiosity peaked, Charlie called from the pilot's chair.

"I have visual on the rover." Law turned and looked toward the front. The rover was magnified on the forward shield. They left the hatches opened as smoke billowed from underneath. "Geez, they did a number on it." Charlie leaned in and inspected the visual. Law agreed and was glad. Their lack of knowledge balanced Law and Xia's disadvantage.

"Bring us in as close as you—" An alarm blared as the rover's cabin began to glow bright red.

"Incoming!" Charlie roared. Xia grabbed her sword from Law and sheathed it as they braced, but the warning didn't come early enough. An explosion to the right of the rover lifted to two wheels, throwing everyone not seated and strapped in, to the left side. Charlie yelled as he fought to correct the rover. "Hang on!" They drove through sand blasted in the air on every side. Law was back on his feet. He tapped at one side of his forehead at what he thought was sweat. Wincing and looking at his hand, he realized it was blood slowly trickling its way toward his eye. He tried to offer navigational support.

"Bank right, Chuck!" Law yelled. The alert system was beginning to triangulate things coming toward the rover. Xia was beside him, pointing at anything Law did not call out.

"There!" Xia yelled as she spotted a small contingency of Jacen'zo fighters at the tree-line of the mountain's forest, flanking what looked to be some sort of turret. Law saw them loading ammunition, one after the other and sending it their way. He turned to Xia, looking for a solution, but Zax was already up, walking to the canopy door with what looked to be an enlarged version of Loxaria's energy rifle. As he threw the door up in to the air, sand sprayed into the cabin, the booms of the artillery blasted into the cabin as it was no longer sealed. Zax threw his legs out the rover, sitting over the edge while Zen grabbed the buckles of his armor, bracing herself with her legs on either side of the doors frame as he started blasting toward Jacen'zo's men.

Charlie rounded the rover wide to dodge the last few shells that came in, but also to give Zax a more direct shot. Law watched as his charged rounds sprayed toward their adversaries, casting shadows against the trees until they started pelting the turret. It exploded shooting a fiery mushroom into the sky. The soldiers immediately surrounding the turret went flying, the rest scattered into the trees like crux beetles fleeing a lifted rock.

"Get us over their Chuck!" Xia called out. Charlie looked at Law with his brow raised. Law returned a similar look as smiles crept across their faces. Though humor was the last thing their current situation warranted, hearing Xia mimic Law, by calling Charlie 'Chuck" somehow squeezed some of the tension out of the rovers packed cabin.

Charlie pulled them up well into the tree-line trying to stay clear of the fire that littered the ground. Xia returned her second blade and its sheath to Law as they prepared to disembark.

"We must move quickly!" Xia proclaimed. "Their commamauds are more advanced. We will have much difficulty tracking him. Getting your sister back. Jacen'zo must not leave this planet." It was not Law wanted to hear. He could not imagine what Jamie was going through right now.

"Then we're wasting time. Let's go!" Law jumped through the rovers open door. Landing beside Zax and Zen. Charlie and Xia followed along with Loxaria and the remaining soldiers. Xia led them into the woods in the direction the fleeing soldiers ran, leaping over patches of fire that lined the divide between blue sand and grass.

The woods at the foothills of the Zoa's mountain range were dense. Law looked toward the sky for any sign of stars or moonlight, only to find darkness. Law and Charlie lit the lights at the end of their CMPs, shining the path forward. Xia and her team had lights on their armor as they methodically made their way deeper into the woods. They had encountered a few more of Jacen'zo's forces that peeled off from the larger group waiting for them. Hand-to-hand, they made quick work of them. Even one handed, Charlie was able to take down one of his soldiers. Though the motivations were clear for them both. If Jacen'zo made it to their commamaud and were allowed to take off, their path to getting Jamie back would become that much harder.

"These woods will only become harder to navigate the deeper we go. How are we sure we're tracking them? There can't be many more soldiers stupid enough lagging behind." Charlie asked the group. Xia was with Loxaria who tried to find a trail with a small instrument she held.

"Would have been good if we brought one of IQ's drones," Law said. He was scanning for any sign of a trail. Maybe there was a struggle from where they had to drag or fight Jamie up the trail. As he alternated his CMP's light from the tree trunks to the wooded floor, something small in the brush threw the light back at Law

"Wait a minute." He said as he bounded toward it for further inspection. Law kneeled in the dirt. It was a reflective piece of Jamie's flight jacket. He picked it up and looked ahead. Holding his arm ahead of him, he stood again and walked ahead. Law focused on the area he shined the light on. Just as he had walked almost deep enough into the unbeaten path, he saw another small torn strip of her white flight jacket.

"Everyone!" Law yelled instinctively before he swiveled his head, scanning around him. Just as he was convinced he had endangered himself by calling out, Xia came, followed closely by Charlie and the others.

"What is it, Law? Are you alright?" Xia asked, scanning the surrounding area as he did.

"I'm fine!" Law reassured her. "We're fine," he added as Xia continued to scan. He held up the two scraps he had recovered.

"Is- is that pieces of a flight jacket?" Charlie asked, taking a piece from Law's fingers.

"It is!" Law said.

"Damnit! They must be ripping it to shreds trying to force her through here." Charlie said. He banged his fist on the tree trunk he was bracing himself against as he, too, began to scan the woods.

"No, I don't think it's that Chuck. There would have been more and concentrated in spots where she fought." The feeling of pride in his chest manifested itself as a smile on Law's face. "She's leaving a trail." Law shook the remaining piece in his hand. "I found these about fifty yards from each other. I'm willing to bet we'll continue to find more in that direction." Law said as he pointed northwest from the group.

"Let's get going then!" Charlie was ready to break out into a sprint before Xia grabbed his arm.

"It is likely they will be waiting with more viciousness than they did before. Tread lightly and be ready for the fight of your life." Xia said, casting an ominous look at Law and Charlie.

"I was ready the moment they took her," Law said. He charged his stun rifle before turning and followed what he believed to be the path his sister left for him.

"There they are!" Charlie called back to the group. The woods began to thin as they made their way toward its edge. Law could barely hear Jamie calling out.

"Charlie! Law!" she yelled before Law could see Jacen'zo snatch Jamie by her curls and pull her down the hill.

"That son of a-" Charlie yelled. Taking off in a sprint after them. As Jacen'zo disappeared from their sight down the hill with Jamie in tow, two of his soldiers appeared and fired

"Get down!" Law yelled, tackling Charlie from behind. He rolled over his friend and fired his stun weapon in the direction of the soldiers as they retreated for cover. Zax and Loxaria sent a barrage of shots in kind. Hitting two of them squarely in the chest while the others retreated. Law turned, offering his hand to Charlie, who was already making his way up. Charlie looked at Law's offered hand. He looked at the rifle he had in his left and waved his right arm.

"Really?" he yelled, returning to his feet and sprinting toward the valley Jacen'zo and his soldiers disappeared down. A bit of mischief in his voice. Law was on his heels.

"Not the time, Chuck!" Law yelled. He checked over his shoulder. "Xia!" he called back.

"Push forward," she commanded as she began to catch up. Zen, who took a shot to her leg, was on Xia's shoulders. Xia ran with her blade in one arm, holding Zen steady with the other. Zen refused to surrender her rifle. Using it to cover their rear as she propped herself on Xia's back. Law turned just in time to see Charlie stop dead in his tracks.

"Holy –" Charlie said as his jaw dropped. The drop-off Jacen'zo took Jamie down and led to a valley that housed what looked to Law like two of the skyscrapers from Earth he had learned about in Cultures and Humanities. Xia and the rest of her soldiers ran up to Law's side. She kneeled, allowing Zen to hobble off her shoulders. "Xia, what is this!" Law asked, trying to comprehend the structure before him. He scanned it end to end while also trying to get an eye on Jacen'zo and Jamie.

"It is nothing like I have ever seen," Xia said. Her eyes darted back and forth as she scanned it with Law. "Is this where he has been hiding? His base?" She called back to one of her scouts. The scout shook his head. "We knew nothing of this, Maheda."

"Why would he lead us here? He's been able to keep it concealed as long as he has." Law followed the energy beam up toward the sky. The concealment canopy had to be ten times the size of the one Xia and her soldiers used. They had not noticed they had stepped through the curtain until they saw its source, instead of a small device that sat at the center of the grove at Xia's base. This one was fixed atop the larger of the two buildings they looked down on.

"Wait a minute," Charlie said as he searched Jacen'zo's base through a pair of binoculars he had pulled out.

"What is it, Charlie?" Law asked. He looked between Charlie and the valley. "Chuck, what do you see?" Law asked more urgently.

"We have to go!" Charlie yelled as he tore off down the hill. Law looked at Xia, seeing the fear in her eyes, before he took off behind Charlie.

"Charlie, wait!" Law called after him, stretching his legs as far as possible while trying not to lose his footing going full speed down the hill. "Charlie!" Law yelled once more as he gained ground on Charlie. He yelled back without stopping or turning to Law.

"It's not a base! It's a ship," Charlie yelled. "We've got to get to Jamie!" The realization almost knocked Law off his already unstable legs. As they reached the base of the hill, they went from looking down at the structure to looking up at it. If these were ships, they would be the largest ever made. They were easily three times the size of the omnitransport and could not only hold the entire colony of people but several other planets' worth. Law searched side to side for Jamie before they came to a stop.

"Where's the hatch? How the hell do you get on this behemoth?" Charlie yelled. Law did not realize how loud the ship was becoming.

"Is it powering up?" Law yelled but could barely hear himself. Charlie didn't answer. They had made their way under the belly of the ship. Above them, spurts of steam and smoke blasted from a mechanized sky that hovered fifty meters above them.

"Law! Take cover!" Xia's voice blared in his ear from the new communicator she had given him and Charlie. Charlie turned and looked to Law. Law turned, trying to look back up the hill before he was knocked off his feet by a force that almost tore his shoulder from his body. A searing pain overtook the entire left side of his body as he grabbed at his shoulder. Charlie dove beside Law. He fired shots back as he slid sideways to partially cover Law. Charged shots rained down the hill. Law looked over and saw Xia and Loxaria running in their direction.

A dozen soldiers emerged from behind two of the massive columnar supports of the ship. They focused most of their return fire toward Xia's soldiers on the hill. Loxaria overtook her leader, holding her forearm in front of her, allowing a forcefield to sprout from her wrist, covering both her and Xia. She grabbed at her belt and threw an orb in their direction on the run. It landed several yards in front of Law and Charlie, bursting like a crystal ball hitting the ground and sprouting a forcefield like the one on her wrist.

As rounds made their way between the fighting groups, a circular opening in the ship sprayed steam in all directions, casting a covering cloud over Jacen'zo's group. A platform lowered from the ship down behind the semi-circle his soldiers had formed. That's when he emerged just as the smoke descended around them, casting a light cover.

"Hold your fire, it's Jamie!" Law forced himself to yell through the pain.

"Hold fire!" Xia echoed. The shots from the hill ceased immediately while Jacen'zo continued. Charlie pulled Law up as he ground his teeth through the pain. He pulled his stun rifle from behind his back. Law adjusted his stun rifle to a lower setting. Even if they hit Jamie, at most, it would only stun her for a short period.

They made their way directly behind the barrier. Law looked toward Xia. She and Loxaria were taking cover behind her forcefield and a rock jutting from the hill.

"Does this thing move?" Charlie asked, slowly putting his hand toward the center of the forcefield. Just before he touched it. A crossbar appeared, inviting Charlie to grab hold.

"Hell yeah, Let's move!" he commanded Law. "I'll shield us, you fire." Charlie handed Law his rifle, grabbing the forcefield and advancing. Law put a rifle on each side and fired indiscriminately toward the fighters who were returning fire. Jacen'zo continued waiting behind the pillar. He was visible, watching, waiting for the platform to finish lowering. It was halfway.

"Xia—I've got eyes on Jacen'zo—He's preparing to board," Law called out in between blasts. "Can you get a shot? Take him out?"

"No Law. We could hit Jamie." Xia responded.

"We're running out of time!" Law shouted. He winced at the pain from holding the weight of the stun rifle in his left arm. "Charlie, we have to move."

They had stopped their progress. Law noticed Charlie's planted foot sliding down into the dirt as the barrier lost ground.

"It's too many. I can't move it!" Charlie yelled. The noise from the ship was almost overwhelming, coupled with the blasts pelting the forcefield like hail hammering against an aluminum awning. Law threw his good shoulder against the barrier. At most, the two of them made it an immovable object against an unrelenting force. A force that had almost taken everything from Law. He couldn't let them his sister too. But it was too late.

Law looked through the crystalized forefield. Jacen'zo walked toward the platform, holding Jamie by her hair like a dog by the scruff of its neck. She alternated throwing blows at his rib cage and clawing at the hand that held her.

"Charlie, look!" Law said. A helplessness that had only resided in his heart found his voice. It also found Charlie's

"No!" Charlie whimpered. His eyes were wide. "Loxaria, you have to take a shot." He demanded.

"Charles, our weapons do not stun. We cannot risk hitting Jamie." Loxaria replied.

"Can we take the ship out? Zax? Anyone?" Law pleaded. A broken voice over the communicator came back.

"We are out of ammunition." Jacen'zo reached the platform that had finally hit land. He stepped squarely into the center. For a moment, Law swore he stared directly at him, directly into his eyes, mocking him. The same eyes he had seen in the playback from the cave. Law stood from the forcefield, allowing it to slide more violently as he shot toward the platform. One of the rifles was shot from his hand, but he wouldn't stop. One of his shots would hit Jacen'zo. He had to hit him. Soldier after soldier threw themselves in front of him the closer Law came. One after one, they tumbled from the platform just to be replaced by another.

Law fired relentlessly, ignoring the stun rifle's beeping, warning him the charge was depleting. He pleaded and prayed. Just let one hit him before it ran out. But nothing came close before a long tone came from the weapon.

Jacen'zo noticed. Law looked as Jacen'zo's spy jumped on the platform with him. He took something from his belt and jabbed it in Jamie's neck as she continued to fight to free herself. Jamie grabbed at her neck where the spy stuck her before she dropped to the platform like a ragdoll. A smirk crept across Jacen'zo's face as he kept his eyes on Law, reveling in the terror on his face. He put the hood of his cloak over his head. Other soldiers jumped on the platform, continuing their fire, but none obscured their leader's line of site.

The platform began its ascent.

"No! Law screamed. He started to run from behind the barrier, but Charlie was able to grab the back of his jacket.

"No Law!" he grunted, trying to maintain the weight of the barrier being pushed back from their fire and hold onto his friend. "You can't save her if you're dead!"

"Let me go, Charlie. Let me go!" Law yelled. He thrashed as he tried to unzip his jacket. He had to get to her. He had to try. Law watched as the platform had made its way halfway up to the ship. The shooting stopped just as he was able to get his jacket off. He ran as fast as he could. They were not too high up, Law thought. Maybe he could jump. Maybe his adrenaline would give him a few extra centimeters that could get him to grab the bottom of the platform.

"Law! No!" Xia yelled through the communicator behind his ear. Out of his peripheral, he saw Xia running from behind the rock. He ignored her. If anything, he ran faster. Law was close enough to see those menacing eyes again before a soldier squared their aim at him. He prepared himself to dodge the shot. Zigzagging a bit to buy himself time. He wasn't going to make it. Law's legs slowed as his mind began to accept the inevitable, eventually causing him to stop and fall to his knees.

Jacen'zo placed his hand on top of the soldier's weapon, causing him to let go of his aim, even though Law invited him to take the shot. He lifted his head toward his ship as the platform closed them off from the ground.

Law cried out as loud as his lungs would allow, but he could not hear himself. So, he tried to scream louder. He wanted his rib cage to crack from the pressure he put into his cries. He wanted to fall to the ground and give up. Just as he was going to allow himself, he felt Charlie's large paw engulf his chest and pull him back up. He looked up at his friend through tear-stained eyes as Charlie let out a roar of agony. Law couldn't hear him either but felt the vibrations through his chest as his friend clasped him close.

An explosion of wind came from all sides, kicking up a dust storm just before Xia and Loxaria threw themselves on either side of them, covering them with their forcefields.

Law watched the ship above rise to the sky.

As the dust settled, Jacen'zo's ship had reached a resounding height. The other joined it. Both ships hovered ominously over the valley for a moment. Law, Charlie, Xia, and Loxaria watched, waiting.

"Please tell me your people are close!" Law said in desperation.

"They are still hours away," Xia said, still staring at the sky.

"Even if they were here, Law, I do not know what they would be able to do against that!" Loxaria answered, pointing up at the ships that had eclipsed the moon.

"Guys!" Charlie said, forcing Law and Loxaria to look to the sky.

This ship Jacen'zo had boarded was starting to point itself toward the moon and began emanating a beacon from its front. It lit the clouds like a searchlight, getting brighter and brighter. At the ship's rear, the five spherical thrusters began to ignite. Starting as small balls of light at the center and gradually expanding into a cluster of giant suns.

"No," Xia said in a whisper.

Jacen'zo's ship was there and then it was gone in a second, leaving a crack of thunder in its wake as it tore off into the sky and out of Aurornova's atmosphere. Law was frozen in awe, seeing a ship of that size disappear so fast.

"Get the fleet on comms paxteek. This is far worse than we feared." Xia commanded Loxaria. "Law, you must communicate with your people as well. I fear trouble will come for them?" Xia said ominously as she pointed toward the remaining ship.

"Charlie, do our ships have any firepower?" Law asked. Could the commander and several omnijets provide any support or any safety for their colony, Law thought. Charlie let out a nervous laugh.

"To do anything with that?" he asked rhetorically. "It would be like mosquitos to a bullmoose."

"I'm sure the omnijets, hell, even the omnitransports, could outmaneuver them." Law grasped for ideas.

"Of course. But the problem is, transports are just that, they have no firepower, they're just meant for carrying people. The jets are armed for cutting through terrain and blasting asteroids out of the way. Not for galactic dogfights." Charlie finished.

Law relented but was distracted by the remaining ship's movement.

"What's going on there?" he asked the group. Unlike Jacen'zo's ship, this one turned toward them, slowly drifting in their direction. As it approached them, the bottom began to open up. Two enormous doors slowly flipped downward. Within, a bright ball of amber light shined, making it look like daytime within the valley.

"We must go!" Xia declared in a panic. "We must go now!" She ran over to grab Zee to throw her over her shoulder, but Zax had already picked her up. Xia and her soldiers made their way for the tree line. Law and Charlie did not waste time questioning. They ran to the woods, zig-zagging around trees. Law held his hand over the wound on his shoulder. Every footfall sent a shooting pain to his shoulder, making it feel like a tiny blacksmith was smacking at it with their hammer.

As he ran deeper into the woods, the trees were not as tightly bunched, allowing Law to look back toward the ship. All Law could see was light, as if it was the middle of the day. Along the ground, they stayed ahead of the line of light that pursued them. Law pushed his weary body faster, turning back to make sure Xia and her people were still ahead. Once he turned, an awful mechanical grinding emitted from behind them before an explosion rang out. The ground shook violently and Law's knees almost buckled under him. The quake threw him into a tree at his side. The pain made him cry out instantly and see stars. As blue and green leaves rained down ahead of him, he could make out Loxaria waving them ahead as she pointed toward a cave. Law steadied his legs and focused his eyes. He ran as fast as he could to catch up with Charlie, who was sprinting to catch up with Xia's soldiers.

At his sides, the trees bent in the direction Law ran. Just as Charlie ran through the caves opening, a force behind Law threw him forward into the cave as Loxaria dove in just behind him. Dust, dirt, and leaves blasted into the entrance as Loxaria landed on top of Law. They both covered their heads and waited out the elemental violence around them.

"Commander, avoid that ship at all costs!" Law pleaded. "Take cover, outmaneuver it, whatever you have to do to get away from it. Can you order our people off-world?"

"Mr. Everstorm, we simply do not have that kind of time." Commander Rell said. She braced herself at the panel in front of her command chair at the center of her omnijets flight deck. She began to pace. "Captain, how far until we make contact?" Rell asked. Folding her arms and resting her chin on her lifted fist.

"T-minus thirty—no ten minutes. Commander!" The captain spun his chair and looked toward her. This thing is moving fast, like nothing I've ever seen. It's coming directly for us."

"Get out of there!" Law screamed into his CMP. His voice reverberated around the cave's walls before it ran off into the darkness the light of his CMP could not reach. The urgency in Law's voice sent a shock to Rell's face.

"Captain, reverse course. Send word to Acting Vice Commander Mina—emergency Code Ro Upsilon Nu. Mr. Everstorm, I'm—" The commander could not finish her sentence before sparks exploded above her. She was thrown to the side, and the transmission was lost. Law, Charlie, and Xia watched the screen for a moment. Waiting, hoping for the comm to return, but it did not. The commander was lost, and Fort Kelly would soon fall.

Law dropped his arm and paced the cave. He couldn't think. He tugged at the collar of his jacket, stretching it to allow him air. His sister was taken off-world and Jacen'zo had left his lieutenant to subjugate his home. Their commander was likely dead, and he was in a cave.

"So, what now, *Maheda*?" Law directed at Xia. He made no attempt to look at her but also did not attempt to mask the venom in his voice.

"Excuse me?" Xia said. Law heard the crunch of her footsteps approaching him from behind. He didn't want to turn and face her because he was unsure if his anger was strong enough to hold back the tears of hopelessness sitting behind his eyes. He spun anyway and let out his frustrations.

"This is all your fault. All of it! If you would do your job and catch this madman, he wouldn't be inflicting his will on my people. So, I asked, Maheda, what do we do now?" Law reiterated. This time, he clearly saw that he had struck a nerve. Then he questioned whether it was the wisest thing to do.

"Watch your tongue, Lawrence Everstorm. If you knew what that word meant, you would not be so bold."

"Law. Take it easy, brother." Charlie said from behind him. "We all need to just cool our boosters." He had stepped between the two of them now. "Xia, what's the lieutenant's play at Fort Kelly? Are they going to wipe out our people? My parents—" Charlie's voice trailed off.

Law's stance softened. Xia's and Loxaria's heads dropped. All this time, Law had been so hyper-focused on what he had lost, what he had been through, and how he was affected he never took a moment to think about Charlie. He had fought and been through everything Law and Jamie had from the moment they left the Oasis. Now, a ship was heading for their home. Charlie had left his parents for the sake of Law and his family.

"I'm sorry, Chuck. I—I've been selfish." Law said. He dropped his head. Why had he not been more attuned to what his friend was going through?

"Look, bud, I get it. No one has gone through as much as you have through all of this. But that doesn't mean no one else is going through it." He lowered his voice and faced Law. "I'm guessing including Xia."

Law saw Loxaria place her hand on Charlie's shoulder as she cleared her throat.

"It is my, uh, speculation that it is not the intention of the second ship to destroy your home or your people." She said tenderly as Charlie moved beside Law. "I believe the second ship will remain here. They will likely look to utilize your people's technology and resources to continue to mine the xenolis and create more destructive weapons similar to what we just witnessed." The lieutenant motioned to the outside of the cave. Thin smoke swirled aimlessly outside as fires cast an eerie glow around where the woods once stood. All the trees they weaved through running from the valley were now scattered like spilled toothpicks, splintering in all directions. Law let out a deep sigh, not before inhaling the smell of charred dirt and leaves. He wondered if this was what would become of Fort Kelly. But he tried to remain hopeful for his friend.

"It sounded like Rell's final command was to Mina, giving him some emergency code," Law said, taking his eyes off the destruction and looking to his friend. Charlie lifted his head and pointed his finger at Law.

"Yeah. She did! It was the evacuation and shelter command. Ro Up-silon Nu is the code for civilian inhabitants to retreat off-world while others retreat to the bunkers we have. Maybe they—" Charlie's voice cracked as he slammed his eyes closed.

"Maybe they had enough time to get off-world?" Law finished the sentence for him.

"We had so many people with that last migration, though, and we only keep one transport on-world during migration season. What if they stayed waiting for me?" Charlie asked. Law didn't have an answer for that. He merely put his hand on Charlie's shoulder and squeezed. Law hoped they were able to get off-world. He needed something to go in their favor. If not for him, then why not Charlie?

"Chuck—" Law said, pulling Charlie aside. "Look, you've been so helpful, and cosmos knows I would be dead if it weren't for you, but you need to get to your family and make sure they're okay. I wouldn't blame you one bit. I can take it from here."

Charlie took a deep breath, rolling his shoulders and steeling his face. He put his large hand on Law's shoulder.

"I appreciate you, brother. My Dad's no slouch. If there was trouble, I have no doubt he had Mom packing long before Rell gave the order." Charlie said, a smile creeping onto his face as he looked off. "They made it. I'm sure of it." Law sighed in relief as his friend stared at him with a steadiness in his gaze. Charlie squeezed Law's shoulder. "You and Jamie are my family, too. I'm with you, whatever comes. They took a piece of us, so I'm going to scatter their pieces across this galaxy and the next until she's back. If that's what it takes."

Law threw himself into Charlie's embrace, who wrapped his arms around Law and squeezed. Law reciprocated his friend's squeeze and muttered softly without lifting his head. "I love you, Chuck." Law felt the rumble in Charlie's chest as he reached up with his remaining hand and patted the back of Law's head.

"I know."

"We're going with you," Law said. They had been over possible scenarios well into daybreak. Most of the soldiers had found a way to get some rest after patching each other's wounds. Even Charlie had managed to settle down and rest after willing him to believe his parents were on the transport and where it would likely take them. Charlie's father had always wanted to sail the pink oceans of Arbitross, the next inhabited planet outside of Aurornova's system. He said they never would have gotten the credits even with him saving to help them, so what better time to take an impromptu vacation? Xia brought Law back to reality.

"That is not possible, Law. You cannot come to Cerbraxia," she said, waving him off before crossing her arms.

"Why the hell not?" Law demanded an answer. His voice was a little louder than he intended, causing a short echo down the cave. He looked to see if he had woken anyone. A few stirred, including Charlie. "Sorry. But I need to find my sister. Apparently, my father is on your world being held captive by Jacen'zo. We're going. Whether you like it or not. There isn't enough of you, space, or time to keep me from finding him. He's—" Law paused. His tone was softer this time. "He's taken too much."

Xia stared at Law with wide eyes.

"I know Lawrence. And I am the cause of it all." She answered him. Xia leaned against the cave wall and slid down, sitting herself on the ground. "I cannot be responsible for you being lost amongst all this. It is not your fight." Law crouched in front of her.

"It became my fight long before I became your problem," he smirked. Xia tried to fight a smile as she turned her head before softly gasping and looking up. He had not noticed Loxaria and Charlie walking over.

"Plus." Charlie said, "It would be my problem if this guy were lost. His sister would take my other hand and beat me senseless with it." he said, waving his left hand around before smacking himself in the face a few times. "Not to mention, you're down a pilot. Law and I can get you home." Law looked at Charlie with an eyebrow raised. He had flown with Charlie dozens of times, but it was a bit of a stretch to say they both would fly them, Law thought.

"Maheda. Both Law and Charlie have proven themselves as warriors. They also have more than enough right to accompany us. Jacen'zo has made certain of that."

Xia chewed at her lip, looking at the three of them as she considered their points.

"Fine!" she said, pushing herself to her feet. Law stood before her, a brief glint of satisfaction crossing his face. Xia stepped closer to Law, putting a finger in his face. "Keep that fire, Lawrence of Aurornova. You will need it for what is to come."

Law stared at the stars outside the observation deck of Xia's commamaud. The vastness of space surrounded them now as Charlie was piloting them away from their home and onward to Xia's. Just before they broke through the upper atmosphere of Aurornova, Xia called everyone to the flight deck. Charlie had kept them in the dense clouds to get a view of Fort Kelly. Hovering over their home was the second ship. On the ground was destruction. Habs were on fire. The hueys were in ruins, but the Admin building and Sci-Rez remained intact. They had invaded Fort Kelly. The single strand of silver lining was Charlie telling Law that he received a comm from his parents on a transport to Tellathia.

Now, here he was, staring at the reflection that the dim lights of the commamaud's passageway presented against the window. It was the first time he had seen himself in days. His hair was matted in spots with blood, as mud and dust intermingled with his brown skin, casting a disheveled mess of a person back at him.

"Lawrence," a voice softly pulled Law from his trance. Xia's reflection was next to his. Unlike Law, she looked much more put together. Her long white and purple dreads were back in a bundle at the back of her head. The jewel at the center of her forehead had been shined. She wore a navy flight jacket and held a bundle of clothing in her hands, like hers, but in black.

"We have assigned you to the quarters of one of our fallen. You and Charlie's are on the same corridor as mine." Xia said, holding the clothes out to him. "You will be able to go and refresh now if you wish." Law took the clothing with a soft smile.

"Thank you, Xia. And respect to your fallen." Law said, offering a slight bow of reverence. Xia gave an appreciative nod.

"We will rendezvous with our fleet within a few hours. They have some promising information of where Jacen'zo may be going with Jamie." Law pursed his lips as the lump in his chest swelled. Xia grabbed his hand and squeezed. That was enough to open the floodgates. The tears ran down his face quickly, giving him no time to wipe them away before Xia saw, likely deciding to give Law some space, she released his hand slowly and made to walk away.

"Hey Xia!" Law called after her. She turned, "What is Maheda?" Law had been meaning to ask for the longest time. It wasn't until he used it to agitate Xia that he remembered how much it annoyed her. But everyone appeared to use it with a tone of reverence.

Xia's shoulders dropped with a huff of annoyance. She walked back toward. Law as he took another swipe at his face, wiping away tears.

"It is a term of respect," she said as she rolled her eyes. "One that I have asked my soldiers repeatedly not to call me." Law shook his head as he tried to wrap his head around what she had just told him.

"It is a term all my people use for me because of my father." She continued. "A term used for the first child of our Mah-Hed. The—" She hesitated. "The leader of our people."

"Wait, what?" Law thought through it. "You're some kind of princess?" Xia glared at him. He wasn't sure if she knew what that meant, but she didn't seem to like what his tone implied. He decided to pivot. "I don't understand. Why would you be annoyed by that?"

"The expectations that come with that word are not me. I do not know." She crossed her arms and shuffled her feet. Law could not help but empathize.

"Well, I apologize for using the word without knowing its weight," Law said. Xia walked to him and placed her hand on his chest. She then reached up and ran one of her knuckles down his nose and chin like she had earlier in the rover. She blinked her glowing eyes at Law and walked off.

Law looked back out the window at the stars that littered the canvas of space. Charlie's voice came over the intercom.

"Preparing to jump, please make your way to designated areas."

Jamie was somewhere out there. The farthest she had ever been away from him in their life. He wiped one last tear from his cheek.

"I'm coming, sis." Law tapped his fist on the window before turning and walking toward his new quarters.

Cy Harold (he/him) is an author whose writing highlights diverse and multi-faceted characters in the science fiction, fantasy, and mystery genres. When Cy is not fully immersed in the world of Aurornova, he allows himself to be distracted with a short story or two.

When Cy is not writing, he is an analytics developer during the day and spends his nights chasing his children, binging Star Trek and other action/adventure shows, gaming, and drinking bourbon. He resides in the Research Triangle Park area in North Carolina, USA, with his wife and children.